Running

Run

ning

NATALIA SYLVESTER

CLARION BOOKS
Houghton Mifflin Harcourt
Boston   New York

Clarion Books
3 Park Avenue, New York, New York 10016

Copyright © 2020 by Natalia Sylvester

All rights reserved. For information about permission to reproduce selections from
this book, write to trade.permissions@hmhco.com or to Permissions,
Houghton Mifflin Harcourt Publishing Company,
3 Park Avenue, 19th Floor, New York, New York 10016.

Clarion Books is an imprint of
Houghton Mifflin Harcourt Publishing Company.

hmhbooks.com

The text was set in Minister Std.
Art by Alex Cabal

Library of Congress Cataloging-in-Publication Data
Names: Sylvester, Natalia, author.
Title: Running / Natalia Sylvester.
Description: New York : Clarion Books/
Houghton Mifflin Harcourt, .[2020] |
Audience: Ages 12 and up. | Audience: Grades 7 and up.
Summary: "When fifteen-year-old Cuban American Mariana Ruiz's
father runs for president, Mari starts to see him with new eyes. A novel about
waking up and standing up, and what happens when you stop seeing your dad as
your hero—while the whole country is watching."
—Provided by publisher.
Identifiers: LCCN 2019029658 (print) | LCCN 2019029659 (ebook)
ISBN 9780358124351 (hardcover) | ISBN 9780358330806 (ebook)
Subjects: CYAC: Fathers and daughters—Fiction. | Politics Practical—Fiction.
Cuban Americans—Fiction. | Conduct of life—Fiction. |
Family life—Florida—Fiction. | Miami (Fla.)—Fiction.
Classification: LCC PZ7.1.S994 Run 2020 (print)
LCC PZ7.1.S994 (ebook)| DDC [Fic]—dc23
LC record available at https://lccn.loc.gov/2019029658
LC ebook record available at https://lccn.loc.gov/2019029659

Manufactured in the United States of America
DOC 10 9 8 7 6 5 4 3 2 1
4500791393

For Nonno

Prologue

Gloria collects the mangoes from the tree in our backyard once they've fallen but before the birds or bugs can get to them. She cuts them into cubes and lets me nibble on the pepa and then she packs them into my lunch in a little Tupperware with a spoon. When I get home from school the first thing she always asks is, "Did you remember to bring back the Taper?" Then she washes the container by hand and leaves it to dry facedown on the kitchen counter.

In the mornings I help her pack me and my brother's lunches while I wait for my mom and dad to get dressed. I cut our sandwiches into triangles and put them in ziplocks. I put the cold cuts back in the fridge and wipe the counter. Somehow, Gloria always sneaks in a note on my napkin. I know I'm too old for them, but they're funny, usually some pun having to do with my food. Like with the mangoes, she'll write, "Man, go eat some frut!" She always spells *fruit* like that. She's learning and she's trying; but it's the words that are similar in English and Spanish that trip her up. She even has a language app on her phone that she plays in the kitchen while she cooks, but only if my parents aren't home yet. It makes her say things like, "The mountain is too far to walk," which cracks me up because there's not a single mountain in Miami, unless you count Mount Trashmore, the landfill we pass on the highway anytime we go to Orlando.

The morning after Papi dropped his bombshell of a plan on our futures, the papaya tree in our neighbor's yard had yielded fruits the size of footballs. It'd grown at an angle so that one of the fruits dangled over our side of the fence. Gloria ran across the grass to get it before the neighbors could see her. That day at lunch, along with a Tupperware full of diced papaya, I got a napkin that read, "Papá ya agradeció a los vecinos."

Dad already thanked the neighbors. It's a play on words, so it loses all its humor in English, which is what I said to Zoey, who speaks so little Spanish that the joke was entirely lost on her.

"Papá and ya mean 'Dad already.' Gloria just likes to make double meanings with different words for food," I said.

"It's not that funny if you have to explain it," Zoey said.

Vivi and I locked eyes and smirked when she wasn't looking, a silent acknowledgment that we, of course, had gotten it. Even though she teases me about the notes being childish, Vivi also thinks they're cute "in a charming retro kind of way." I told her about the stolen fruit and the mango tree that's ours and how Gloria jokes there's so many mangoes, we should sell them off the side of the road. Vivi only laughed and said, "Oh my god, Mari, that's so reffy."

Papi got home late that night, so we waited for him to eat because he kept calling to say he'd just left the office, he was just five minutes away, he was just eight minutes away. When he arrived twenty-five minutes later, I got so upset watching him take off his tie and unbutton his shirt at the table that I blurted out, "Oh my god, Papi, that's so reffy."

He stopped and gestured to me with his right hand balled up in a loose fist, his thumb sticking out. "Mariana. We do not talk like that in this family. What would people say?"

People. He's always saying that, like there's some invisible audience watching us at all times. When I was little I thought these people were on the other side of every mirror in our house, even the bathrooms, so I'd never undress in front of them. I'd brush my teeth, twenty seconds on each side of my mouth exactly, just like the dentist ordered, thinking people were judging my every move.

"Why not? What does it mean?" my brother asked. Ricky's seven years younger than me, but his question made me realize that I didn't know what it meant either. Not really.

Mami cleared her throat and wiped her mouth with the napkin on her lap. This is her not-so-subtle way of warning my father to be careful. I've gotten this look so many times, it might as well be a neon light flashing CUIDADO across her forehead. "It's . . . it's a horrible thing to say about people who've been through difficult times."

"It's short for refugee," Papi added harshly. "And very insensitive."

"I'm sorry," I said. "I didn't know."

"You know better than to be so careless with your words," he said.

3

"That could be your grandparents," Mami added. "They fled Cuba not even a week after they were married, leaving everything."

My dad set his hand on the table, rattling our silverware, the salt and pepper shakers. "We don't make fun of people like them."

When Papi says *people*, there's a hierarchy: first it's his campaign manager, then his biggest donors, then the news anchors and Twitter and Facebook and, basically, the entire internet. People we can't see but who can see us. People I'm devoting my life to, he always says.

That's why my father's running for president.

To make things better for everyone.

Except, it turns out, me.

one

"I'm Anthony Ruiz." My father pauses, widening his smile. "And I approve this message."

From behind the camera, the director says, "Just a few more times."

"I'm Anthony Ruiz, and I approve this message."

Someone holding a light over me and my family coughs. Papi leans forward and looks across the couch at Mami before trying again. "I'm Anthony Ruiz and I approve this message."

"Not so fast, Tonio," she says.

"I'm Anthony. Ruiz. And I *approve* this message."

Ricky tries to keep from laughing, but ends up sounding like he sneezed with his mouth closed. I shoot him my most stern don't-laugh-at-Papi look, but I fail miserably at keeping a straight face.

"You sound like a robot, Papi," he says.

"It's super unnatural," I add.

"I'll try it one more time. We don't have all day," he says, but I think he's trying not to laugh too. The dimple on his left cheek—the one that, according to Mami, makes the focus group of women her age melt—starts to peek through.

"Actually, this is going to make great blooper reel footage," the director says. "The PACs will love it."

At the mention of PACs, my mother clears her throat and turns her nose up, away from the director. It's no secret that she's not comfortable with what we're doing. When I asked her why before the shoot, she said that Political Action Committees can help the candidates they're supporting, but they can't donate more than five thousand dollars directly to their campaign.

"It's to keep super-wealthy people from buying influence in an election," she said. "But outside of that five thousand, PACs can do other things with the money they raise, like make ads and buy airtime on TV for their chosen candidate."

"So we're shooting these videos for the PACs," Ricky said matter-of-factly. I raised my eyebrows and gave him an encouraging smile. It's cute how he acts like he knows what he's talking about, even though I suspect he thinks there's a giant yellow Pac-Man doing Papi's bidding. Still, he catches on to more than my parents give him credit for.

"No no no no no," Papi replied, very quick to contradict him. "We're not shooting footage for the PACs. We're putting these on YouTube. Whatever anyone does with all the video is completely up to them."

Mami glared at my father.

"What?"

"It's too gray, Tonio. You know how I feel about shady tactics."

"It's common practice. All the other candidates do it."

"That's not the kind of reasoning I want to teach the—"

She was interrupted by one of the assistants asking us to take our seats at the dinner table.

Not that we actually ate dinner. It's noon on a Saturday and we've been up since five in the morning for makeup and to catch what they call "good light." Papi said grace twenty different ways over a meal we didn't eat, then we played catch in the backyard. Correction: Papi and Ricky tossed a football back and forth while Mami and I sat on beach towels by the pool, laughing like we were in a 1950s toothpaste commercial. We walked around the neighborhood holding hands as a family, and now we're here: all four of us on the couch in the living room. Mami sits next to Papi with Ricky to her right, and I sit to Papi's left. He puts his arms over our shoulders and squeezes.

"I love you all so much."

"Nice, that's really nice," the director says. "One more time?"

"Gladly," Papi says. "I'm just so proud of my family." We all look at him and smile, but his gaze remains steady on the camera until he finally catches my eye and says, "I love you, hijita."

I smile back despite the awkwardness. Between the film crew and Papi's campaign staff, there are at least fifteen people watching us. There will be who knows how many million more, once the videos are online.

I try not to think about it.

"Okay, now let's try the approval a few more times, but this time the kids join in and say 'we approve this message.'" The director takes off his Marlins cap and runs his hands through his hair. I can't remember his name, just that Papi was really excited we got him for this shoot because he did a bunch of spots for a Mitt Romney PAC in 2012. *When politics was still about honest men running,* he always says.

"I don't think that's a good idea," Mami says.

"¿Por qué no?" Papi lowers his voice even though we're all wearing mikes.

"It's tacky, dear. Leaning on the kids so much."

"I think it'd be sweet. Ricky, what do you think?"

That's messed up and my father knows it. Ricky's only eight, which means he does anything Papi asks, no questions. He'll figure out he has a choice in things eventually. For now, he nods enthusiastically.

"Mariana?"

I'm surprised Papi asks me. Has he forgotten the fifty-three hundred times I've begged him and Mami to leave me out of this? My father acts like I'm still eight years old and dreaming of being an actress. He caught me rehearsing my Oscar acceptance speech in front of the mirror with a hairbrush as a mike the *one* time and he's just never been able to drop it. He put me in front of the cameras every chance he got, calling me his Best Supporting Actress. But back then his campaigns were different. For one, I had no lines. Mami was in charge of everything and she insisted it was for our own protection that Ricky and I should be "seen but not heard." Besides, people weren't exactly tuning in by the millions to watch footage of their local elections.

This, though. This is on a totally different level.

Before he announced he was running for president last fall, my father made a really big deal about getting me and my brother's support, and of course I was excited for him—I still am. But guess who froze on camera during her first channel 39 appearance when the anchor asked the simplest question of all time? Turns out a mike is *not* the same as a brush. Turns out it makes "Are you excited for your father?" sound like "What is the square root of seven hundred forty-nine thousand?" Papi knows I can't handle the public speaking thing. He knows that inside I panic Every. Single. Time. Still, he can't accept the fact that I'm not a crowd-pleasing natural like him.

Mami cuts in before I can answer. "You don't want to look like a local mattress store salesman, do you?"

She gives me a subtle wink. At least she remembers that Papi promised to use Ricky and me as little as possible. "Only when it's absolutely necessary," he'd said.

Except who gets to decide what's necessary and what's not?

"Don't exaggerate, Juliana. It's just a few simple words." He smiles, but his dimple isn't showing anymore. He taps me on the chin and says, "Right, chiquitica? It's not like we're live."

I wave his hand away like it's a mosquito that landed on my face. He's making things so much worse. We may not be live, but everyone's watching us. If I contradict him in front of the crew, I can already imagine what his assistant, Joe, will say when it's over: every time you undermine your father, you make him look like less of a leader. But if I stand here another second, I'll feel my throat turn into a giant suction cup, like in those nightmares I always have where I've lost my voice.

"Can we take a break?" I finally say. "I need to use the rest-room." I don't wait for the director or my dad to say yes or no. I walk out before they have a chance to stop me.

I use the half bathroom downstairs because the camera crew is blocking the way to my bedroom and bathroom upstairs. It's smaller than my closet but at least it's quiet. I check my phone and see that Vivi texted me a bunch of screenshots and links to articles in support of my father.

See? It's not so bad. She adds a bunch of smileys and the lady-dancing-in-red-dress emoji. That's her trademark.

Thanks, I text back. Still trending, tho.

Last week, during the primary debate, Papi messed up bad. I could tell by the way Mami, who sat in between me and Ricky in the front row, squeezed my hand like she was making orange juice.

The moderator had asked my father about climate change, about why the party is so averse to using those two words when Miami Beach is already being affected by sea level rise.

"That's not entirely accurate," Papi said, in this vague, could-mean-anything way that I'm starting to realize is prob-ably the point. He added that the weather patterns are not necessarily manmade and that what's happening on the beach shouldn't be blown out of proportion.

"When a hurricane blows our way, do the other forty-nine states duck for cover? No, because we're talking about Miami, not the whole country," he said. Then, maybe out of nerves, or maybe thinking it'd be funny, he chuckled and added, "We can be our own Latin American bubble sometimes."

By the end of the debate, #BubbleBoyRuiz was trending and people from both political parties were saying that comments like my dad's are what enable our government to abandon its own people in times of crisis, like they did Puerto Rico after Hurricane Maria. Others were calling his Latin America sound bite *controversial* and *insensitive*, which everyone knows is code for racist. Joe started freaking out that my dad's campaign would have to go into crisis mode. *Jesus. He just made all of South Florida think he doesn't think they count*, is what he kept repeating, over and over. The primary elections are less than a month away; other states like Arizona and Illinois are voting on the same day, but my father's team is hyperfocused on Florida because for him, it's make or break. He can't win the GOP presidential nomination without winning his home state; it's worth way more votes than most. Pissing off the city with his highest number of supporters was a really stupid move.

Even the kids at school were upset. In the halls, I counted four girls who walked by me popping their gum in huge, loud bubbles.

"Ignore them," Vivi said. "They'll be over it by tomorrow. They're so full of shit, pretending they care about politics."

But it's been five days and things have only gotten worse. I click on the hashtag and scroll. People accuse my father of turning his back on his own community. A headline from the *Miami Herald* reads RUIZ BURSTS OWN BUBBLE AMONG HISPANIC

VOTERS. An opinion piece is titled HERE'S WHY SENATOR RUIZ'S COMMENTS PERPETUATE WHITE SUPREMACY. One of the most popular tweets (a thread shared twenty-two thousand times and counting) is by Jackie Velez, a senior at our school. She has a huge following because she's the editor of the school paper, and she interned at *Teen Vogue* one summer. The only person in a bubble is @SenAnthonyRuiz. He seems to have forgotten that Latinx people are Americans too. What makes him think we'll support him at the polls when he so easily turns his back on his own community?

Jackie's avatar is a picture of her leaning against a mural of the Puerto Rican flag, screaming. Half her head is shaved and the rest of her hair is dyed bluish-black. It cascades diagonally over the left side of her face, accentuating her cheekbones and dark brown eyes in a way that makes her look like some sort of postapocalyptic Disney princess. I take a screenshot of her tweet and send it to Vivi.

Did you see?

I watch for the "Delivered" notification under my text to switch to "Read," but Vivi must have gotten distracted, because nothing happens. Instead, a follower request pops up on my screen, and I almost drop my phone into the toilet when I see who it is.

Jackie.

The Jackie Velez.

Requesting to follow *me*.

It's like she knows we were just texting about her. I take another screenshot.

WTF?

Still no reaction from Vivi. I dim the screen on my phone and tuck it into my back pocket, ignoring Jackie's request. Or at least, trying to. For once I'm actually glad my parents made me set all my social media accounts to private at the beginning of Papi's campaign. What could Jackie possibly want with me, and why now?

I take a deep breath and brace myself for whatever fresh hell awaits in the living room. Judging by the way Joe hovers over his phone, shaking his head, he's seen the latest tweets too. "It's not good," he says to Papi. "But it's still fixable. On the bright side, it'll only help the ratings for the interview on Friday."

My stomach clenches. Three days ago, my dad's PR guy booked us all for a *Meet the Candidates: Home Edition* interview. It's this new thing where one of the major news networks doesn't just interview the candidate and the family—they get a tour of their whole house. Even the kids' bedrooms. When I asked my parents if they were fine with millions of strangers knowing where their kids slept at night, they agreed to leave me and my brother's rooms out of it. But then last night, one of the other candidates' Home Invasion interview aired. He has five-year-old twin daughters who wore identical yellow dresses. The whole family sat in their living room while the little girls took turns sharing stories of how their father plays hide-and-seek with them on weekends and never misses an imaginary tea party. Then they went into the girls' bedroom and poured pretend tea for the host. Now the news won't stop commenting on how cute and well-behaved they are. How the congressman should be so proud of his daughters. I think the part that got to Papi the most, though, is that they keep saying the congressman is such an involved father. So my dad decided the full home tour was back on, our rooms included. He insisted I was overreacting and that it'd be too risky for the campaign not to do it.

"You have to understand, sweetie," he said. "We can't have people thinking we're hiding something. And you and Ricky are ready for this. Or was all that money we paid Jamie for nothing?"

I wanted to tell him that yes, in fact, all my twelve weeks of training sessions with a media coach have accomplished is that I'm now hyperaware of how many *ums* and *you knows* I say when I talk, making me so much more insecure than before I started. And it's different for Ricky. An eight-year-old could do nothing other than blink on national television, and he'll be cute and endearing. Just look at the congressman's twins: they sipped on air and people lost their minds over their natural charm. Meanwhile, I have to be perfectly composed, enunciate every word, and make sure I sound smart but not robotic, sophisticated but not elitist.

It made me wish Jamie had trained me in how to tell my dad no. How to speak so he would listen. By then, though, nothing I could say would have made a difference.

Mami had been oddly quiet. Now she stands behind him and rubs his back in small, firm circles. "Are you sure this won't backfire?"

Joe sends off a quick text. "Juliana, trust me." He always

says her name with a hard *J*, like it's a longer version of Julie, instead of the soft *J* our family uses. "Even the people who hate-watch it won't be able to resist your charms. Let alone Ricky and Mariana's. You show some Miami pride, get back in touch with your local roots . . . convince them you're just like any other American family."

We *are* like any other American family, I want to say. At least, I thought so until we started visiting Papi in DC every spring break. But other American families don't roast entire pigs in a hole dug in their abuelo's backyard on Christmas Eve. They don't make their ringtones play Celia Cruz or get their son's portrait painted for his first communion. Mami feels guilty that we never got mine painted when I was Ricky's age because we didn't have as much money back then, but you'll never see me complaining—it's creepy the way his eyes follow you down the hall and his little fingers clutch at the rosary.

Joe looks my way like he just noticed I'm here. "Mariana! Why don't you show your parents what we've been practicing? For the interview?"

I should have stayed in the bathroom longer. Joe's been writing out these notecards with lines that he thinks will make my dad sound good. He wants me to memorize them without seeming too rehearsed. Papi looks at me wide-eyed with his mouth half-open, the same way Ricky looks when he's playing video games, like he's expecting something spectacular. Mami sighs and says, "Go on, hijita."

I feel every muscle from my stomach to my toes tense, and I take a deep breath.

"I know my father will make a good president because . . ." I pause. It's hard for me to get the words out. They've been shoved down my throat for so long now, saying them feels like regurgitating. Even worse, Joe thinks I've paused because he taught me to. Said it makes me appear more genuine, like the thoughts are just occurring to me. "Because he's my hero and he's never let me down."

My parents look like they're about to cry. I feel like I might too. It's not that that the words are a lie, it's just that, who even talks like that? When Joe originally asked me the question, I answered, *because Papi works super hard. Like, night and day, he's working his butt off.* And yeah, I know that's not exactly presidential daughter material, but it could've been finessed. Joe didn't even bother. He didn't even butcher what I said. More like he took an order for ham and offered up sliced cheese. And now I'll be humiliated in front of 2.5 million people. That's the show's viewership, one of the highest, if you ask Joe. Or even if you don't. He'll still brag about it to anyone who'll listen.

"That's excellent. Excellent," Joe says. "Just don't be afraid to be yourself, okay? Just act natural."

He's always saying that. Joe talks like we're close friends, when in reality he barely knows me. He just thinks he does.

We shoot footage for another hour and a half. If this shoot and the interview go well, Papi and his staff plan on launching a livestream of his campaign. There'll be cameras everywhere he goes, which means everywhere we go when he's with us. I can't imagine anything worse. Our lives are being turned into a cheap presidential election version of *The Bachelor*. Would Jackie start writing about me then, too, with so much fresh material to pick through? I pull out my phone and hit decline on her request. Whatever it is she wants with me, it can't be good.

Joe scribbles another line on a pink notecard and hands it to me. It's about how much Papi loves Miami—real subtle. I fold the notecard in half, then into quarters and eighths until it's a tiny wad so thick it won't bend any further. Papi glances at my hand, but I hide the paper in my palm before he can see what I've done to it.

"You'll be perfect," he says.

Perfect. No pressure or anything. Just perfect.

two

My father has been a politician for as long as I can remember. It's not something I ever had to get used to. It just was.

When I was in kindergarten, Papi led my whole class on a field trip to Parrot Paradise. It was just a few blocks down Old Cutler, so the teachers got a long rope and had each of us hold on to it as we walked down the street, which was lined with so many trees, their roots cracked open the sidewalks.

"Look up, Mari. You'll miss everything," he told me. He stopped at a crossroad and everyone stopped behind him. He turned his head left, right, left, and we followed. Mami was all the way at the back, walking next to my teacher, who kept reminding us not to let go of the rope.

When we got to the park, the first thing I saw was a man in a khaki uniform wearing thick black gloves, and a bright red parrot, the size of a blender, sitting on his shoulder. Her name was Giselle, and her feet looked like they were made of dried leather and bubble wrap. The man let us each take a picture with her on our heads, but when it got to be my turn, Giselle's nails dug into my skull so hard, I couldn't tell if the drops on my forehead were sweat or blood. I was terrified I might cry and humiliate myself in front of the whole class, humiliate my father. But he came over and placed his hand on my shoulder. "I'm right here with you. I won't let anything happen to you," he said. "See? Everything's fine."

The next Sunday, the picture was published in the lifestyle section of the local paper with the caption: BIG BIRD: COUNCILMAN ANTHONY RUIZ AND HIS DAUGHTER, MARIANA, SHARE A SPECIAL MOMENT WITH THEIR NEW FEATHERED FRIEND. In the picture, I'm grimacing and my shoulders are scrunched up all the way to my ears, but Papi holds me, looking proud. I'd thought we were taking a family photo. Somehow it got sent to the press.

On weekends we'd go door-to-door with Abuelo and Abuela to hand out Papi's pamphlets. While my father talked to voters, I'd play tag with the neighborhood kids. After my brother was born, I'd help Mami watch after him. I'd change his diaper if she was in the middle of a conversation with someone. I'd carry him in my arms when she needed a break and he'd cry if we put him in his stroller. By the time Ricky learned to walk, we realized people loved seeing us holding hands down the sidewalks. The adults would call us darling, or precious, or model children.

Weekend rallies were like huge family get-togethers. There were the six of us, plus a bunch of people I didn't really know but felt like I should know, or had to pretend to know, because they'd say things like they'd last seen me at my father's very first election, and did I remember them? I'd nod and smile even though at my dad's first election I was like two.

When Papi was done speaking, he would play with us

—catch or soccer—and of course, we danced. He'd salsa with Mami first, and then the two of them would bring out my brother and me. Papi knew all the best spins, and he always joked that I was his favorite dance partner because I just went whichever way he turned me. He said letting someone lead requires trust. We'd hold hands and he'd bring his arm over my head, across my back, over my chest, until he'd tangled us into a knot I knew he'd get us out of. Papi's confidence when we danced was on another level. There was a lightness to it, a spontaneity I never saw anytime else. It's not that he wasn't sure of himself when he spoke to constituents or did inter-views—on the contrary. But that version of him was always measured, always planned far in advance. For two or three minutes at a time, when the music kicked in, I got to hang out with just him, no matter how many strangers were watching.

Weekdays were different. We never ate out and Mami cooked every meal and we'd eat at the round kitchen table in the apartment while she set aside two plates to reheat when Papi finally got home. On the days he got off work before din-ner, we went on bike rides together, down the same road that led to Parrot Paradise. Somehow it wasn't as exciting. There were no crowds or cameras watching. Everything just felt bet-ter when we were in a big group. Whenever it was just the four of us, it felt like something was missing.

The years when my father was a county commissioner and then a Florida legislator are honestly kind of a blur. Like a long road trip, how when you finally arrive you can't pick apart exactly how you got there. What I do remember vividly is the day he told us he was going to run for the US Senate. I was eleven and Ricky had just turned four. Papi told us to sit on the couch, the beige one in the new house we'd moved into just months before. He stood in the center of the rug in front of us and clapped once.

"Tonio, espera. Help me in the kitchen first," Mami said. Ricky and I sat waiting, marveling at how the couch seats were so deep, our feet just bobbed over the edge of the cushion.

My parents came out of the kitchen holding two bread bags full of end slices. They told us to tear them into little pieces, and we got into the car. On the way to the park by the canal, Mami said, "You know how Papi's been working really hard to make Miami a better place for people to live?"

We smiled and nodded. I didn't understand much about his job, but I knew enough to know that he helped a lot of people, and that's why so many of them liked him. People were constantly telling me how I must be so proud of my father, and I was.

"Well . . ." Mami reminded me of soft-serve ice cream, the way she was sitting in the front seat, twisting around to look at us. She leaned her head toward my father.

"Well, I'm going to try to help even more people now." he said. "I'm going to run for the US Senate. Which means I'd represent all of Florida."

"Cool!" Ricky said. "All of it?"

"The whole thing," Mami said.

"Even the tippy-top?"

"Yes, papito. Even the panhandle." Papi laughed and glanced at me through the rearview mirror. "What do you think, Mari? Do I get your vote?"

I'd been busy looking at the crumbs in our bags, trying to guess how many ducks we could feed. "Always," I said.

He stopped at a red light and looked right at me. "This is a really big deal for me." Maybe he didn't think I was excited enough, or fully understood. "I'd represent our whole state. In Washington, DC."

"We're moving?" Ricky asked.

"No. I would just work there. And here, too, sometimes. It's exactly like when I go to Tallahassee."

"So *you're* moving? Out of Florida?" I said.

"You know that where I work and where I live are two different things, Mari. This will always be home. And I'll visit every week."

"You'd visit Washington?"

"He'd visit home, sweetie," Mami said.

I didn't understand. I thought visiting a place meant going somewhere that's not home. But we'd gotten to the park, to the edge of the canal, and by then the conversation seemed over. Papi filled each of our hands with breadcrumbs and we took turns sprinkling them into the water, waiting for the ducks to come, one by one, to peck at the pieces before they got soggy and sank. My brother tossed in his entire fistful, and out of nowhere, the ducks swarmed us. It made Ricky laugh about as loud as the ducks were quacking. Maybe that's why my parents thought I wouldn't hear them as they stepped away from the water's edge.

"I'm scared we're losing sight of the things we stand for," Mami said.

Their voices grew lower, but even though I could only make out Papi's every few words, I'd heard some version of them enough times to fill in the blanks. "I'm just trying to make this a better world for all of us. For all the families that started out like we did, with nothing."

"We never had nothing," Mami said, raising her voice. "We had each other." Ricky turned around.

My father smiled like nothing had happened and rejoined us. "How's it going? Where'd the ducks go?"

The ducks had lost interest a while ago when we ran out of crumbs, but we hadn't wanted our parents to know. Instead, we watched the sunset ripple over the water's surface as the ducks swam farther and farther away.

three

We're spending fourth period in the library because the guidance counselors are preparing us to write our community service project proposals for next year. We sit at tables in the center of the room with rows of computers all around us. Even though they split the sophomore class into four groups to fit us in, it feels like everyone in the school is here. They're all staring at me, but not like they did in the beginning of the year. Back then, I was the new girl whose father was running for president. Vivi would post clips from his speeches online, with little arrows pointing at me clapping and smiling. I'd walk down the hall and overhear students' excited whispers. Nobody bothered covering their mouths or looking away because they weren't saying anything bad. Now, though, they all do these subtle double-takes. I feel people's stares wash over me the way a warm undercurrent brushes against your knees in the ocean. It leaves me with the same uneasy feeling of suspecting someone peed in the water.

This morning, all anyone can talk about is the op-ed Jackie Velez published in the school paper. She basically turned her tweet into a five-hundred-word manifesto about how Miamians represent the best of what our country has to offer. "Not a bubble, but a sea of diversity," she wrote. "Our voices are a current, strong and unstoppable."

Maybe it's just like Joe had feared—people are blowing Papi's one misspoken comment out of proportion. *It hasn't even been a week but the situation completely snowballed and spiraled out of control like some sort of viral tornado,* he said. Which kind of made me wish he would calm the eff down, and maybe learn not to mix his metaphors while he's at it.

I'll never admit this to his face, but I can kind of see where Joe's coming from. I mean, Papi already apologized. And yeah, for someone who's always telling *me* how I need to choose my words carefully, he really failed miserably at picking the best phrase to say on national TV. But, the nerves. The pressure. It's not like I can't relate.

I look around and catch girls rolling their eyes at me. I don't even know most of their names, but they know mine. That's what's weird about going to a school with twenty-five hundred students: every day is just a bunch of strangers' faces mixed in with a few that you more or less recognize from one or two classes. My last school was much smaller because it was private, and in each class there were maybe twelve of us. We all knew each other. Not just each other's names but that Jason Burman was super into photography and Anita Valdez was vegan, and that the twins Blake and Hannah Cohen had a younger sister two grades below named Rebecca who looked nothing like them. Everybody knew everybody's business. Then Yvette Martinez's parents lost their house, and she said they blamed it on my father breaking his promises about property taxes years ago. That was all it took for the whole class to turn against me. Yvette made freshman year such hell for me, I was actually relieved when my parents decided to put me back in public school sophomore year. They said it'd look better to working-class Americans, and they figured I'd adjust easily since I'd gone to Grove Elementary up until fifth grade.

It was kind of working, too. Vivi reconnected with me right away; we'd been best friends until we were ten, but the second I was back she acted like we'd never drifted apart after I switched schools. The first week of the year, she introduced me to Zoey and told me to sit with them at lunch. Even though the whole student body had been gossiping about seeing me on television with my dad, neither one of them brought him up, not even once, until I did a few days later. I was starting to think I had a chance at carving out my own identity, until Papi's debate debacle happened. Now I'm back to being Senator Ruiz's daughter and everyone besides Vivi and Zoey hates me for it.

"Mariana, how are you, dear?" So, maybe not everyone hates me. Ms. Lindeli is super nice because she was Papi's guidance counselor when he was a student here years ago. She has a picture of the two of them at his first town hall on her desk. He signed it, *Thank you for believing in me.*

"I'm okay. I mean, I'm fine," I say.

She claps her hands to get everyone's attention. We're supposed to take this period to research organizations or causes we can volunteer for. Vivi, Zoey, and I have agreed to do our service project together. The computer desks get taken before we can grab one, so we decide to look through magazines and papers for ideas. We head toward the stacks, which are all the way at the back of the library, away from all the chatter.

"I don't see what everyone's so worked up about," Zoey says. "Isn't it a compliment? To say Miami's not like any other place in the country?"

I can't help but laugh. When she puts it like that—with her voice super hissy in a loud whisper—it doesn't sound like a compliment at all.

"It's complicated," Vivi says. "But anyways, it's not fair that people are taking it out on you. You're not the one running for president, you know?"

"At least *you* think so," I say, even though we both know it's not that simple. In some twisted way, who your parents are matters, at least it does if they're a big deal. It's why everyone knows that Dania Charles's mom is an anchor on Channel 7, and Patrick Franco's dad is this super-in-demand plastic surgeon. People say he's done Ariana Grande's Botox, which is ridiculous because she doesn't need it, and even if he had, none of us would actually know. There are laws against doctors disclosing who their patients are; it's just like attorney-client privilege. I heard Papi say that to Joe a few months ago, but they changed the subject as soon as I walked into the room. I don't know what they think I'd do. Tell the world on my private Twitter account with all of four followers? Give an exclusive interview to Jackie?

We wander through the aisles until Zoey stops so abruptly I bump into her. "Oh my god," she says, gasping. "Check it out."

There's an entire shelf filled with nothing but old school yearbooks.

"What class was your father?" Zoey whispers.

"Z, we're supposed to be keeping her mind *off* her dad, remember?" Vivi says.

"Ninety-three." I never thought to look for his yearbook before. Papi speaks with such pride about being a Grove High alum, but I've never actually pictured him here.

Zoey runs her fingers through rows of burgundy, green, blue, and black leather spines. She finds the 1993 book and hands it to me. The pages are yellowed along the edges, and they smell like cardboard boxes and shoe powder. I flip until I get to the *r*'s in the senior section. It's easier than I expected to spot him.

In the black-and-white picture, Papi's mouth is curved into an awkward half smile. His face is smaller and his eyes are open wide in a surprised expression. He has the beginnings of a mustache on each end of his upper lip, though the patches of stubble don't connect.

We begin to giggle and then our eyes must arrive at the same spot at the same time, because we all go quiet.

There's a caption below his picture that reads "Most Likely to Become President." Below that, someone wrote in a blue pen in all caps: "BIGGEST JERK THAT EVER LIVED."

"Oh, Mari. Don't let it get to you. People were immature idiots in the nineties, too, you know?" Vivi says.

I pretend to agree with her. There's no telling how long the yearbook's looked like that. Either someone who went to school with my dad hated him way back then, or someone really hates him now, enough to go through the effort of trashing his yearbook picture instead of saying something to my face. Maybe it's a kid whose parents went to school with Papi and couldn't stand him, and now their kid detests me too. Passed down through generations. How sweet.

I slam the yearbook shut and it makes a deep, hollow sound. I stick it back on the shelf. Vivi and Zoey move on to a stack of *People* magazines, but I can't stop thinking about my father's picture. I can't stop wondering who did it, and what they'll write on mine in a few months. Behind us, a hush comes over the library as Ms. Lindeli tries again to get everyone's attention.

"One of our seniors, Jackie Velez, has an announcement she'd like to share with you all."

"She's here?" Even whispering, there's no hiding the trepidation in my voice. Zoey practically trips over herself as she rushes out of the stacks, but Vivi and I stay behind, watching Jackie through the tiny spaces between the shelves. Jackie paces around the computer desks, handing out a bunch of seagreen flyers. Her voice is deeper than Ms. Lindeli's, and as she moves farther away from where we're hiding, I only catch every few of her sentences.

"This is really important . . . We're going to be choosing a new president, a new vice president . . . see how you can get involved." She pauses to run her fingers through her hair and I swear her eyes travel over all the desks, all the computers, and land right on Vivi and me. I duck so fast I feel a nerve in the back of my neck snap a little.

"Mari, don't be ridiculous. She can't see you," Vivi says, right as the bell rings.

Even so, we wait until she and everyone else have left to make our exit. When we step through the double doors of the library into the outdoor hallway that overlooks the courtyard, Vivi goes first, then Zoey, then me.

"Mari?" Jackie's voice is velvety and melodic, and it travels up my neck like nails digging into my skin. I swear, this girl is everywhere. Without saying a word, I hug my books tight and turn to face her.

"I've been trying to get ahold of you. I thought you'd make a great profile for this article I'm working on."

"No, thanks," I say, before she even has a chance to explain what it's about.

"Really? With everything that's going on, you don't want to add your side of the story?"

"I don't want—I don't have anything to say about that." Never mind that I have no idea what *that* is. I try to channel my father's confidence, the way he firmly but politely shuts a conversation down when he no longer feels in control of it. Jamie explained how he does it during one of our first training sessions. "Remember you have power too. Remember you can choose to engage or disengage."

Jackie raises her eyebrows and uses her thumb to fan the corner of the pile of sea-green papers she's been handing out.

I want to know what's on them—something horrible about my dad, I'm sure—but instead of asking her I square my shoulders and decide to quietly stare her down. Thank god I'm holding my books across my chest, otherwise she'd probably see my hands shake. Jackie looks at me vaguely confused, like I'm a blurry picture on her phone and she's waiting for me to load. I give her nothing, afraid to even blink, until Zoey clears her throat and asks if we're going to lunch or not.

"That's fine. You have such a unique perspective, but suit yourself . . ." Jackie lets her voice trail off as she starts to walk away, but then she turns back around. "If you ever want to talk, Mari—"

"It's Mariana," I blurt out, breaking my silence to correct her. I pronounce the vowels and the r softly, so it flows the way it's meant to. "Only my friends and family call me Mari." I say it in Spanish, like sea, like mar. My name is like the ocean.

"I'll remember that," Jackie says, smiling like she's pleased with something, though I can't figure out what it could be. She rushes off without another word. We watch her turn the corner at the end of the hallway.

"That . . . was intense," Vivi says.

We head to our usual lunch spot in the school's central courtyard. By the time we sit down, I feel dazed and like I just finished darting up a flight of stairs. I try to catch my breath as I take out my lunch. Taped to a bag of Ricky's Goldfish that Gloria packed because we're out of chips is a napkin note that reads, "Sea you soon, Mari Mar." Underneath it, she drew a school of fish. For a second it makes me laugh, but then it dawns on me.

The sea. Jackie's sea of diversity. Strong and unstoppable.

"Oh my god. Of course. You guys, it was her." Vivi and Zoey stare at me blankly. "Jackie. *She's* the one who wrote on my dad's picture."

"I don't know, Mari," Vivi says gently. "It doesn't really seem like her style."

"Yeah . . . she doesn't exactly hide her opinions. Why would she put it in an old yearbook?" Zoey adds.

I don't know. Maybe I'm jumping to conclusions. All I know is I feel unsettled after our encounter.

"I think I should talk to her," I say, gathering my things.

"What? Right now?" Vivi asks.

"She's registering students to vote outside the gym," Zoey says. We both look at her, surprised that she would know this, but she just shrugs and takes forever to chew a bite of her sandwich before adding, "She said so. At the library. You didn't hear?"

I must've been too busy hiding to catch the last part of her speech. If Zoey's right, that means she's not far—just a quick walk across the courtyard and through the science building, and I'll be face to face with the one person I've been avoiding for days.

"Come on." I start making my way before I can change my mind. Before I even think of what I'll say. This is probably not the best move, but I'm just so anxious to do something, anything, that doesn't involve me hiding or shutting up that suddenly no other plan really matters. It's kind of like that moment before you jump into a freezing pool, when you know it's going to suck but you're already committed and running, unable to stop and both scared and excited at once. Like maybe you're only doing it for the impact.

We turn the corner toward the gym and follow poster boards that read, ARE YOU 18 OR WILL BE BY ELECTION DAY? REGISTER TO VOTE TODAY. A small group of students stand in a line and at the end of it, there's Jackie. Filling out forms and stacking them into neat little piles. Flashing each student a crisp, white smile and high-fiving them like civics is the most exciting thing in the world. She has a whole setup with her table and a blue canopy that's plastered with signs and stickers, which show the date of the election, the last day to register, and a bunch of GET OUT THE VOTE logos. By the far-off end of the table, away from Jackie and all the students, there's a poster that has the words KNOW YOUR CANDIDATES in big block letters. A neon yellow arrow points down at what looks like a stack of sea-green papers, but as I get closer I see they're actually baby blue. So, not the forms Jackie was handing out at the library. I pick one up and see that it's a voter's guide.

DO YOU KNOW YOUR CANDIDATE'S POSITION ON THE ISSUES THAT MATTER TO YOU?

Below the headline, a chart lists each candidate and their stance on several issues, everything from foreign policy to taxes to immigration and LGBTQ rights. The columns are tiny, so it only lists their last names. I scan it and find RUIZ four squares from the top.

"Mariana!" I set the paper down at the sound of Jackie's voice. "You came. Did you change your mind?"

"What? No. No. I was just . . . looking?" My tone rises at the last syllable. I sound like a shopper talking to an overeager salesperson. To make matters worse, just to have something to do with my hands, I start straightening up the stack of papers.

"You can take one of those, you know."

I wonder what she's trying to get at. Does she think I actually *need* one? As if I don't know my own father. "No, thanks. I'm good."

"Okay . . . well, can I help you with anything?"

"Did you write in the yearbook?" I blurt out. "About my dad?"

She looks as confused as I must sound. "The yearbook? I write for the paper. That's why I wanted to interview you—"

"About my father?" I say again.

"I don't think you get what I'm trying to do."

"I'm pretty sure I do. I wish you'd just leave me out of it."

She studies my face. I can feel the edges of my lips start to shake, so I turn away and go back to fixating on the papers. I can't stop staring at the little square with Papi's name on it. Our name on it.

"Seriously, take one. They're free."

"I'm fine, okay? It's nothing I don't already know." I step away, afraid if I say another word Jackie will know I'm lying, will know that she's already won whatever game it is she's playing. Her face turns into a semifrown and then she kind of just shakes it off before quickly turning her attention to someone else in line.

I find Vivi and signal for us to go, grateful that she knows me well enough not to ask how it went. I'm so embarrassed that I begin to feel lightheaded, a clump of regret climbing up my spine and blocking all the air from my brain. It courses through my blood and my veins, a nervous energy that I can't get rid of no matter how much I try to focus on anything else.

I get to class and tap my pencil against my notebook, waiting for today's lecture to begin. When it finally does, none of what Ms. Walker says registers. All I can think to write at the top of the page is the one question I haven't been able to get out of my head since I saw it.

Do you know your candidate's position on the issues that matter to you?

I spend the rest of the period trying to list the answers, but I come up completely blank.

four

The Florida primary elections are in exactly three weeks, and the big home interview is this Friday, just three days away. I know this because Joe wrote a countdown on the mini whiteboard that hangs on our fridge. Joe has been on Papi's staff for years, and he's always stopping by the house to pick up things that he says are for the office, but that are actually personal things for Papi like an extra tie or his blood pressure and allergy pills. It wouldn't bother me so much, except for the fact that we also use the whiteboard to set reminders for Papi's medications, and every time Joe changes the numbers for the day's countdown, he smudges the dosage information. Papi's going to have a massive sneezing fit and a mild heart attack one day because Joe can't be bothered to use a calendar.

This afternoon I find Joe standing against the sink, eating a bowl of leftover picadillo that Gloria made last night. He's got a paper towel tucked into his collar, and in between bites he checks his phone.

"Hey. What brings you here this time?" I ask. It's not the way it used to be, when Papi ran his campaigns out of our apartment. There are no yard signs to pick up here, no boxes full of files or mailings that need to be collated.

He swallows a mouthful of beef. "I told your mom I'd take

Gloria to Publix. Then I gotta get back to campaign HQ to prep for the rally tomorrow."

He actually says HQ instead of headquarters. Then he looks at his watch and points at me with his fingers in the shape of a gun. "Two forty-five sharp. Remind your mom for me?"

"Yeah. Fine." Mami is the last person who needs reminding. Sometimes I think Joe makes up tasks just to feel useful.

"Do you know what you're wearing yet?" He says this like he thinks we're bonding, like choosing a new outfit is the only way I'd ever get excited about Papi's campaign.

"I'll figure something out."

"Don't be nervous. Remember what Jamie taught you. Your role is a supportive one. You'll just be in the background." Joe is always repeating Jamie's media coaching tips to me, which makes me wonder if Papi told him about my stage fright. I begged him to keep it a secret, but I guess even Joe doesn't have to be a genius to figure out that I'm uncomfortable in front of the camera.

You know what I never noticed until I got on TV? It's not just that my palms sweat almost as much as my armpits or that my pulse is suddenly louder than a Nochebuena party right before someone calls the cops with a noise complaint. It's that I forget how to be human. I have to remind myself to breathe, to put one foot in front of the other, to keep my weight evenly distributed so I don't just suddenly fall to the ground, even if I'm standing still. And making my face look natural is really hard. There is either smile or don't smile, nothing in between.

It's the same with my hands—nothing I do with them feels right when people are watching. Essentially, my body shuts down, and everything that happens next is a blur. No matter how much I focus on the present moment, or try to "be here now" like Jamie says, I inevitably go on autopilot like some kind of robot. A nodding, smiling, clapping teenage robot.

"Do you think he'll get a big crowd? With everything that's going on?"

"Big, yes. Good? That's the real question."

"Hi, Cup of Joe." Gloria rushes into the kitchen rummaging through her purse. "Sorry, sorry." When she looks up and sees me, she asks me in Spanish, "You're coming with us?" in a tone that I know is asking not *if* but *will you please.*

I smile at Gloria and nod. No one but her gets it. No one else will admit that Joe can be creepy. It's as if every minute you talk to him, he's trying to test the boundaries of what he can and can't say to you. Or maybe he's just one of those people who is deep down insecure and struggles to hide his awkwardness. That's still no excuse for the time he asked if I had body piercings he couldn't see, or told Gloria that the pictures of her school days in Nicaragua were nice because she was so much thinner back then.

It's why Gloria calls him Cup of Joe. When she learned it was an idiom for coffee she said, "That makes sense. More than one cup and he gets on your last nerve."

Gloria puts the grocery list in her purse and ties her hair up in a messy bun. Joe's gaze travels up and down her neck and

I push my chair back under our glass table. It scrapes against the marble tiles and startles him.

"We going? I need to be back soon too," I say.

While Gloria and I do groceries, Joe wanders to the deli section and orders himself a sub. Chicken tenders and honey mustard on a whole wheat roll with pickles, onions, oil, and vinegar. He says it like it's all one word.

"You guys want? I can wait for yours to come out while you shop," he says, pointing at a green wire table by the deli's café. "I have a bunch of messages I need to take care of anyway."

"Thanks. I'll have the same but with muenster and tomatoes," I tell the woman behind the counter.

"Tell Gloria not to take too long," Joe says. I shoot him an annoyed look and he adds, "You don't want your sandwich getting soggy."

I chuckle at the thought of Joe thinking he knows what I want or don't want. It's so typical of Papi's staff. I'd hate it if it weren't for the fact that it's nice to know some things are mine. They can tell me how to dress, what to say, and how to act, but they can't control the things I feel and want. Even if it's just a Publix sub that's a little soaked with tomato juice around the edges.

I grab a basket, find Gloria by the produce, and ask her if I can help.

"Of course. Gracias, Mari." She tears off a section of the grocery list and hands it to me. It's all written in Mami's perfect, nearly microscopic cursive. "Actually, if we hurry, I can convince him to stop by my apartment on the way home. I have some books I need to pick up."

The thought of seeing Gloria's apartment excites me. In the four years she's worked with us, I've often wondered where she goes home to on the weekends. The most she's ever told me is that her place is tiny and she shares it with her room-mate, Amarys, who's from the Dominican Republic and plays practical jokes like putting decals on the windows that make it look like the glass is broken. Amarys loves to make her worry, is what Gloria will say, though she never looks worried, just amused.

We load the groceries into Joe's trunk and Gloria sits in the front so she can give him directions to her place. It's a few minutes from the Publix, off a back road that hugs the edge of US 1, right around the corner from the Metrorail station. Joe rolls down his window to spit out his gum and the sound of the train rattling overhead fills the air. We pass a small strip of stores with a Domino's, a barber shop, and a nail salon with $27 MANI-PEDIS written in blue letters on the glass. Gloria's place is in the last building on the street, which is about a third the size of the others. It's shaped like a U that someone divided into several units, and the center courtyard is filled with overgrown palm trees.

Joe parks at a spot marked RESERVED and Gloria and I snap off our seat belts at the same time.

"Entro y salgo. Just wait here," she tells me. I watch her dash off and disappear behind a staircase as she makes her way up. Through the bars of the hallway balcony, I catch a glimpse of the purple scrubs she wears as a uniform, but I can't make out which door she goes into.

Joe drums at his steering wheel with his thumbs, even though the radio's turned way down.

"You okay?" I ask.

"Yeah. Just staying alert. We don't exactly blend in around this neighborhood with my car, you know?"

I get what he's implying. "You drive a Subaru, Joe."

"It's brand new."

I roll down the window and let the breeze massage my hair. The driveway is full of potholes and the buildings look nothing like the new ones being constructed in our neighborhood. These have stucco walls and terra-cotta tiles on the roofs, but they're faded and cracked in places. "It reminds me of one of our old apartments. We lived on the first floor of a building just like this."

"Bet your parents are glad that's behind you now."

"I liked it," I say, still looking out the window. "I like it."

What I remember most was all the noise. Kids actually played on the sidewalks, and because our air conditioner was never working, my parents would leave the windows open. I used to stare out at the streets through the screen and pretend the little squares were pieces of the world I could place in my pockets.

Gloria bounces down the steps hugging a stack of books. She's been studying to take her citizenship exam in a few months.

"Ready to go, *muchachas*?" Joe emphasizes this word like it's a joke to him, so exotic. He loves referring to me and Gloria this way, except for when it's just me. He calls me *muchachita*, which is even creepier. I'm no one's little girl. Least of all Joe's.

"Sorry," she says, even though she didn't even take five minutes. "Amarys te manda saludos."

"Really?" A giddy smile spreads across my face. If Amarys had meant to say hello to both me and Joe, Gloria would've said so in English, but she didn't. "I wish I could meet her."

"Maybe one of these days," she says.

I gasp in excitement and cover my mouth.

"What? What?" Joe startles, looking over his shoulder as he pulls out of the parking lot.

"No, nothing. I thought I had to sneeze."

"Promise you won't do that during Friday's interview. It makes you seem flaky."

Sometimes, and I mean very rarely, I get so annoyed at Joe that I almost feel bad about it. He tries so hard to make everything perfect for my father that he goes too far. And he's so excited about this nightmare of an interview you'd think it was his dream come true. Well, it definitely wasn't mine. I never asked to be paraded around in front of millions. I never agreed to offer up my bedroom for the world to dissect. My life is not some throwback *MTV Cribs* episode.

"How are today's polls looking?" I ask.

He answers the same way he always does. "Unreliable."

five

When I get home, the smell of paint hits me as I climb the stairs. A rustling, crunching sound, like packaging paper being stepped on, is coming from my room.

"After this room is done, I left some blue paint in my son's room down the hall." Mami's voice sounds rushed but focused. Even before I walk in, I picture her texting with one hand while the other points in the direction of Ricky's room. It's exactly how I find her, along with two men in work clothes. One of them kneels on the floor, running tape over the edges of the walls. The other pours a can of pale purple paint onto a tray.

"Mami, oh my god! What are you doing?"

My bed, my desk, and my dresser have all been pushed to the center of the room, huddled together like they're chatting. My bookshelf has been shoved a few feet off the wall, and my vintage Lucille Ball Barbie is tipped over, facedown, on the floor.

"Mami! A little respect for my space, please." The doll is protected in its box, but that's not the point. Mami should understand my *I Love Lucy* obsession better than anyone—she was the one who got me hooked on Lucy's boxed set of DVDs years ago. I've seen all the episodes, even the one-hour specials, multiple times. "You know I don't let anyone touch this." While she's still turned around, I check the space on the shelf where the box used to be. My journal's dark wooden cover sits face out, totally exposed, in the same spot I've been hiding it since freshman year. I feel my face get hot, blow up like a balloon, as I casually place the box back in front of the journal.

"I'm so sorry, Mari. I told you, we're doing touchups around the house."

"You never said that included my room."

"Of course I did. It must've slipped your mind." A look of dread sweeps over her. "Ay dios mío, or did it slip mine? I'm so sorry, I thought I . . ." her phone beeps and her voice trails off into Spanish.

There's a pile of folded clothes on my bed that Gloria probably left there—bras and panties are lined in colorful, neat stacks next to a bunch of notebooks and picture frames that the painters must've taken off my desk when they moved it. Everything's just clustered together like it's nothing, like no boundaries exist anymore. "How could you just let people go through all my stuff?" I gather as much as I can into my arms and walk into my closet, shutting the door behind me.

Through the white wooden panels, I hear my mom's voice grow soft and singsongy. "Mari. Don't make this bigger than it is. It's just paint. It's the same color."

"It's Purple Majesty," one of the painter guys says in a deep, croaky voice.

I remember. I picked it out when I was eleven, thinking the name would make Papi happy. It reminds me of those mystery ice cream flavors they pump full of food dye. It'd look so ridiculous on television.

"It's not just paint," I shout as I begin stuffing my underwear into its drawers. Out of habit, I check the very back for the glow-in-the-dark thong that Vivi bought for me online as a joke. It says "angel" and then "devil" when you turn off the lights. "Because you're the pure and innocent one, get it?" she said. I wore it once, and then I washed it by hand and hung it to dry underneath a hand towel in my bathroom so that Gloria wouldn't find it in my laundry basket. The next day after school, I found the hand towel on my bed, washed and folded with the thong tucked into it. It was weeks before I could look Gloria in the eyes again.

"What do you want me to do, Mari?"

I groan loud enough so she can hear me. "Can you at least make it an off-white?"

Mami whips open the closet door, startling me. "Fine. You're lucky we have Cinnamon Oatmeal in the garage." She turns to the painters and adds, "She grows out of everything so fast. Acaba de cumplir quince."

Even though I turned fifteen last month, my parents decided against throwing me a quinceañera in the middle of election season. Papi suggested waiting until next year instead —*What could be more American than a sweet sixteen at the White House?* Mami warned him not to get overconfident, but in the end she agreed. She'd been planning on helping me shop for my dress and choreographing my court dance. She'd even saved a bunch of YouTube videos for ideas. To be honest, though, I was relieved. Where was I going to find fourteen girls and guys to dance at my quinceañera? I would've been too embarrassed to ask anyone but Vivi and Zoey.

Mami regretted it the day of my birthday, though. After I blew out my candles over an ice cream cake that was partly melted because Papi was late from work yet again, she pulled him into the hallway, pretending they were getting my gift. Of course I got up to eavesdrop.

"We'll never get this moment back," she said to him. "How much more of our lives will we give up before it's no longer worth it?"

I think of that question constantly. Like right now, when Mami looks super tired but also super wired, as if she's afraid that if she stops moving, she'll never start again. She takes a deep breath and signals for me to walk with her into the hallway. "Your father wanted you to have these. For your room." Resting against the wall are a couple of framed pictures of our family—the day we all went to the beach for Father's Day, and the four of us backstage before he announced he'd be running last year. There's also a giant, red-rimmed photo of a sunset over a lake and the words WISH ON THE SUN. ONLY THE BIGGEST STAR FOR YOUR BIGGEST DREAMS.

Where does my father find these things? I hope this was another one of those personal errands he sends Joe on when he's too busy to make "thoughtful" family gestures. I can live with Joe being unoriginal and cheesy. ¿Pero Papi? Please. Just, no.

"Seriously? Just tell them to skip my room," I say. "Tell them to skip *me*. I beg you."

"Mariana. You know how important it is that every step of his campaign go smoothly."

"Me not being there is not that big of a deal."

"We have to do what we can to help his chances . . ."

"Even give up your kids' privacy? Honestly, Mami, is it even worth it?"

Her head jolts back a little, like she's dodging a punch, and she begins to blink. "Please don't make me seem like the bad one. It wasn't my first choice, but it's our final decision."

"*His* final decision. Why does *he* always get to make them? Why not *you*?"

Mami looks stunned. Seriously hurt to the point that I almost apologize. Then I remember that even if she agreed with me, she'd never go against my father's wishes to say so.

"You know what? Tell them to hang these up wherever you want when they're done," I say. "It's not like you care what I think."

"Hijita . . ."

The painter comes back upstairs with the can of paint and asks her if it's the right color.

"That's the one," she says, way too cheerfully.

"Yeah. Go to town." I step into my room one last time, grab my laptop and leave them to it.

• • •

There aren't a lot of places in my house you can go to be alone. Everything is exposed, and one room kind of flows into the other. "Open-spaced floor plan" is what the real estate people call it. Sunlight everywhere. Columns and arches instead of doorways. I used to love it because the house felt cheerful and warm, like summer, but lately it just leaves me with the sense that I'm on display.

I head outside. The canal that runs behind our backyard is extra calm today, but looking at it doesn't bring me any sense of peace like it normally would. I sit along the edge of our pool with my feet in the water, wishing I could jump inside and scream. Instead I FaceTime Vivi. My laptop screen is dim from all the sunlight, but I can tell right away that she's been crying. Her voice is nasal and she's slouched over her desk, rubbing her forehead and blinking like eight hundred times a second.

I almost don't want to ask. Vivi's parents are going through a divorce, and they're being horrible about it, always fighting in front of her and making her a go-between for their arguments. "What's wrong?"

She grabs a tissue and blows her nose like she's an elephant. "We're moving. My parents are selling the house. They couldn't agree on who gets to keep it so now nobody does."

She's full-out crying by the time she stops to take a breath. I think I might cry, too, but I try to hold it together for Vivi's sake. We can't both break down at the same time. That's essentially the one rule in our entire friendship: we can be vulnerable in front of each other because we're strong for each other, in the moments we each most need it.

"Oh, Vivi. I'm so sorry." I know it's not much, but it's the only thing I can think to say.

"It's not fair."

"Where will you guys go?"

"Probably Miami Beach for now. With my aunt and Abuela. My mom doubts we'll be able to stay in South Miami. It's too expensive."

My breath catches and I almost drop my laptop into the pool. "Does that mean . . . would you have to switch schools?"

Vivi breaks into a loud sob and I cringe for having asked. "Maybe. I don't know. Mom says she's looking at apartments. You know the ones on Eighty-eighth? Right by the Dairy Queen?"

"We actually lived there," I say, "when I was little." My brother and I used to sleep on the couch cushions on the living room floor. It was a one bedroom, and my parents couldn't afford another mattress while my dad finished law school and my mom worked to pay our bills.

"Yeah, well, apparently they're super expensive now. My mom says the owners remodeled the units and suddenly they think they're like South Beach. So who knows."

"But . . . in the middle of sophomore year?" I can't bear the thought of facing school without Vivi, not after she's back in my life again all these years later.

"Ugh, Mari! Stop asking me so many questions. I don't

knowww," she says, with a whine that stretches out her words. "Let's just change the subject—what's up with you? You looked upset about something when I answered."

That's the thing about Vivi. She never hesitates to call me out on things, and it's mostly a good thing. But how spoiled would I sound, complaining about how my mom is getting my room painted?

"I was just thinking about Jackie Velez. I wish she'd keep me out of whatever it is she's doing," I say instead.

"But you told her no. And you held your shit together. You should be super proud. I am. My Mari is ready to take on the world," she says in a cutesy voice. Vivi is only six months older than me, but she loves to joke that I'm like the little sister she never had.

"Not helping, Vi. I swear, at one point I thought I might cry from embarrassment. I barely held it together."

"Did you or did you not *not* have any bodily fluids leave your body during your interaction?"

I giggle. Vivi can make anything sound sexual. "Maybe a little sweat."

"Doesn't count. Nobody saw or smelled it."

"Gross, Vi!"

"Oh my god, don't be so squeamish! I'm just saying, it felt good, right? Not letting her intimidate you?"

She has a point. Still, it doesn't solve my Jackie problem. Just because I turned down being interviewed doesn't mean she won't write about me, or about Papi again. I take my feet out of the water and let the breeze and the sun dry them off. "I should've asked about her story more." Until the Bubble Boy fiasco, Papi had never showed up on Jackie's radar. She's usually tackling bigger political issues, and not just online either. The first week of school, she almost got expelled for setting up a giant mirror in front of the school entrance. She had painted "We are all complicit" across the glass, and then she'd written things like *racism, police brutality, femicide, xenophobia, Trump, homophobia,* and *climate change* over and over until you couldn't see your reflection without seeing the words first. It was actually kind of cool until the wind picked up and shattered it to pieces. I guess Jackie didn't take into account that it was still hurricane season.

Principal Avila said she could've killed someone. I wouldn't go that far, but there definitely could've been real blood instead of the cheap red acrylic paint she probably stole from the art lab. Literally everyone and their mothers were talking about it, calling for her to be expelled. Even Papi heard about it, to the point that he felt the need to text me several times to stay away from her. The PTA complained that the school can't allow student protests if they endanger student safety. By lunch, Jackie had posted a picture of the shattered mirror online with a super-long caption explaining that its destruction symbolized how we all must work to dismantle oppression. And then Jackie wrote a piece in the school paper about First Amendment rights and then that went viral because one of the editors at *Teen Vogue* retweeted it, and it became this huge weeklong drama that ended with Jackie getting three days of in-school suspension but also permission to create her own student activist group that'd be recognized as an official school club so long as a teacher volunteered to advise it.

So yeah, that's how I first learned about Jackie Velez. When she sets her mind to something, she's pretty much unstoppable. Which was fine until she set her mind on me.

six

My father's campaign slogan is *Rebuilding America*. Before he officially announced his candidacy, my mother spent months trying to come up with it. She's written all his other campaign slogans, so it only made sense, but then my father insisted on hiring an ad agency.

Sometimes he'd run their ideas by us. I was studying for midterms when he popped his head into my room and said, "Integrity First, what do you think?" and before I could answer, he shook his head and said, "It doesn't say anything about my plans. We need to be less vague."

Mami was the one who suggested *Rebuilding America* after he turned down countless others and spent thousands. The agency took the idea and ran with it. They created a logo with the *America* much bigger than the *Rebuilding*, so it looks like one word is propping up the other.

He showed it to me and my brother one night when he was actually home for dinner. "What do you think?"

"Cool! It looks like Legos," Ricky said.

"It's very nice, but no work at the table," Mami said.

"Of course. And you know, it's just a rough concept," Papi said. "But the agency did a great job." Then he kissed my mother on the forehead. "What would I do without you?"

"No tengo idea," Mami said, which is how she always responds when he asks.

I like the slogan because it feels true to our roots.

It reminds me of my great-grandfather, who died before my grandparents left Cuba, but who built the house my mother's father was born in with his own hands. When Abuelo arrived in Miami, he worked in construction for years until his back gave out. Then he went to trade school and became an electrician.

He took pride in the kind of work that makes our country run, Papi always says.

I first heard these stories in Papi's early speeches, but I know the details no one else does. That Abuelo's electrician's toolkit, a thick canvas bag made up of tightly packed compartments, used to be navy blue. It's now faded and sits by his television, the color of the sky. It's the size of a shoebox and heavier than a gallon of milk. I know every bank, strip mall, car dealership, and home Abuelo helped build in Miami, because he always points them out to me as we drive past.

According to Papi, Rebuilding America is both a vision and a plan. It's literal and figurative.

It's about erecting buildings and bridges, roads and homes, and knowing that what makes them stand strong is the American spirit.

I know that Abuelo's back has never stopped hurting him, even though he won't admit it. After Abuela died five years ago, he asked me to help him plant avocado trees in their garden in her memory. He took the seed from the last meal they shared, and with a couple of toothpicks he submerged half of it in water until it sprouted. Months later he dug a hole and planted it. Now there are three trees, each grown from the seed of the other. Abuelo speaks about them like they are a family: abuela, mamá, hija.

Rebuilding starts at home, at the dinner table, with the whole family.

Once, while Mami drove us to one of Papi's weekend rallies, I asked him why he never talks about my abuelos on his side of the family during his campaign speeches, or at all, really. He said that just because he doesn't talk about his parents doesn't mean he doesn't think about them every day. He got quiet and started pinching his thumb like he was trying to make his fingerprint go away. I wondered if this was the end of the conversation, and then his phone rang.

"Trust me," Mami whispered. We were at a red light, and she caught my eye in the rearview mirror. "What happened to your abuelo and tío abuelo in Fidel's prisons . . . your Papi's only heard stories, of course. Your grandmother was pregnant with him when she got here. But even so. It stays with a person. Sometimes the things you don't remember are the things everyone else tends to forget."

Maybe he heard us. Maybe he'd kept thinking about his father the whole time he discussed whatever very important topic he was talking about with his staff. When he hung up, Papi started searching for something in the center console. "Some stories you just don't pass down," he said, never looking up at me. "It's not worth the pain, hijita."

Then he popped a mint and began rehearsing his speech in the car.

Our country has been hurting, and now we must heal together.

It's the night before the big Hialeah rally and we haven't had dinner yet because Papi's flight home from DC was delayed. He'll be in town just a few days—for tomorrow's rally and Friday's Home Invasion interview—before he heads out on the campaign trail again. Mami wants us to all eat together given we have so little time as a family lately, but Ricky's hunched over the table with his head on the glass, clutching his stomach.

"I'm suuuper hungry . . ." he says.

"Have a snack. But please, papito, no te quejes. I had my fill of complaints at this afternoon's meet-and-greet," Mami says.

"Are people still mad about Papi's debate comments?" I ask.

"Not as much. Now they're back to their usual gripes."

"Like what?"

"Ay, Mari. You know I don't like talking about these things at the table."

At dinner, at lunch, or any other meal for that matter. I once heard a reporter ask Mami how she balances the duties of motherhood with being a politician's wife. She said that she keeps the two separate. "We don't talk politics with our children."

It never used to bother me, but lately it seems hypocritical. Don't talk politics with your kids, but make them pose for your campaign pictures. Don't talk politics with your kids, but have them say they approve your message in sketchy videos that maybe are or maybe aren't for the PACs. Don't talk politics with your kids, but expect them to support your policies.

Our food is on plates in the oven waiting to be reheated. Gloria finished eating an hour ago, washed the dishes, and went to her room for the night. The dishes are all piled up and drying on the counter because Gloria never had a dishwasher back home, and though she's learned how to use ours, she doesn't like it. She's never told me why, but she says a person's habits are a person's habits, y ya.

The alarm chimes and I hear my father's footsteps making their way through the living room and into the kitchen. He's trailed by Joe, who picked him up at the airport. Ricky dashes out of his chair to give my father a hug. He's at that cute, awkward height where his arms wrap around my father's butt, but he's too young to be embarrassed by it.

"Say hello to your father," Mami whispers. Before I can get up, he's already standing behind me. He bends over and kisses me so hard I feel his skull dig into my cheekbone.

"I missed you," he says. "I was starting to wonder if I'd ever be home." I hate it when he jokes about this, because I sometimes wonder the same thing, except for real.

While we eat, Mami fills him in on how the home improvements are going, and how they finished painting my room today. Joe sits at the end of the table, a few seats away from us, scribbling on a stack of pink and green notecards.

"What are those? Are those for me?" I ask.

"Just some last-minute edits for Friday. You won't have to

memorize anything new," he says. "It's all the same talking points, but a little more refined."

I set my fork on my plate, letting it clank as I sink into my chair.

"What's wrong?" Mami asks.

"So now I'm not refined enough? This is so ridiculous. I'm tired of pretending to be someone I'm not."

Papi looks at me, confused. His ears droop down along with his whole face, and then, as if he just figured something out, he smiles. "Hijita, no one's asking you to be someone you're not. We're just helping you to be the best version of yourself."

"No, you're asking me to be the version *you* want. No one ever asked me what *I* think about the issues. No one ever tried to get *my* side of the story."

The second the words are out of my mouth it hits me: no one except Jackie Velez.

"¡Que your side ni que your side!" Papi says, like it's cute.

I sit up straighter, leaning toward him. "I'm serious. If everyone's going to be judging me, then at least—"

My father laughs and, immediately, Joe joins him. "Sweetie, if anyone's being judged here, it's me."

Don't call me sweetie, I want to say. *Don't you dare laugh at me and call me sweetie.* But I know by the look on Mami's face that now's not the time to talk back to my father. Like it ever is. I take a deep breath and try to keep my voice calm, even though inside I'm shaking. "So then I shouldn't have to do it. I'm going to the rally tomorrow. I'm going to be standing behind you on stage like always. But this interview. Please . . . please don't make me do it."

He doesn't find this funny anymore. Good, because I'm being serious.

"You're just nervous. For no reason. How many times have we told you not to be afraid?"

But all I hear is: *How many times have we not listened?*

He sets aside his plate, stands up, and takes a manila folder out of his briefcase.

I'm so mad my fork shakes in my hand. I let my teeth scrape across the metal as I place a way-too-large bite of rice and pork in my mouth. I know what he's doing. He thinks if he ignores me long enough I'll eventually get tired of protesting. That's what my father says about anyone who criticizes him. *In the end, it's about stamina.*

My father takes more than a few seconds to glance over the papers and slaps the folder shut with both hands, as if he's trying to kill a fly that landed on its pages. "Mija, I have an idea. How about when this is all over, we take a day off, just the two of us, to have fun and just relax?" He tucks my baby hairs behind my ears as he sits down next to me.

"Where?" I ask.

"Your choice. But give me three guesses."

I take a sip of my water, pretending to ignore him.

"The beach," he says.

I shake my head.

"Venetian Pool."

Wrong again.

"The Everglades."

"Like you didn't know," I say.

He laughs so loud I almost do, too, but instead I just raise my eyebrows at him. He's not off the hook. Yet.

"You sure you're not part fish, hijita?"

I grin, puckering up my lips like a fish blowing bubbles, just twice. It's an inside joke we have, since Papi's the one who taught me how to swim when I was little. We started with me lying over his outstretched arms at the steps of our apartment building's pool, kicking and splashing, then eventually he taught me to swim in the ocean. To make me laugh anytime I got nervous, Papi would make a fish face. Just like he is doing now, right before he kisses me on the forehead.

"I'll make it up to you, I promise. For now, we need to focus on the rally tomorrow. I'm going to need all the moral support I can get. You know Harrison will be there, right?"

My face drops and I let out a sigh. Does he even hear himself? Does he even hear me? We're back at square one again, him only caring about the campaign above all else.

"Yeah. Whatever."

Harrison Irving owns the second-largest construction company in Florida. He never misses my dad's events if he can help it. We're supposed to be on our best behavior at all times, but the pressure feels extra whenever Irving's around.

Rebuilding means American steel, American workers, American grit.

It means putting up a facade of the perfect family even when inside you're falling apart.

I don't say good night, and Papi doesn't notice because he's wrapped up in some loud-whispered conversation with Joe. I go to my room—with its beige walls and cheesy posters—and plop down on my bed. The painters didn't even bother putting it back in its place.

I open my fourth-period notebook to do some homework, but it's pointless because I won't even be in class tomorrow. Still, if I don't do it now, tomorrow I'll have to do whatever makeup work I missed, and then Friday, I'll miss class again for the Home Invasion interview, and everything will just keep piling up, all on top of Joe's ridiculous notecards that I'm supposed to study like there's a final exam I have to pass, just for Papi to get all the credit. It's messed up and exhausting.

There's a light tap at the door and Mami comes inside my room. "¿Qué haces, Mari?" she asks, starting to look over my shoulder. I cover the paper with my arm. So far, all I've managed to focus on is drawing flower petals around the holes in my notebook paper, and tiny waves on the first blue line. I can't help that I doodle when I'm stressed. I stress-doodle.

"Just math stuff," I say.

"Well, don't stay up too late." Mami rubs my back and kisses me on the forehead. "We have a big day tomorrow." It irks me when she does this, acting all sweet and supportive after I've argued with Papi, even though all she did was stay quiet. Saying nothing isn't the same as taking my side. If anything, it leaves me feeling like she secretly agrees with him.

I wait until she leaves to take out my phone. I think about calling Vivi, but she's got enough to worry about with her parents splitting up. Feeling resigned, I plop onto my bed and start scrolling through my friends' posts. It's not even fun anymore because I'm not supposed to like anything. Before my dad announced his campaign, my mom took my cell and said we needed to set some ground rules for my online presence. Which basically amounted to: I'd have none. No liking posts that could be interpreted as endorsements. No posting pictures that might cause Papi problems down the line. Then —and here's the worst part—she purged nearly my entire history.

"This isn't fair. You might as well pretend I don't even exist. That'd be better than you invading my privacy like this."

"Sweetie, on the contrary. I'm protecting it."

"I don't even post those kinds of things. I'd never." My voice became a rage-filled whisper.

"Yo lo sé, preciosa. It's not you. But not everyone gets it. Tú sabes . . . when you're in politics, people will turn any innocent little thing into some huge horrible thing."

She deleted so many pictures so fast, I didn't have a chance to back them up. They were mostly selfies of me or me and my friends, but also a bunch of others: my favorite dishes, books I've read, places I've been. By the time she finished, my feed was just a bunch of sunsets and flowers. It looked like the kind of thing a bot would put together. You'd never believe there was a real person behind it.

I didn't talk to Mami for nearly a week after that. I don't know if I'll ever forgive her for making me feel so invisible. For making me feel erased. If she can delete parts of me in an instant—all because of *What will people think?*—then how is this even my life anymore? How do people I've never met get more control over it than me?

I scroll through what little survived in my library. By some miracle she missed my Favorite Videos folder at the very bottom. In it, there's a video from the last time my father and I took a day off, just the two of us, and went to the Everglades. That trip changed our lives and all I have of it is this forty-three second clip.

The sound of the breeze and birds chirping is like a song I've memorized by now, and then Papi smiles and begins talking about how beautiful it is out there. It's green everywhere. Saw palmetto leaves jut out of the water in clumps so dense, it looks like we're surrounded by land instead of water. Every once in a while, a soft-shell turtle pokes its head out and stirs the surface, but then it's quickly calm again, like a hiccup.

My father's voice doesn't boom like when he's trying to speak to a whole crowd.

These moments are everything, hijita.

The video stops and the screen goes black. I'd stopped shooting because he'd seemed nervous all of a sudden, which was so unlike him, it made me nervous. I remember thinking he was going to tell me he and Mami were getting a divorce. They'd spent so much time away from each other lately.

"I've been working really hard this year, Mari. Trying to see what the next step is for me, for our family. There are some things in this world . . . they're bigger than us, you know? That's why I love bringing you here." He went quiet and looked out at the horizon.

"It's our special place," I finally said.

"It really is." He put his arm around me; the movement made the boat rock gently, like a cradle. "I know I haven't always been a perfect father, but I'm trying. In my own way, I'm trying to make this world a better place for you and Ricky."

We took a deep breath in unison. The air smelled like a fish tank, like dampness stuck in the back of your throat.

"I've decided to run for president, Mari. Your mother and I have been exploring the possibilities, and it looks like I have a chance of winning. But I need to know you're okay with this. That we'll have each other's backs."

"What? Wow." I'd known this day was coming, but my parents always talked about it like some far-off future. I'd be an adult and Ricky would be in college, with our entire childhoods and adolescences behind us.

Papi smiled and hugged me so tight, I pushed away the small part of me that was afraid. The wind picked up, drying my eyes until they burned and filled with tears. I let the tears fall on his shirt so he would only see me smile when I finally pulled away.

"I'm really happy for you," I said.

"For us," he corrected me. "Hijita, everything I do is for us."

We went back to scanning the mangroves for alligators, and every once in a while we'd see one, its tail slivering by so quietly, it barely disturbed the water. We counted thirty-four turtles and sixty-seven white ibises, and even spotted two of their nests. The baby ibises had brownish feathers and sleepy-looking eyes, and Papi started naming each one after me, my brother, and my cousins.

"You're that one," he said, pointing at the biggest of the little ones, standing at the very edge. It had more patches of white than brown, and it looked the most like its parent, which was covered entirely in plumes the color of clouds. "Esos otros, they all look a little lost," he said. "But I have faith that that one will find her way."

seven

Papi has already left for the rally by the time I wake up in the morning. That's an upside of his busy schedule; if we're ever mad at each other, we get to skip the tense breakfasts and the good morning kisses on the cheek that make me feel like a fish being reeled in.

Mami texts me from downstairs to make sure I'm up. Normally, I consider sleeping in and missing the occasional school day a perk of the campaign, but today I resent it. I don't know how many days I have left at school with Vivi. How many more lunches watching the cafeteria marquee scroll happy birthday messages to students, painfully slowly, and seeing who can guess their names with the fewest letters?

Ven a mi cuarto, Mami texts. She wants me to get ready in her room because she has today's outfit in her closet waiting for me. I picked it out from a pile of clothes she bought weeks ago. It's a navy dress with white, swirly accents around the neckline and a matching patent leather belt around the waist. It's kind of old-fashioned, but in a cute way that reminds me of something Lucille Ball would wear in *I Love Lucy*. Mami likes the dress because the designer is American and the colors look patriotic. It's one of those Target special edition brands where they team up with a really chic label to make less expensive clothes.

"That way we won't be seen as elitist," she says as we get dressed. "They notice everything, you know."

I can't tell if she means voters or the press. I picture the cameras getting close enough to zoom in on a tag that's hanging out of the back of my dress, and just in case, I check one more time to make sure it's not.

Ricky wears the same suit he always does and changes up his clip-on tie, which is the most effort he ever has to put into his clothing. To me, he looks just like Little Ricky in those episodes where he plays the drums with his father. Mami parts his hair down the side and pats him on each hip, a silent gesture that means he's done. He sinks into the love seat in my parents' room and starts watching something on the iPad. I wait for Mami to tell him to sit up straight or he'll wrinkle his suit, but no one ever gets on his case about how he looks. Instead, Mami's eyes are fixated on my eyebrows. She moves her head side to side like a confused cat, then tells me to look a little to the left.

"I think they might be uneven," she says, grabbing a pair of tweezers. I tell her I just did my eyebrows days ago, but she holds my forehead and starts plucking.

"Ow!" It's like getting hit in the face with a bunch of ice cubes. My eyes begin to water immediately, and I try to rub them but she pushes my hands away.

"Just these two little ones right . . . here."

"Mami, they're fine." She never cared about my eyebrows before all of this. Now she's always looking at me like I'm a project that needs to be fixed.

"Maybe just a tiny bit of foundation. And mascara. What do you think?" The excitement in her voice reminds me of how she used to talk about my quinceañera, like turning fifteen meant I'd become a whole new person. I wonder how long Mami's been wanting to make me over. It's not that I don't wear makeup; I just would never wear this much. "They'll want to do your full makeup on Friday for the network interview. We might as well do a test run."

"They're going to make me look fake, aren't they?"

"You know, most girls your age love wearing makeup. It makes you look older."

"Not older, Mami. Just old."

"Ay, Mari. That's not nice."

I take a deep breath. "Can't I just sit in the background, like at the rally this afternoon?"

"I don't understand you sometimes. Why are you obsessed with hiding from the world?" She yanks a hair above my left eyebrow from the root.

I hiss in pain, but stay still. "I'm not. I'm just . . . it never bothered you ever?"

She leans back, tweezers still in hand, and looks right into my eyes. "What never bothered me?"

"Everyone watching you. Judging you." I close my eyes. Mami applies shadow on my lids in tiny, fast circles. "And it's not like *we're* the ones doing anything. It makes me feel like a prop. Like we're just a couple of trophies for him to display."

Her brush strokes become harsher, somewhere between tickling and pain. "We're not props, Mariana. We're supporting him. There's a difference."

"What if I get sick to my stomach? And you still haven't given me one good reason why they can't skip going into my room. It's *my* room."

She snaps the eyeshadow case shut and places her hand on my shoulder. "First of all, your father and I have faith in you. Just remember there's nothing to be nervous about. It's all in your head."

I've never understood why people say this last bit like it's helpful. Of course it's all in my head. Along with my entire consciousness and sense of reality.

"Second of all, the home tour . . . people just want to see that we're a normal American family, Mari. Just like any other. Mírame."

"Do they *not* think we're normal? So we have to prove it to them?"

"It's an election. It's not always going to be fair, okay?"

That's the most ridiculous thing I've ever heard my mother say. Literally nothing makes sense unless she means the opposite.

"Pero, Mami—"

Her fingertips land cold and soft against my chin. "What did I tell you last time?"

I don't answer. I look down and pick at the lint on my dress. When I first became obsessed with *I Love Lucy*, it was because Ricky Ricardo was Cuban. I liked to think he was like my father, but that only lasted a couple of seasons. Ricky Ricardo wanted Lucy out of the spotlight, while Papi kept putting us into it. I was more like Lucy, really, with no choice in the matter either way.

"Mírame," she says again, until I have no choice but to meet her eyes. "It's not just Papi running for president. It's all of us. Sometimes I don't like parts of it either, but we promised we'd support him."

"Like what parts?"

"What parts what, Mari?"

"What parts don't you like?"

"That's not important. The point is, you'll be fine. You'll be great. They'll have one or two questions for you, máximo."

"See? Why do you do that? It *is* important. Why are we just automatically supposed to agree with everything he says? No one ever asked what I thought about the issues. They just had Joe hand me a card with lines on it."

"What has gotten into you? We agreed we'd do this as a family. Did we or didn't we?"

But *agreed* implies I could've disagreed. I don't know how to explain it to her, or why, but that never felt like an option to me. Not even a little bit. I let out a sigh, tired of arguing in circles. "You used to be on my side."

"What did you say?"

I know I mumbled, but I also know she heard me. She leans into the mirror to wipe any runny eyeliner from her lashes.

But it's true. She used to listen better. She used to speak up more. Before my father's last press conference, Mami suggested keeping me and Ricky off camera. Papi wouldn't hear of it. "These beautiful, intelligent children of mine? How are you going to keep a proud father from showing the country what great kids he's raised?"

"Co-raised," Mami said.

Now she just looks at me like I've grown horns out of my head. "What's gotten into you lately? Te lo juro, sometimes I don't even recognize you anymore."

I look in the mirror, at all the crappy makeup Mami's making me wear.

Same, I want to say.

Same.

eight

Before the Bubble Boy fiasco, all you'd ever hear on the news was that my father was the party favorite. That he was exactly what they needed in order to push the reset button. Joe is convinced the public will come back around again. This morning, someone leaked a cell phone video of another candidate flirting with a thirteen-year-old girl at a gas station, and now Joe is practically giddy as we wait for Papi's rally to begin.

"It's not about the other guys being bad candidates, though. It's about your father being a great one," he says. Then he lists all the reasons Papi is so likable, as if his own daughter wouldn't already know. It's always the same spiel too—the party sends it out in a mass email so their spokespeople always hit the same talking points.

Anthony Ruiz is a young, fresh face. A Hispanic whose family epitomizes the American dream, but he's not wishy-washy on immigration. He's a self-made man who knows what it means to work hard for every cent he ever earned, not a billionaire out of touch with middle America. He hasn't been in DC long enough for it to go to his head, but he has enough government experience to lead with competence. Being from Miami and growing up among so many different cultures makes my father worldly but not elitist. Best of all, everyone sees a bit of themselves in him: every race, religion, gender, class.

"He has a way of making none of those things matter," Joe says. "He doesn't care about identity. He only sees *people*. I mean, just look at this diverse crowd. Beautiful!"

We're standing at the foot of the steps to the stage, minutes after the rally was scheduled to start, and Ricky and I have the luck of being the only people still around to hear Joe give his usual pre-rally pep talk. Everyone else is cordoned off in a grassy area near my dad's RV. I start to feel myself get pre-stage sweaty, my skin dewy like the moments before it rains. I look over and catch Papi shaking hands with his donors. Harrison Irving hasn't arrived yet. That explains why we haven't started.

"If none of that stuff matters, how come almost all his donors are rich white guys?" I say.

Ricky laughs. "Dad's a rich white guy. Is that bad?"

I shake my head and turn his shoulders so we're facing the audience again. Ricky, like my father, has pale skin that momentarily turns paper-white and then pink if you push down on it with your thumb. It's like the opposite of a bruise. But Cuban white isn't the same as white people white. Ricky's too young to remember Papi's earlier campaigns, when people used to say things like, "I'm voting for that young Spanish fellow," or "He speaks such good English. No accent or nothing." Once, a white woman at a rally told us that if it wasn't for his last name, she wouldn't have known Papi was Hispanic, and regardless, she didn't really think of him that way. I was eight, the same age Ricky is now. I asked Mami if our heritage was a bad thing, if it was something we should hide. She said no, but that some people aren't comfortable talking about race or ethnicity, so they try to pretend these things don't exist. She pointed out how our skin's darker than Papi's and Ricky's, but it's also much lighter than a lot of Cubans who are Black or indigenous. *None of this makes us any less or any better than anyone,* she said, real emphatically so I wouldn't ever forget. But I wonder when Mami slathers Ricky's face with sunblock (like she'll probably do any minute now) if it's really so his cheeks won't burn, or if it's so his features won't "get too dark," like she says ours get when we've spent a lot of time in the sun.

"You guys hot?" Joe asks. "You want something to drink?" He gives us an uneasy look and grabs a couple of small water bottles. It hasn't escaped me that the bigger the campaign gets, the smaller Joe's responsibilities. To compensate, Ricky and I have become his pet project. Yesterday, Mami told me that Joe would be taking us to school now that she'll be traveling more. They're heading to Arizona the day after the dreaded Home Invasion interview, which is now only two sleeps away. Then they'll hit Illinois, West Virginia, and Wisconsin, so Gloria will be taking care of us after school during the week. On the weekends, Abuelo will be spending the night.

"Dammit. We're behind by seven minutes." Joe raises his voice to no one in particular. "Seven minutes!" He runs off, leaving my brother and me just five steps away from the stage. I imagine climbing them, walking to the very center, alone.

Suddenly everything seems to slow down, and I feel far away, like I'm floating out of myself.

You know how when you're on a high-rise balcony looking over the glass railing, and you imagine, just for a tiny second, what it would be like to jump? Not because you really want to, but because you're curious, because there is so much space between you and the ground, it's practically unreal?

It's like that. I picture myself in front of this crowd of very important people, announcing the campaign has been canceled, and we can all go back to our previously programmed existences. It's like that because it would thrill me. It's like that because Papi would kill me.

Despite everything, when he gets onstage, it's true. He's a star. He starts by making fun of himself and they love him for it.

"You know, when my family and I launched this campaign, I had all these big dreams about doing the perfect things, saying the perfect things. And then that bubble burst." The crowd erupts into laughter and I play along, shaking my shoulders as if I'm giggling. I'm like a nervous kid in a choir, moving my mouth with no sound coming out. Papi waits just the right amount of time for the noise to die down. "So now, I think I'll just speak from the heart."

He thanks everyone for being here and for the warm welcome home. He switches to Spanish to tell a corny joke about the weather and how nobody knows how to prepare for a storm like Hialeahans, with their duct tape, nail guns, tabletops that serve as plywood, and a tin pan full of arroz con mojo heated over a can of Sterno.

"You know, the essentials." Everyone laughs again, but no one more loudly than him. It makes his whole body shake; his face brightens and his shoulders bounce toward his ears like those dancing Halloween skeletons. He makes it impossible to stay angry at him. I cover my mouth as I laugh, and then I remember Mami once told me to never be ashamed of my smile, so I lower my hands and clap instead. I let out the same deep breath I always do, the one I hold before all his speeches, the one that escapes me when he begins talking—like I'm surprised that this is who he is.

Papi walks across the stage, holding the mike close to his chest like it's always been a part of him. When he says that things will be better soon because he has a plan, it's hard not to believe him. He makes everyone feel protected. He convinces us he'll never let us down. Papi's voice echoes through the loudspeakers and the bass catches in my throat. I can't remember a time when I didn't think my father was the most powerful man in the world. Maybe soon, he will be.

nine

I'd hoped to see Vivi before going into first period English, but only Zoey is at our usual spot in the courtyard. She's eating a bagel she bought from the band members that sell them every morning, but it's so windy that her hair keeps getting caught in the cream cheese. It makes me wince; she has beautiful reddish hair that she normally wears in a bun, but today she looks oddly disheveled.

"Where's Vivi?" I ask.

"Didn't you hear? Her dad changed the locks to their house yesterday, so when she and her mom got home last night, they couldn't get in."

"Oh my god. After dance class? Poor Vivi."

"I know." Zoey's whole body slumps toward the ground. We're sitting on the cement bench beneath the stairwell of the science wing, and I scoot a couple of inches toward her and put my hand on her back. It feels awkward there, but she looks like she's about to cry, and I don't know what else to do.

"They had to sleep at her aunt's house last night. In Miami Beach," she says.

"Oh my god."

"It's horrible, right?"

I nod and wrap my arms around my stomach. I'd hoped

to ask Vivi to come over to my house for the Home Invasion interview. I figured if anyone can help me not spiral into full panic mode, it'd be her. But those plans are evaporating faster than a three o'clock rain shower, all because her dad decided to be a jerk.

"She must be crushed."

"Right? I mean, it's so unfair."

This isn't about me, but still, the timing could not possibly be worse. The interview's exactly thirty-one hours away.

"She didn't even have a change of clothes," Zoey says. "That's why she's not here today. You can't exactly show up to class in pink tights and a leotard."

"I would've lent her clothes." My mind is having a hard time catching up with my words. What if my last day at school with Vivi already happened?

"Vivi said her mom didn't want to bother anyone. And she told me to tell you that her phone's dead because her aunt doesn't have the right chargers in her house."

"This blows. It's bad enough they have to move, but to lock them out like that?"

Zoey looks over her shoulders and leans in, so close I see her pupils dilate. It occurs to me that this is probably the longest conversation we've ever had, just us two; Vivi's always been the glue that holds our trio together. She whispers, "My mom says her dad probably has some young girlfriend already, and that's why he's in such a hurry."

"What? No. That's pure speculation." Then I gasp and cover my mouth. "Oh my god. I'm starting to sound like Joe."

"Who's Joe?"

"He's this guy that works for my dad. It's nothing." The bell rings. I stand up and gather my bag. Vivi would've known what I was talking about.

When I walk into first period, Ms. Walker is writing on the whiteboard: COMMUNITY SERVICE PROPOSALS DUE TODAY!

All my blood rushes up to my face as it dawns on me that I forgot to do mine. Of course. Why wouldn't this week get worse and worse? There are signs and flyers plastered all over the school, and for months we've been getting worksheets full of questions like, *What changes would you like to see in the world? What role can you play in this change?*

I place both hands on my desk, like Jamie taught me to in our media training sessions, because she said this would help ground me in a moment. I will most definitely be very grounded very soon, which isn't fair because I've never missed an assignment before. I don't even know what excuse to give Ms. Walker, or my parents, for that matter. Mami's constantly logging into the school's site to check on my grades. There's no way she won't notice an "incomplete" and immediately tell Papi. I picture him slapping his palm on the table, saying *School is your one responsibility,* even though this is really all his fault. If I'd been in school yesterday instead of at his rally in Hialeah, somebody would have reminded me.

I sink deeper into my chair, trying to ignore both Vivi's empty seat next to mine and the one behind me, where Patrick

Franco is sitting. He lets out a burp and our whole side of the classroom giggles except for me.

Ms. Walker shoots him a look, but otherwise ignores him. "Who would like to share with us today? What do you want to do and why?"

When nobody answers, she tilts her head up and scans the room, as if she's sniffing out someone to pick on. I pray that she won't pick me. "Justine?"

From all the way in the back, a timid, high-pitched voice says something about animal shelters. "They need people to walk and play with the dogs," Justine says. I catch her eye and smile, and she turns bright red.

"That's a wonderful idea. Anyone else?"

A couple more kids volunteer before Ms. Walker can call on them. One of them plans to help write captions for YouTube videos at the School for the Hard of Hearing. Another has signed up to be a mentor with an organization that helps young refugee girls from Syria adjust to life in the United States. There's even a kid who's forming a grassroots effort to protest the use of certain soaps and chemicals in our school district.

It's becoming painfully clear that she's going to make everyone in the room share their project. I hate raising my hand in front of the whole class on a normal day, so the fact that I haven't done the work makes this exponentially worse. My heart starts to race as I try to think of what I'll say.

I'm still in shock that all three of us dropped the ball on

this. Vivi, I get. She has enough problems to worry about at home, but Zoey? Last time I checked, she's not on the verge of being homeless or navigating her father's campaign horrors. I actually don't know what's going on in her life since we're not that close, but still. What's her excuse? I lock eyes with her in the back of the room and she just raises her shoulders without a clue, like a living freaking embodiment of the shrug emoji.

"Mariana? How about you?"

This is my nightmare. My second worst nightmare. "Me?"

"Yes. What's your cause?"

Before I can say anything, Patrick scoffs behind me. "Lemme guess, you're running for president too?"

"That doesn't even make any sense," I say.

"Neither does your father."

The class erupts into a collective *oooh* and Ms. Walker tries but fails to get them to settle down.

"That's enough, Patrick. Mariana, you were saying?"

I wasn't. My mind is a complete blank. I start to wish Patrick would make another inane joke just to cause a distraction. My mouth goes dry and my words feel like rubber bands wrapped in a ball that's being stuffed down my throat.

I go through my backpack blindly and reach for my phone. It lights up and when I quickly check it, there's a text message from Papi. I dim the screen without reading it and blurt out, "Protecting the environment."

"A very important cause, Mariana. We need more environmentalists like you." Ms. Walker stands over my desk, waiting.

"I left the proposal at home. I'm sorry. My dad had that rally yesterday and . . ." I stop myself midsentence. I know how this sounds.

The whispers start up again. Behind me someone says, "That's no excuse," and some other kid mumbles something about special treatment.

"Email it to me," Ms. Walker says, loud enough for the whole class to hear. "No later than tomorrow morning. If I don't get it by then . . . I'll be very disappointed, Mariana."

Tomorrow. As in the morning of the Home Invasion interview. Ms. Walker can't imagine that my life could possibly be about so much more than school and this community service project. People like my father are trying to change the world for real, and she calls me out in front of everyone for not BS-ing a couple of aspirational paragraphs?

The whole rest of the period, I can hear Patrick breathing through his mouth behind me; he sounds like a tiny dog snoring. When the bell rings he stoops next to my desk and whispers, "See you tomorrow night, first daughter."

I roll my eyes and jam my books into my backpack. What he meant doesn't hit me until I'm halfway down the hall.

Tomorrow night. He meant tomorrow night on TV.

I walk as fast I can to the bathroom. I think I'm going to be sick.

"See you tomorrow night," he said. Because bringing a news crew into your bedroom is bringing everyone else in with it. It's like having Patrick Franco peering over my shoulder, seeing where I sleep, where I dress, where I keep my underwear and my journal and all my most private thoughts. It's like having Jackie Velez there to judge me, telling me all the ways she hates my father every time I look in the mirror. The whole world will be watching, listening, just waiting for me to mess up.

I make a run for the last stall in the girls' bathroom and close the door. Squeezing my eyes shut, I take a deep breath. The air smells like a candy version of lavender, like Abuela's house used to on Sundays, after she'd mopped the floors with Mistolín. It soothes me. I can still feel my heart pounding in my chest, but it's slower now, steady.

I hear my phone buzz in my backpack.

Papi again. There's his first text, sent thirteen minutes ago, that I ignored:

Don't be nervous about tomorrow. You're prepared. You've got this.

And then his second text, just now.

Hope you're having a good day, hijita.

It's ok, I text him back. I'm about to leave it at that but for some reason I add: Just chose my service project. Gonna help protect the environment.

That's great. We can do a beach cleanup again. I'll take a day off after FL primaries.

I smile and nod, alone in a bathroom stall. Ever since the summer between fifth and sixth grade, Papi and I have collected trash and debris that washes up along Biscayne Bay as part of a beach-wide cleanup. We pick up tons of plastic soda rings tangled in the mangroves, and bags that look like jellyfish along the shore until we get close enough to poke them and they crinkle. We do the cleanups every year, and Papi has started helping me reuse all the glass bottles in our house. Sometimes I catch him after dinner, scrubbing off the label of a jar of pasta sauce so we can use it to store other food.

That'd be cool.

Proud of you, he responds.

Me too.

ten

"She looks perfect. Doesn't she look perfect?" Mami asks no one in particular. It took the network's hair and makeup crew forever, but apparently I'm now camera-ready. My face feels like it got coated in cake frosting. They put a sealant over my lipstick that pulls on my lips when I smile. They even dabbed the bags under my eyes with green goo that blended into my skin to make the dark circles disappear.

"Here, you might need to reapply later," the makeup artist says, handing me a small tube. She places her hand under my chin and turns my face side to side to get one last look at it. "She was so excited about the interview she didn't get any sleep," she says to the hair stylist, talking like I'm not even there.

I resist the urge to tell her I was up past one in the morning last night researching the Everglades for my community service proposal, and when I finally got to sleep my brain couldn't shut up about all these facts and figures—how the swamp's shrunk to half its size, how even the alligators are not fully grown because they're short on water, how the Everglades is becoming saltier, which is bad for our drinking water. I ended up dreaming I was being chased by mini gators and giant salt shakers through Jackie Velez's home. Jackie hasn't tried to contact me again, but last I checked she's oh-so-subtly throwing me shade on Twitter.

Am looking forward to @SenAnthonyRuiz's interview tonight & a real conversation on climate change. Voters want to know what candidates will do about the issues, not what kind of toys their kids play with.

It's obvious she's hinting at the last Home Edition interview, when the congressman had a tea party with his daughters, but I know it's a dig at me too. All her talk that day outside the library about her wanting my side of the story was just that: talk. It was stupid to even entertain the idea that my thoughts on this campaign mattered. Sitting here in my overdone makeup and a dress hand-selected by my mom, I feel as powerless as those two little girls playing pretend with their father.

I try to shake myself out of it. It's too late for second guessing. I was so busy with schoolwork last night, I didn't get to rehearse Joe's edited lines more than the five or six times he made me say them. It doesn't matter, anyway. It's like cramming for a test: I'll either nail the answers in the moment, or I won't be able to retain them even if my life depends on it. Which it kind of feels like it does.

I get out of the chair and mumble thanks to the makeup artist, but she's already moved on to my mom, who's directing her to the bedroom.

"There's better light."

I take deep, chest-expanding breaths as I make my way to the kitchen, catching a glimpse of myself in the hallway mirror. Seeing my face in a handheld mirror in the makeup chair was one thing, but taking it in as a whole is bizarre. The crew insisted on making me wear fake eyelashes. They curl so far back they practically touch my eyebrows. When I'd asked them if the lashes were really necessary, the woman just looked at me and said, "You ever see a woman on television without them? Trust me, you want them."

Maybe she has a point. I once read that in the "Quiz Show" episode of *I Love Lucy*, you can tell when she's about to get her face doused with water because they're the only scenes where Lucille Ball's not wearing fake eyelashes. She looks strange without them, which has always made me sad. The camera has a way of making the real seem fake and the fake seem real.

There's no time for vanity, though. All around me, production assistants are setting up cables and lights, and Papi's staff is buzzing about like the sky's falling. I've seen my dad for all of five minutes today. Ricky, as usual, is dressed and ready, playing games on his iPad in the kitchen while Gloria makes him a snack. He seems so excited and carefree, looking at him actually brings me a bit of comfort. Then I remember the other candidate's twin daughters, with their matching yellow dresses and smiles. They're not much younger than him.

"Hey. What are you up to?"

He pauses his game and folds his hand over the tablet. Any other kid would probably never take his eyes off the screen, but Ricky has a sweetness about him, a genuine interest in paying attention to people first.

He takes one look at me and his eyes practically pop out of

their sockets. "Oh my god. What'd they do to your face?" His words are low and shaky, like he's worried my features won't ever go back to normal.

"I know. I can't wait to take it off. What about you? You okay?"

He nods. "I was just about to beat this level."

"How's school? The kids being nice to you?"

"Yeah. Why wouldn't they?"

"And Andrew? Is he watching tonight?" Andrew is the only real friend he's made this year. It must be odd being the new kid in third grade. Probably not as odd as being a new sophomore, but still.

"I don't know. We don't really talk about it."

"You don't really talk about Papi and the campaign?"

"No. It's just our parents' jobs. That'd be weird, right?"

Andrew's mom is a vet, and his father is a cop. Maybe to Ricky it'd be like asking him how many dogs his mom saw that day, or how many traffic tickets his dad gave, but this campaign is different. Huge. And definitely not your everyday job.

It always startles me that Ricky thinks this is all normal. The cameras. The rehearsing. The constant pressure of knowing any little mistake can cost Papi an entire election. "Listen, if you're ever not . . . that excited about any of this, you know you can tell me, right?"

He leans in close. "Why are we whispering? Oh my god! Are you changing your mind? Are you not going to vote for Papi?"

We have these fake ballots that Mami makes us every

election. I keep wondering when my parents will realize I'm too old for them. Clearly Ricky is still very invested. "What? No. I'm just saying . . ." I let my voice trail off. "Just have fun out there. During the interview, okay?"

He nods and goes back to his game. Our senses of reality exist worlds apart.

I'm about to head to my room to get dressed when Joe starts following me up the stairs.

"Do you need something?" I say, stopping halfway.

"Oh. Right." He backtracks and gestures silently for me to follow as he hoofs it to the kitchen and then down the narrow hallway that leads to the garage.

"What are we doing here?" I don't like how secretive he's being.

He brings his fingers to his lips, like he's about to shush me, then seems to think better of it. "It's just that I've been thinking about what you were saying the other day at dinner. About no one ever asking for your thoughts on the issues."

"You mean . . . what I said to *my dad?*" He nods and completely misses the point of what I'm implying. No one ever invited him into the conversation, but he feels free to insert himself anyway. Sometimes I wish my parents would care half as much about my in-person privacy as they do about my online privacy.

"Yeah, that. And I think you're right. I think it'd be so much more impactful if the senator's daughter was opinionated."

"You do?" What the hell. Of all the times for him to actually listen to me. We go on the air in under an hour and he thinks now's a good time to change course?

"Totally. No other candidate has a kid your age, so they wouldn't expect it. But you—"

"But that's not what I meant. I'm not ready. And I've never had a chance to talk to Papi about his policies . . . Mami doesn't like us to bring his work home, so I'd have to do more research. And, of course, it's nice to be asked, but couldn't we have prepared for this like months ago? I still don't know if I want to talk to anyone. Or if I have anything to say. Oh my god, what if I'm scared of public speaking because I have nothing to say?" I'm rambling now, spiraling through a cluster of words that make absolutely no sense until I start to see little spots in the air.

Joe waves his hands in front of me. "No no no no no! You've got this all wrong. It's fine, it's totally fine." He reaches into his shirt pocket.

"I made these for you," he says, fishing out a couple of pink notecards. "See? They're just new lines. Super simple ones. About your dad's policies. You don't have to do any research or anything. I did the work for you."

"You . . . wrote down my opinions."

"No. I mean, well, they're your dad's positions. Why wouldn't you agree with them?"

"You're serious right now. You're actually serious."

"Mari. We have no time for games. Just take the cards. I know it's last-minute, but it's for the good of the campaign."

For the good of the campaign. What about the good of

me? I snatch them from his hands just to get him to shut up. They're super thick stock, but in my hands they shake like flower petals.

"You'll read them? It's all stuff you've heard him say before. Shouldn't be hard to remember. Even just one."

I raise one finger in the air and nod. He takes my silence as agreement and gives me a thumbs-up as he walks away, leaving me alone in the empty hall. I feel like I'm going to be sick. I have to lean against the wall to catch my breath, and when I finally start flipping through the cards—catch glimpses of statements on things like property taxes, healthcare, and the importance of protecting human life—my whole body freezes in place as my heart starts racing uncontrollably.

He just assumed he could tell me what I believe. He assumed I was some thoughtless sponge that absorbed everything my father's ever said without question.

What if he's right?

I think back to all the conversations my family's had, talking about the campaign but never actual policies. To the handout Jackie insisted I take, so I could know each candidate's position. To all the times I've applauded every word of my father's speeches, too zoned out and nervous to listen.

My pulse is between my ears now, pounding against my skull. It's hard to breathe, impossible to think straight. This isn't going to end well. This isn't even beginning well. I close my eyes and think of Jamie's advice for when my nerves are through the roof. *If your body goes into overdrive, give the pent-up energy an outlet. Do some jumping jacks. Jog in place. Make giant circles with your arms. Go for a run. Do whatever it takes. Move.*

So I do.

I dart into the garage, out the side door, and run. As fast and as far as I can. I just go.

I'm at least ten blocks away from my house before I feel calm enough to stop. My lungs are burning and my heart feels like it could burst, except now it's just from the running. My body's working again. It's as if I turned it off and turned it back on. I place my hands on my hips and keep walking in the same direction I was headed. Without even thinking, I've somehow made it halfway to Vivi's house.

Except she's not there anymore, and I don't know if she ever will be. I have no idea where I'm going, no idea what's waiting for me if I head back to the house, and no other option than to keep going.

My phone buzzes in my back pocket. Shit. It's Joe.

Lmk if you need help with the cards.

I turn off the phone, squeezing the power button so hard it temporarily makes my fingers pale. If I'm going to do this —whatever the hell *this* is—I can't have Joe or my parents tracking me. I keep walking, keep trying to think. I have four one-dollar bills in my pocket and a phone that might as well be dead. It doesn't even matter that I don't know what I'm doing next. All I care about is what I'm *not* doing next. I'm not doing that damn interview.

• • •

It comes to me when I'm just a couple of blocks away from the Metrorail station: a not-so-perfect but good-enough-under-the-circumstances plan. In the time it took me to get here, the sun has already begun to set. A cluster of people wait for the light at the intersection to cross US 1, and when they walk I follow them, assuming they know where they're going more than I do. Even though we live close by, I've never actually taken the train. I don't know anyone who does, except for Gloria.

Everyone here looks like they're a regular, though. They all have cards that they swipe at the gated turnstiles before making their way in. Just like that. Como si nada.

I walk up to a turnstile to check if there's a slot for dollar bills or coins.

"You going or what?" a man behind me says. "The train'll be here any minute."

I step out of the way to let him through, and it's only then that I notice an automatic ticket booth to the side of the entrance. It's labeled EASY CARD and a bright turquoise screen guides me through a process that is anything but. It keeps freezing on me, and when it doesn't, it only gives me the option to buy a monthly pass. Overhead I can hear the heavy, windy sound of a train approaching, and from the corner of my eye, I see a security guard making his way toward me. Shit.

"What do you need?" he says, gesturing at the screen.

"I'm just trying to pay fare for a ride. Two rides," I add, realizing I have no idea how I'll get home when this is all over.

"Do you have an EASY card?"

Does it look like I have an EASY card? I want to say. Instead I shake my head no, afraid I'll sound as clueless as I feel.

He pushes a bunch of buttons and gestures for me to insert my cash in the machine. "Ahí lo tienes," he says, smiling just as the kiosk dispenses a blue card with green dots. I mumble thanks and run through the gate and up the escalator so fast, I almost go past the yellow line and over the edge of the platform. Beyond the tracks, the tops of a row of palm trees peek over the edge of the rail, and the neon lights of a strip club on the other side of the highway dot the horizon. When the train finally comes, people wander in without any sense of urgency. I stay by the doors, clutching the leather handle that hangs from a metal bar, not wanting to stand too close to anyone or miss my stop.

"Dadeland South," a voice through the PA announces as we finally arrive. Outside my window, a building flashes the words *Bare Necessity* in neon cursive letters. If I didn't know any better, I'd think I'd just gone in a circle: a strip club when I started, another when I arrive. I take the escalator down to the ground floor, where a Metrobus lets out its exhaust so loud it's like a giant sigh of relief. I finally let out a deep breath too.

In a weird way, at this moment I'm kind of grateful for Joe. If it hadn't been for him driving us to Gloria's place a few days ago, I'm not sure where I would've gone. As it is, I have no idea which apartment is Gloria's, or if her roommate is even home. I try to remember which way she went. Upstairs.

Past the palm tree that leans over the roof. I have to grab hold of the railing at the top because the realization rushes at me all at once. *Holy crap, Mariana. You really blew off this interview.*

All the apartments have identical doors and a window to their right or their left. I pass one with a "Wipe Your Paws" welcome mat. Gloria never mentioned having a pet. The next door has a potted bamboo in a square-shaped steel pot and a plain black mat. I don't know Gloria's décor style, but I know that's not it.

I stop at the end of the hall, where the railing curves around the building and looks out to the courtyard and the parking lot. The corner unit has a window that's covered by thin white blinds and there's a sticker on the glass that says PRIVATE SIGN. DO NOT READ.

It makes me chuckle as I knock on the door. It makes it so I don't even hesitate.

"Mariana?" The woman who answers is tall and slightly round. She's wearing drawstring pants and a yellow tank top, and she looks surprised to see me, but also not.

"Amarys?"

She gives me a look of a hundred questions, but asks none of them. Instead she steps aside and gestures for me to come in.

"How did you know it was me?" I don't know why, but suddenly I feel shy.

"You think Gloria never talks about you?" she teases. "And I do watch the news."

"Oh. Right." I wonder if I'll ever get used to having people I don't know feel like they know me.

"You're taller, though. In real life." As Amarys studies me, I try to imagine which news clips she's playing in her mind.

"Yeah, well . . . everyone looks short next to my dad."

She nods, but she has a look like she wants to disagree with me. "¿Entras, o no? You're gonna let the mosquitos in, mami."

I step inside. Their apartment is dark for this time of day. Aside from a small tiled entry by the door that extends into the galley kitchen, the floor is entirely covered by a shaggy beige carpet. Amarys is barefoot, so I take off my shoes before walking into the living room.

"I'm sorry to come over uninvited," I say.

She pulls out two glasses and a pitcher of filtered water from the fridge. Half her braids are tied in a bun at the crown of her head, while the rest of them sway gently over her back as she moves. "Unannounced isn't the same as uninvited. Pero ¿qué haces aquí? Don't you have someplace to be right now?" Her Dominican accent makes it sound like she's in a hurry but also really excited.

Even if I wanted to lie to her, I can't think of a story fast enough. "I just wanted to get out for a bit, go someplace quiet." This much is true, at least a really simple version of the truth. No need to get into messy details.

Worry washes over her face. "Do your parents know you're here?"

"They're too busy to notice."

She pulls out her cell phone and starts texting someone.

"Please . . . don't."

"Pero . . ."

"It's just for thirty minutes. They don't even know I'm gone." I try to sound casual and convincing, but even I don't believe the words that are coming out of my mouth.

The clock on the microwave reads 7:25 p.m., just five minutes until they go live.

"I'm just texting Gloria. In case your papis are worried."

Maybe, if I'm lucky, Gloria left her phone in her room, like she usually does, because my mom thinks it's unprofessional to be distracted by your phone while you're working. Maybe by now, she's finished helping Mami get ready and they've sent Joe looking for me. Everyone else is being told to be quiet before the cameras roll.

I take the glass of water and walk around the living room. They have a gray futon in the center of the room, and a flatscreen TV on the wall surrounded by framed pictures of Amarys and Gloria. There's one of them sitting across from each other under a tiki hut, their glasses clinked together in a toast. Another one is just of Gloria, midspin, as she's dancing in a club with lights of all colors illuminating her figure like a Christmas tree. The next one up is of Amarys and Gloria hugging two teenage-looking girls with deep brown skin and amber eyes. Amarys and Gloria are each kissing one of them on the cheek, their eyes closed, while the girls purse their lips and make a peace sign with their fingers.

"Those are my little sisters, Angela and Eva," she says,

anticipating my question before I can ask it. They look just like younger versions of her.

The top picture, the biggest one, is of her and Gloria holding one another in a restaurant booth and smiling. Gloria's hair is chin-length, much shorter in the picture than it is now, and Amarys wears hers in an afro with a purple scarf twisted like a headband.

"How long have you and Gloria lived here?"

"Four years. We moved when she got the job at your house. But we've been together eight now."

"Oh, cool." My cheeks turn warm. I can't remember if it was Gloria who called Amarys her roommate, or if it was me who just assumed. "It's nice to finally put a face to all her stories."

"Only the good ones, I hope." Amarys sits on the futon and gestures for me to do the same. The coffee table in front of us is covered with a bunch of notebooks, binders, and textbooks thicker than a Bible piled one on top of the other. There's a guide to passing the bar exam and a plastic-bound copy of the Florida constitution. Amarys clears half the space and places her phone face up in the middle of the table. I try not to look at it, though I keep it in my peripheral vision, hoping it'll stay dim and free of notifications. "Gloria's told me all the chisme about you."

"Really?"

She shakes her head and laughs. "Nah. Just that you're a smart girl who the world's gonna have to listen to one day."

I've never wondered if Gloria talks about me, but hearing

Amarys describe me like that is like getting a gift I didn't know I wanted.

"And that you're well-behaved, but only because you wanna be. She likes that."

It's weird. To have people see things in you that you don't see. I don't know how to respond, so I point at the constitution and tell her my dad has the same one in his home office.

"Don't ever read it unless you can't sleep. I swear it'll bore you to death," Amarys says.

I take another look at the clock and ask if I can watch TV.

"Dale. Put on whatever you want."

I flip to CNN just in time to see the newswoman I met a few hours ago introduce Papi and thank him for welcoming her into his home.

"It's so lovely to meet your family. I was so sad to hear your daughter Mariana was not feeling well tonight. On behalf of our entire team, please wish her our best."

Papi nods graciously. Mami looks stiff and tightlipped, like she's sucking on a piece of ice. She has one hand on his knee and the other on Ricky's, as if their bodies were a chair she's clutching. But my father . . . my father has never looked calmer. Like Joe would say, he's in his element. He answers every question like it's the beginning of the most fascinating conversation he's ever had.

I slide off the futon and inch toward the screen until I'm sitting on my knees and his face looks bigger than mine. He doesn't seem to have a care in the world.

"Your Papi's a natural," Amarys says.

"He's been preparing practically his whole life for this," I say. Despite the awfulness of the situation, I can't help but feel proud.

The newswoman chuckles at whatever it is he just said. She turns and looks down at my brother. "And what do you think about that?"

"Papi always does what he says he'll do." Ricky sounds like a gruff-voiced, child-size robot.

They go to a commercial. Amarys checks her phone again and out of instinct, I check mine. Except it's just a dark black box when it's turned off.

"Mariana, you okay?"

I hadn't noticed until she asked that my breathing is quick and heavy again.

The interview comes back on and I turn up the volume in hopes of drowning myself out. The newswoman sits on one of our beige couches while my parents and Ricky sit across from her on one identical to it. They're all squeezed together like they're about to hug.

"In just a few moments, we'll receive a tour of the Ruiz family home. But first," she crosses her legs toward my family and opens her mouth to say something, but instead she goes quiet. Her hand comes to her ear like she's swatting away a fly. In the background, I hear Papi clear his throat.

"Oh," she finally says. "Oh." She looks up at my family. "Senator Ruiz, were you aware that, for the duration of our interview this evening, your daughter has been missing?"

eleven

It's chaos. Onscreen, everyone starts talking at once. Ricky begins to cry. Mami stands up and starts yelling *What is going on?* in Spanish while Papi won't stop saying *There must be some misunderstanding, there's nothing to be concerned about,* and the news lady keeps asking him to clarify, keeps asking him where I am, keeps asking my mom to please sit back down, and everyone's talking over everyone until all I see are my mom's legs in her navy blue skirt, pacing across the screen, and all I can hear is my own breathing and Amarys's voice like it's behind a thick glass saying, "Mariana? Are you okay, mami?" and "Coño, answer your fucking phone, Gloria," and then finally, "Aquí está. She's been here the whole time. I was trying to call you! Esto es una vaina."

And then they break to commercial again and for half a second, everything goes quiet, and that's all it takes for what I've done to really sink in. I feel my blood rush away from my face, and I think I might cry, or vomit, or both. I must look pretty scary because suddenly Amarys gets really quiet and sits next to me on the floor. She places her hand on my shoulder.

"Mariana? Listen to me. I need you to breathe. Close your

eyes. Inhala. Exhala. Inhala. Exhala. Everything's going to be fine, okay?"

I do as she says, taking one deep, long breath, but when I exhale it's like I'm a balloon that someone let go of before tying the little knot. I can't control the words, or the tears.

"I just couldn't do it. I couldn't say their fake lines which I was probably going to mess up anyways in front of the whole freaking country, and they were going to go into my room, did you know that? They were going to go into my room with all their cameras and zoom in on the pictures on my desk and the posters on my walls, even though Mami replaced them with these horrible motivational posters that made my room look like a freaking fifth-grade classroom, it's like, is nothing sacred anymore? Like I don't feel constantly on display enough already. Not even this one space that's mine is mine anymore.

"I don't want to do this. They can't make me. I just wanted them to leave me alone. Just this one time, just for this one stupid interview. I begged them and they wouldn't listen. What was I supposed to do?"

By the time I'm done, Amarys is holding me, and I just know I'm like one breath away from ugly sobbing.

She hugs me so tight she rocks me side to side. "It's okay, nena. It's going to be okay. I'm not gonna lie to you . . . it's probably going to get a lot worse first. ¿Me entiendes? But you're strong and you're gonna keep being strong, and it'll get better, you got it?"

There's a knock at the door. Neither one of us moves.

Another knock, angrier this time.

"¡Ya voy!" Amarys pulls away from me so she can look me straight in the eye. "I need you to be ready for whatever happens next because it could be anything. But you're gonna get through it, okay, mami?"

I nod and try to pull myself together.

"Acuérdate lo que dice Gloria. The world's gonna have to listen to you one day. Not the other way around."

"Yeah. Okay."

She dashes for the door and opens it. Joe barges in without even looking at her.

"Jesus Christ, Mariana. Let's go. Right now. We gotta go."

He pulls me up by the arm and covers me with a black coat like I'm a fire that needs to be extinguished. I can't even feel my legs move as we rush down the stairs and toward his Subaru. Overhead, a helicopter hovers in the sky and beams a spotlight on us. I try not to look, but I can't help it. We're surrounded by microphones and cameras being shoved in our direction, and their flashes are blinding. People call out:

"Mariana, what happened to you?"

"Mariana, did you run away?"

"Are you trying to sabotage your father's campaign?"

That last question gets thrust back at me by Joe once we're safely in his car.

"What the hell were you thinking? Do you have any idea what you just did to your father? To his poll numbers? Did you even think about anyone but yourself?"

No no no no no.

This wasn't supposed to go down like this. All these people

and their questions . . . they weren't supposed to care about me. I'm just his daughter; I'm not the one running for president. I turn away from the car window, from the silhouette of Amarys watching us pull away from behind her bedroom curtain, from the reporters who have now begun shifting their attention to her apartment while the other half get in their vans to follow us.

"I thought you said the poll numbers were unreliable," I say.

"Not as unreliable as you."

That's when the tears finally come. Not the ones I've been holding in, but the ones that come rushing in their place. Hot tears. Angry tears. The kind that would never hide afraid.

twelve

Amarys was only half right. Yes, everything goes really bad, really fast, but I can't see it getting better.

The whole ride back to my house, Joe and I are followed by the news crews of the local stations. One of their vans passes us and parks across from our driveway. A reporter gets out just as Joe pulls in.

"Don't move. I'm coming around to get you," he snaps.

He opens the passenger door and holds his coat over my head again. As we run across the cobblestone, I catch a whiff of his sweat mixed with fabric softener, a whole workday's worth of body odor and stress. Mami opens the front door to our house before we've even reached it. She makes like she's about to run out, but then someone holds her back.

I hear my father yell, "¡Juli, no! Las cámaras!"

They wait until I'm inside to confront me. Mami grabs me, hugs me, and shakes me. "Do you know what you put us through? Gracias a Dios you're home. Let me get a look at you. What were you thinking?"

She runs her hands along my clothes, squeezes my arms, my face. Behind her, Papi stands rigid, waiting his turn. He looks back at everyone still in our house and yells at them to give us some privacy. "This is off the record," he says. "Mariana." It feels like forever that he just stares at me. "I don't even know what to say to you right now." He curls his right hand into a fist, his thumb sticking out in that half-raised, half-pointing way that he uses when he's addressing an audience. It makes me so angry I can't even think straight.

"Good. I don't want to hear another one of your speeches anyway," I say. The room goes quiet just as Ricky lets out a deep, breathy gasp.

"Go to your room. Now."

"As long as they don't follow!" I jerk my head toward the newswoman as I walk past and climb the stairs. She's sitting on our couch, tinier than I'd imagined she'd be, with her mouth hanging open. I slam my bedroom door as hard as I can, then press my ear against it to hear what they're saying. To my surprise, they go back on the air.

They actually go back on the air.

My father apologizes for the interruption and insists the whole thing was a misunderstanding.

I turn on my laptop to watch the rest of it live. It's just him now; Ricky and Mami are nowhere to be seen. Every time the newswoman asks about me, Papi changes the subject to family values, or how we have to provide working class families with the support they need to raise their children. His voice is flat and monotone, but he still punctuates each statement with a smile. He drones on and on until I realize he's going to keep saying nothing. I snap my laptop closed and listen to the muffled voices through the walls. The interview only lasts a few more minutes, but it takes them forever to pack up all their equipment and leave. The whole time, my father and Joe spew apologies and awkward jokes about teenagers and their mood swings.

It's only when they're gone that I remember I've had my cell phone off this entire time. I turn it on and my notifications go out of control. There must be at least thirty messages from Mami, Papi, and Joe, and a bunch from Vivi around the time the interview started.

You okay? My mom and I are watching at my aunt's. Where'd you go?

And then . . .

Got a charger, btw. The judge ordered my dad to give us keys to the house! Mom said he was soooo pissed.

Followed by . . .

You watching? This news lady is totally crushing on your dad.

And then finally . . .

OMG MARI PLEASE ANSWER U OK? THEY SAY UR MISSING!

I'm freaking out.

Where R you?

Omg Joe just called please please call me back.

I skip all the other text messages and voicemail and call Vivi. She picks up on the first ring completely out of breath.

"Please tell me it's you this time."

"Who else would it be?"

"Oh my god, Mari. Mom! It's her, it's her!" I hear footsteps clack against tile and then her mother's voice in the background thanking god and asking if I'm okay. "I don't know, let me hear!" A door slams and it goes quiet. "We thought you were kidnapped or something! Were you? Did the Secret Service find you?"

"What? No. I snuck away to Gloria's."

"Seriously? You just . . . left?"

"I told you I didn't want to do the interview."

"Yeah, but I didn't think you'd skip it! I mean, you would've been on TV."

"That's the whole point, Vivi."

"I know, but . . . wow. That is so badass, Mari."

"No, it's not. I'm going to be grounded forever. I just didn't know what else to do."

"Bet it'll make them think twice before the next interview, though."

"I guess. I hope." I let out a long, deep breath. "But what if—" I can't bring myself to ask the question out loud. What if I ruined my father's chances at the presidency? And worse . . . what if I actually feel a little relieved about it?

"What?" Vivi says.

"Nothing. I'm just tired, that's all." My body feels heavy and my leg muscles are sore from all the running. I sink into my bed, face down, leaning over the edge to let my fingertips dangle along the tile.

"Well, you won't believe who called me," Vivi says. "I was on my mom's laptop trying to see if you were online, and then you FaceTimed me and when I answered, it was Joe. He was calling around asking for you."

"He was on my laptop?!" My parents must've given him my password when they realized I was missing. Nothing is mine anymore. Maybe it never was.

"It was super awkward, Mari. He told me not to tell anyone you were missing."

"All he cares about is how things look." I think of my parents scrambling around the living room, right before the interview cut to commercial break. "How *did* it look?"

"I don't know. Like your parents had no clue what was going on. You know?"

I can't even wrap my head around it. I've never seen my parents not in control of a situation. Or at least, not pretending to be. "It's such a disaster. And none of it would've happened if they'd just left me out of it in the first place."

"It's not as bad as you think. You'll see. Everyone will forget about it in like, a week."

I wish I could hug her right now. With everything she's going through, Vivi's still trying to cheer me up. Even when I know not everything will go the way she says it will, it makes me feel better knowing that she'll have my back.

There's a knock at my door and my father walks in before I have a chance to answer. He mouths at me to get off the phone and points his finger at the ground. Right. Now.

"Vivi . . . I'm sorry. I have to go. My dad's here."

I can still hear her voice as my dad takes the phone from my hand and hangs up.

"I'll be keeping this," he says. "And you're not leaving this house unless it's to go to school. ¿Me entiendes?" He paces my room silently, squeezing his lip between his fingers like he's about to bite his nails. The makeup he's been wearing all day is clumpy, like someone sprinkled eraser dust across his cheeks. Papi doesn't just look exhausted, he looks defeated. By me. I start thinking of ways to apologize, but no words come.

"I was counting on you, Mari."

But you weren't listening, I want to say, but don't.

"Tomorrow, I'm going to clean up this mess you made." His voice is low and calm. I close my eyes and hear Mami's heels approaching. Their sharp, quick rhythm sends a shock through both of us, and we sit up, waiting.

Mami doesn't bother knocking, she just barges in full of questions.

"¿Qué pasó? How did you . . . What were you thinking? Do you know what you put this family through?"

One after the other after the other. She doesn't even give me a chance to answer. She sits on the edge of my bed across from me, but I just stare at the wall, at this one spot the painter must've missed where the purple still pokes through.

"Your mother's right. This stunt of yours has put everything we've worked for in danger."

"More important, it put *her* in danger, Tonio. Wandering around the streets. We were worried sick, weren't we?" She crosses her arms and shakes her head at him, furious.

"Of course. That goes without saying." My desk cracks under Papi's weight as he sits against the edge and places his hands on the wood.

"Then can we focus, please? On our daughter?"

"I had it all under control. I sent Joe looking for her the second I realized she'd left."

"And it didn't occur to you to tell me she was missing?!" Mami stands up and he pushes off the desk, suddenly more alert.

"I didn't want to worry you. We were about to go on air."

She brings her hands to her stomach, letting out a feeble gasp. "¿En serio? You actually knew all that time and you . . . unbelievable."

"Juli, trust me."

"No me digas trust me."

Now Papi is fuming. Maybe because he knows he can't win with her right now, he turns to me and points at Mami. "See? Look what you've done." She throws her arms in the air and turns away from us. I follow her cue and start arranging the pillows on my bed so I can go to sleep.

"¡Mírame!" Papi pulls away the comforter. "Look at me when I speak to you."

"It's so unfair," I say under my breath.

"What did you say?"

"It's not fair," I say, louder. "Why do I have to look at you when you won't even listen to me?"

"Mari, por favor. Stop being so dramatic." He always says that. To me, to his opponents. If we're not being dramatic, we're being hyperbolic. The only way he knows how to argue is to make you feel small.

"I told you I didn't want to do it." But they just wanted me to obey. So much for democracy.

"This isn't about what you want! It's not about what either of you want!" Mami raises her voice so loud, it startles both of us. "We agreed—*I* agreed—to sacrifice for the greater good of this country. Tell me if that's changed, because I won't do it for anything less."

She holds both hands on her hips and Papi nods. "Of course it hasn't."

"Good. Now, Mari . . . apologize to your father."

But I'm not sorry. I'm spent and hurt and scared and miserable, and I wish he cared, even for a second, about how I feel instead of the status of his precious campaign.

I say nothing. The room grows so still I hear a ringing in my ears, louder with every second my parents wait. I feel the tears burning and brimming in my eyes, but I blink them back. A whole minute passes and we don't say a word. Mami sighs as she reaches for the light switch by my bedroom door and Papi follows her out. They leave without even kissing me good night.

thirteen

When I wake up the next morning, the house feels quiet and unfamiliar. My parents left hours ago, and Gloria's probably in her room getting ready to go home for the weekend. Things fall back into their regular routine but everything feels like it's changed. In the kitchen, I find Ricky eating a bowl of cereal. He sets his spoon down, letting tiny bits of milk and crumbs splash all over the kitchen table. "Papi's really, really mad at you. What did you do, Mari?"

He knows, of course. What he's really asking is why I did it. "You wouldn't understand. Maybe one day when you're older."

He looks so hurt. "You're the one who's acting like a baby." He makes a point out of stomping up the stairs and slamming his bedroom door. Ricky's tiny for his age, but he makes up for it with his temper. He loses it when things don't go his way, and his way usually overlaps with Papi's. My brother may pretend the campaign isn't a big deal to his friends, but I know that privately, he follows every detail he can like it's the Super Bowl of his lifetime. And I just dealt a huge blow to his defense.

Gloria walks in, picks up the bowl of half-eaten cereal he left on the table, and starts washing it. It's Saturday, which means technically it's already her day off, but she usually tidies things up before she goes.

"You okay?" She's wearing jeans and a gray T-shirt cut along the neckline so it nearly hangs off her shoulders. The knot she tied in the back makes it so the shirt hugs her curvy figure. A University of Miami Law School logo stretches across her chest, and in the back it says: Year 3, baby. I've seen Gloria wear this shirt before, and I'd just assumed it was a friend's or something she got at Goodwill, but now I know it belongs to Amarys.

I tell her I'm fine and turn on the morning news. The TV hanging from a corner in the kitchen is small, white, and currently set to a twenty-four-hour news station. I've been afraid to watch anything, wondering if the footage of Joe whisking me into his Subaru has gone viral. What they keep playing instead is the video of Papi the moment the newswoman asked if I was missing during the interview. The words BREAKING NEWS: SENATOR RUIZ'S DAUGHTER RECOVERED SAFE AFTER BRIEFLY MISSING scroll across the screen, followed by NO STATEMENT YET FROM FLORIDA GOP CANDIDATE. The segment plays two or three times in the next half hour.

Finally, around eleven in the morning, my father holds a press conference.

"On behalf of my entire family, I'd like to apologize for this misunderstanding that unfortunately caused much panic and concern. Yesterday, not long before my wife, Juliana; my son, Ricky; my daughter, Mariana; and I were scheduled for a live interview on CNN's *Meet the Candidates: Home Edition*, my daughter told me she wasn't feeling well. My wife and I agreed that Mariana should rest at the home of a dear family friend for the duration of the interview. Our daughter was never missing. We always knew where she was. Unfortunately, amidst all the preparations for the interview, not all of my staffers received the memo, and they immediately began searching for Mariana. I am grateful for their prompt action and concern. They did what any parent would want them to do had the circumstances been dire. Thankfully, they were not.

"Mariana is safe at home. She is feeling much better and will resume her normal activities at school on Monday. As always, my wife and I ask that you respect our family's privacy and especially that of our children. In addition, we would like to thank everyone who sent us their thoughts and prayers during this brief misunderstanding; it warmed our hearts to feel the love and support of so many Americans across this great nation of ours."

When Papi is done, he takes no questions from the press. He walks away from the podium, smiling and waving as if there's nothing to be concerned about, as if he can't even hear what they're saying.

Joe arrives at the house soon after. He's Gloria's ride to the Metro station.

"Am I interrupting anything? Are you two planning Mariana's next big escape? You don't know the night I had thanks to you. I need coffee."

Gloria makes like she's about to grab him a mug, but stops. She points at the cabinet where they're kept instead. "You sure you're okay?" she asks me again. Seems like no matter how many times I tell her I'm fine, she'll keep giving me this look. Like she's sad but also upset with me.

Finally, when I can't take their silence and the sound of Joe slurping his coffee anymore, I pull up a chair and let out a sigh. I'm afraid to ask, but I have to know. "So . . . how *did* everything play out after I left?"

What happened is this: Joe and Gloria were on their way to Dadeland Mall because Mami needed a specific shade of lipstick. Surprisingly, my father was the first to notice I was gone, and he texted Joe to come back right away. He told him not to tell anyone, because he didn't want Mami to freak out before the interview, or worse, cancel it. So Joe made up a lie about there being so much traffic they would've never made it back in time. The network's makeup artist ended up mixing a color that matched the one Mami had wanted, according to Gloria. But basically, Gloria was running around helping Mami, and it wasn't until ten minutes before they went on the air that Papi texted Mami that I wasn't feeling well, and that he'd sent me to my abuelo's house down the street so I could rest somewhere quiet. By then, the news crew was already seating my family on the couch, testing the lighting off their faces, and asking them to hold still or be quiet.

Meanwhile, that whole time, Joe was looking for me. All by himself. Like he had any idea where to start. But he'd been warned to keep it on the down low, and under no circumstances could he involve the cops unless it became necessary.

So Joe went to my school, which was closed except for the gym for a basketball game. He checked the South Miami library and the park where my father first told us he was going to be a senator. He came back to the house, went into my bedroom, texted Papi for the password on my laptop and Face-Timed Vivi, who told him she hadn't even been to school in two days, and then he called everyone in my history from the last two weeks, even random kids who aren't my friends at all, but who I'm doing a group project with in biology. Joe swears it's one of those nosy little jerks who opened their big mouth to the press.

"I'd bet anyone a million dollars it's Dania," I tell Gloria when Joe leaves to use the restroom. "Her mom works for Channel 7. And Dania hates me. Last week she told me there's no way her dad's voting for mine because he's 'morally bankrupt.' What does that even mean?" I don't know how to say 'morally bankrupt' in Spanish, so I say it in English instead.

Gloria shrugs and says, "No sé, nena. ¿Bancarotta? ¿De morales?" She turns away from me to wash her hands at the sink, but I see her reflection in the window right above it.

"Gloria?"

"Hmm?" She still won't look at me.

"I really liked meeting Amarys."

"She really liked meeting you too."

"Did I . . . did I get you guys in trouble?"

"What? No, of course not."

"There were a lot of cameras outside your apartment when Joe and I left."

"Yeah. But they'll get over it. They'll move on to some bigger story soon. Ya verás."

"Did they ask your names?"

She sighs real quick and turns around. "No te preocupes. Amarys didn't open the door. They went away eventually."

"Pero ¿y mi papá?" I'm careful with how I ask because I'm afraid I'll sound just like him. "Did he know about you two?" I hate how it comes out. Know about you two, like there's something wrong with them.

"He never asked, so I never told him. Of course, Amarys didn't want me working for him, you know?"

I nod, remembering what my father used to say before gay marriage became legal, that marriage was a holy thing between a man and a woman. He hasn't talked about it in years, but there it is. Of course, Gloria would hide it; he's always saying he doesn't care what people do with their lives so long as they don't do it in front of him. Looking at Gloria, the way she leans back into the counter with her elbows jutting out casually, pretending that all these years, it has been no big deal to live and work here, I feel the part of me that has always made excuses for him begin to sink into a pool of shame. Not caring isn't the same as supporting someone. Not seeing is the opposite of accepting them.

"I'm sorry."

"No, no, no, no . . . none of this is your fault. You've done nothing wrong."

"I've made everything worse."

"You dared to be honest," she says slowly, "and it only feels like you made things worse because you've made it harder for others to keep telling lies." Her lips press together and her face turns red. "And anyway, you'll see. This will all be forgotten before you know it. Como si nada." She snaps her fingers and giggles, but I'm not convinced.

"Will you and Amarys be okay?"

"Yes. Eso sí lo sé," she says, nodding. She looks like she's about to say something else, but just then Joe comes back into the kitchen.

"Vámonos," he says. I don't appreciate his mocking accent and tone. Gloria presses her lips together and raises her eyebrows at me as she hikes up her purse. I wonder if she wishes she could say something to him, but worries like I do it'd make things worse. We decide to stay quiet, but it doesn't sit well with me. It feels like we have no other choice.

fourteen

On Sunday, I call to check in on Vivi. Abuelo gave me back my phone and said Mami told him it's for emergencies only, but the situation with Vivi is urgent. Her mom still hasn't gotten back the keys to their house, and she's worried soon it won't even be theirs.

"It's already up for sale. My dad says they're staging it. He hired a realtor and everything."

"What does that even mean?"

"It means we have to get out so it looks like other people could live there. My mom and I are moving here, as soon as we can get all our stuff."

"To your aunt's? In Miami Beach? But that's super far." It's at least a forty-five-minute drive from the beach to Grove High. "How will you get to school?"

"You're not getting it, Mari." She pauses as if she's waiting for it to sink in. "I'm transferring."

"What? Starting when?"

"Monday."

"But why—why so fast? Why not wait till you find a place closer?"

"I'm not sure we'll be able to. It's the worst, Mari. Everyone talks like living on the beach is paradise, but my life is literally shit right now. Some sewage pipe burst in the ocean the other day, and now you can't even go in the water, and the second you get on the sand, it smells like caca everywhere."

"Oh my god."

"I know. My aunt says at least now we can help her take care of my grandmother, but we're all apretadas. My mom's sleeping in my aunt's room and I'm on the couch but the living room is stuffed full of cases of bottled water because my aunt thinks our drinking water's contaminated."

"She's probably just being paranoid, Vi."

"I don't know. I just wish I could get out of here. My mom's running errands by your house. Is it okay if she drops me off?"

"I say hell yes, but let me check with my abuelo real quick and I'll text you."

He looks at me puzzled when I ask, a hint of mischief in his smile. "Well . . . your parents said you're not allowed to go over to friends' houses. Y bueno . . ." He shrugs innocently. I give him the biggest hug and text Vivi.

Get your butt over here!

The first thing Vivi wants to do is lie out in the backyard to tan. She says she's hardly seen the sun in a week because it's been raining nearly nonstop on the beach.

"Not that anyone can get on the beach by my aunt's anyways. They're closing it off so they can plug the sewage leak," she says as she rubs tanning oil onto her shoulders. "Okay so yesterday, right? The garage in my aunt's building started flooding. Like, the whole first level below ground. She says it gets like that every full moon. The ocean tide rises so high they have to park their cars up higher. So by this morning, it's all full of water, which is all full of . . . grossness." She fake gags and it makes me shudder. "And then my mom and I got in this huge fight, because I can't believe she's really okay with me and Abuela and my aunt living like that. And then she was like, if you hate it so much, why don't you go live with your father? And that's basically why she agreed to let me come over, she said she couldn't deal with me right now."

"Wait . . . how'd you get out of the garage if it was flooded?"

"I told you. It floods every full moon. So my aunt told Mom to park her car two blocks down last night."

"The builders never planned for that?"

"Mari, you're not getting it. The buildings are like, decades old. It didn't always flood. It's because of climate change," Vivi says. "And we're all living in a shithole because of it."

It's like in those articles I read about the Everglades, though I have a feeling it's more complicated than that. There's no way the city would just let something like this happen. If things were really that bad, wouldn't the story be all over the news? Wouldn't Papi be working with the government to fix it?

"It'll get better," I tell her. "It has to."

We grow quiet and lay in the grass with the sun on our faces. No one is outside today, not even our neighbors across the canal, though for a second I think I see a curtain shift.

The grass pokes through my towel and itches my back, but it's still better than lying on the pool deck because the mismatched bricks file your skin down to bone when you press against them.

"I hope my shoulders burn," Vivi says. "Not like a bad burn, but just enough to get rid of these tan lines." I nod like I agree, even though I barely have any tan lines. Vivi's skin is a much darker bronze than mine; the lighter tint of her palms is the same color as my stomach. She undoes her straps and tucks them under her armpits. You can see the sides of her boobs peeking out, squished like a melted marshmallow between two graham crackers. They're so much paler than the rest of her, they make me feel like I shouldn't be seeing them. I flip over and undo my top, too, and wonder if mine look similar.

"Look what Jorge posted," Vivi says, holding her phone close to my face. Jorge is Vivi's ex, though Zoey and I both know it's more complicated than that. They had an ugly breakup at the beginning of the year, but then they hooked up on the bus ride to Key West during our class field trip to the Hemingway House, and ever since, they haven't gotten back together so much as they *get* together. A lot. The thing is, Jorge's only into Vivi when it's convenient for him, when he has no other girls all over him. I've told her this a million times, but she insists it's no big deal, that the sex is good and the arrangement is mutual, even though I don't see *him* hearting all *her* updates within minutes of her sharing them.

The video is of Jorge at South Pointe, rushing the pier from several feet and jumping over it like it's an Olympic hurdle. He clears it but nicks his foot against the wood, and everyone *ooohs* and laughs right before you hear the splash.

"*Oof.* That sounded painful," I say.

"He's such an idiot," Vivi says. The camera zooms in on the water just in time to see his face pop out, his hair glistening and black. "But a super cute one. I'll miss his stupid face." She flips over and switches her camera to selfie mode. Both our heads are in the frame, silhouetted against the summer heat.

"Vivi . . ."

"Sorry, sorry, I forgot." With the slightest tilt of her wrist, I disappear from view. Her head blocks the sun behind her, so now she's bright and in focus. Even though I look away, I know she's using the kitty filter by the noises she's making. When she smiles, she giggles and it comes out sounding like a mix between a meow and a purr.

"Hey, Mari?"

"Hmm?"

"I'll miss *your* stupid face too. But you already knew that."

"Yeah. I guess I'll miss yours . . . eventually."

Vivi smiles and puts her phone back in her bag and begins rummaging through her things. It's nearly three o'clock. Inside the house, Abuelo has probably dozed off on the couch watching the Heat play. In a few minutes, the cable news networks will switch to a live feed of my parents in Arizona for Papi's speech. I'm sure Ricky is propped on their bed, waiting—seeing them on TV has not gotten old for him yet. I know I'm supposed to be grounded, but it doesn't feel as though I am right now. It's nice just to be in this moment. There's no telling what school will bring for Vivi and me on Monday, so there's no point in talking about it. She's the only person in the world who makes me feel comfortable in silence.

Eventually I get sleepy. A breeze comes by in lazy waves, and beetles and lizards scurry past us. Everything is fine until a buzzing noise comes over us. I flip onto my side, holding my bathing suit top against my chest, and come up on my knees to see what all the commotion is about.

There, two or three stories above us, a small drone hovers in the air, sounding like a loud, angry hummingbird.

It takes me a moment to register because of how it floats side to side. But when I finally get a good look, I realize I'm staring straight at a camera, straight into the lens.

fifteen

At first I freeze. I can hardly breathe, let alone move, but thank god for Vivi. She grabs her towel and starts swatting the drone away. It's a good fifty feet above us but she jumps up and down like it'll make a difference, cursing at it to go away.

"Comemierda. ¡Vete p'al carajo!"

"Nosy piece of crap!" I add, still blinded and dazed from the sun.

All this does is make the drone zoom in closer. With my one free hand I grab my towel and swing it at it, swapping it away like it's a mosquito out for blood, but it hovers just beyond my reach, eerily still and focused. I give it one more try, flinging my towel so hard it escapes my grasp and falls into the pool with a splash. Drops of water land on my feet and calves, and a sudden rush of cold travels against my skin.

My skin. "Vivivivivivi!!!!"

Vivi's on me, towel and arms wrapped around my shoulders, so fast I nearly stumble into the pool.

"Just run. Go, go, go," she says, over and over as we make our way across the yard and into the bathroom at the back of the house. It's dark and dank and it smells like chlorine, because no one ever uses this bathroom unless they're coming in from the pool.

"What the hell was that?" Through the door, I can hear the drone is still out there, and it makes me wish I'd thrown a rock instead of a towel—just one perfect, forceful blow to its pathetic plastic mechanisms.

"Oh my god, Mari. You okay?" Vivi asks.

I nod because I'm breathing so hard I almost choke on my own spit. My hands won't stop shaking and every hair on my body feels stiff, cold, and exposed.

"They can't just . . . fly over my house and take pictures, can they? How is that even legal?" I want to scream but I'm scared I'll wake up Abuelo.

"I know. It's bullshit. Your dad should—"

"My dad's not going to do anything but blame me. I can just hear my parents now. *You should've covered up more, Mari. You need to be more responsible. But here, put on some more makeup for this TV show.*"

"They can't possibly put this on you. We're the victims here."

Only then do I realize I'm still holding the two triangles of my bathing suit top against my chest with my forearm, pressing so hard my ribs hurt.

"I just wanted one afternoon. One hour left alone."

"I doubt it's that bad," Vivi whispers. "It's probably just some kid who doesn't even know how to use that thing. I bet he doesn't know who you are."

"I guess we'll find out soon enough."

It takes sixteen hours and thirty-seven minutes. The next morning, I'm on my way to school in Joe's Subaru when his phone, which is mounted onto the a/c vent, dings and lights up with a Google alert. I can only see the first few words of the subject line, which reads *Senator Anthony Ruiz's daughter caught.*

Joe's eyes dart between the road and the screen. Mami's warned him about texting and driving when we're in the car with him, so he looks like he's having a mild panic attack.

"Can you just read it to me? The code's oh-six-oh-three-nineteen."

The day my father announced he was running for president. Wow. This campaign really is his whole life. I can't decide if that's nice or sad. Probably tragic, considering what the notification says.

I read it to myself first. It's not from one of the major news networks—it's from a celebrity gossip blog, the kind that doesn't even pretend to be real journalism. But still. They have pictures. "In the near-nude," is how they describe me. They say it looks like I'm "recovering just fine" after missing my father's interview on Friday. *The fifteen-year-old, who was supposedly feeling under the weather, just needed to get a little sun.*

They don't share the whole video, just several still images.

The first is of me and Vivi lying on our stomachs in my yard. Our backs are completely bare, and it looks like we don't have tops on, because the untied strings blend into our beach towels.

The second is of me getting up. I'm on one knee, my back still to the camera, but my face is turned enough to identify me. I look older. For the first time in my life, I think I look like Mami. Our noses and shoulders curve the same way.

I keep scrolling until I get to the third image. The air catches inside of me, hard as an ice cube slowly pushing its way through my chest. There are pixels—so many pixels—across my torso. In that flesh-colored blurry blob, everything is lost. You can't see my bathing suit top. You can't see my hands trying to cover up. It looks like I'm not wearing anything at all.

What's clear is my other arm, waving in the air, right at the camera. And my face. Oh my god. My face.

As every tiny muscle contorted itself into a look of horror, they captured the one millisecond when it looks like I'm smiling. I was grimacing. I was shocked. The sun was in my eyes, but none of that is the story these blogs will tell.

Here is the fifteen-year-old daughter of the Florida Senator running for president, waving and smiling at the camera in the near nude. Wanting the attention, welcoming it. It's clear as daylight, but it's a lie.

The notifications on Joe's phone start going off again.

"What? What is it?!"

I can't bring myself to tell him. I put the phone face-down on my thigh, shaking my head no.

"It's nothing," I croak. My face is burning, my throat still frozen. I feel everything and nothing. Shame and numbness. Rage and sorrow.

"What do you mean, nothing?" For the second time this week, Joe bombards me with questions I don't answer. The car begins to slow as he makes his way into the drop-off line at the front of my school.

"What did you do now? Give me the phone, Mariana. You can't keep playing these games."

The car stops completely, enough for him to look me in the eyes.

"Jesus. Is it that bad?"

"For me, or for the campaign? Like you care about anything else."

"Just give me the phone, Mari."

He's not supposed to call me that. Only my family and close friends call me that, and Joe doesn't even pronounce it right.

But nothing is really mine anymore.

I throw the phone at him. It lands by his foot next to the brake, and as soon as he bends down to get it, I jump out of the car and run.

sixteen

I'm completely winded by the time I get to school. Even though I got out of Joe's car only half a block away, my heart's pounding harder than it does in PE. I slow down, trying to look a little less desperate as I get to the main doors.

The best way to describe Grove High is that it looks as if it's going through an identity crisis. The entrance is covered in red brick and surrounded by thin, tall palm trees that lean into one another like they're telling secrets. The second story looks nothing like the first. It's all cement walls and blue-tinted windows framed in gray metal, like someone built a new floor without caring if it matched the original.

I've been walking through these doors without pause all year. Now I brace myself for whatever awaits on the other side as I approach them.

The images of my bare back and my pixelated torso won't stop flashing through my mind. In the car I didn't have time to notice, but now I wonder how detailed they are. If you zoom in, would you see the line of freckles on my back that Mami says look like Orion's belt? When I was little she used to trace them until I fell asleep. She'd tell me to wish on the stars I carry, to never forget that they are a part of me.

As I step into the main hall, a gust of air hits me and

people's faces turn to look at me, one after the other after the other. I wish on every star and every freckle on my body that I could disappear.

The a/c clicks off. I hear whispers crackle, loud yet indecipherable. To my right, by the giant trophy case that displays Papi's Senate portrait smack in the center, Stephanie Lyndon pulls her ponytail loose and shakes her head, never taking her eyes off me. Her friends, whose names I don't know, are huddled behind her and look away when I try to meet their eyes.

I keep my head down and keep walking. The floor is lined with linoleum—three pale pink squares for several randomly placed white and gray ones—and it looks thin enough to crack beneath me. Up ahead, Patrick Franco leans against the lockers and smirks. True to stereotype, he's wearing one of those V-neck Abercrombie sweaters with a stiff white shirt collar jutting over his chin. His dirty toes bulge out of his plastic green flip-flops.

"Bro." He smacks Jorge on the chest with the back of his hand. "Mira la modelo. Nice pictures, Mari."

To their credit, a couple of people hesitate to react for maybe half a second. But all that means is everyone erupts into laughter at once. It's like he gave them permission. Jorge gives me a slow and squinted look, the kind that feels like a million tiny hands slithering over my skin. I wonder what Vivi would say if she knew her ex was looking at me this way, but a part of me is glad she's not here to see it.

Boys whistle and ask me for more. Girls jeer and look me

up and down. Some guy I've never met before stands in the middle of the hallway, covering his torso and yelling "Uy, a camera!" before striking an exaggerated pose with both hands on his hips, chest pushed up and out. Someone else shouts, "Vote for my Papi," in a high-pitched, baby-like voice.

Later, I'll probably think of the most pointed, perfect words to throw back at them. But right now, I feel like my voice has left my body, and all I want to do is run after it.

I keep walking. People I kind of know become busy looking for something in their lockers or backpacks when I try to meet their eyes. I look down at my phone and notice the screen is lit bright green with texts from Mami, Papi, and Vivi. I debate reading them, knowing they'll only make this nightmare worse.

Breathe. Blink. Breathe. *Visualize yourself overcoming.*

I focus all my energy and attention on the door at the end of the hall, trying to imagine myself stepping through it. Just then it opens and its handle clangs, loud and sharp. A gust of wind pushes against my face.

Jackie Velez walks through the door that was supposed to be my escape. Not this again. Please, not now.

She looks right at me, her eyes narrow and her jaw tight. She's nearly half a foot taller than me; her stance is so purposeful it makes me want to step aside as she approaches.

"Hey!" she yells.

I stop walking and she closes the space between us. I've never felt so small and yet so conspicuous in my entire life.

"You think this is funny?" She's still yelling, loud enough for the whole school to hear, even though she's inches away from me. "You think this misogynist attack on Mariana's body and privacy is funny?" Her gaze shifts away from me and scans everyone around us. "Your laughter makes you complicit. So does your silence."

I have zero clue what's going on anymore—should I be scared? Relieved? Jackie has this badass-hero vibe that makes everyone want to be around her and no one want to piss her off. Her words are like an invisible chancleta being thrown through the hall. Nearly everyone stands up straighter, pretends to look busy, and scatters within a few seconds.

"You okay?"

I shake my head no and say yes. "But you hate me," is all I manage.

She looks confused and then amused. Her face is bright and striking and contains every emotion at once. "Says who?"

"All those things you wrote. About my father . . ."

"Are you your father?"

"No, but—"

"Then why would you think I hate you?"

She's actually waiting for me to answer. All I've got is a sad, half shoulder shrug and what I imagine sounds like a toy Chihuahua whimpering.

Jackie laughs and smacks open the door again. "Come on. I wanna show you something."

seventeen

We cut through the courtyard and walk to a far-off corner of campus I've never been to. We pass the picnic tables where the varsity baseball team congregates. Not too far from them, a row of kids lie face-up on the thick cement plant beds. They've all got headphones on and they're using their backpacks as pillows. Out of instinct, I look across the courtyard for Vivi beneath the stairwell, but of course, she's not there.

"Where are we going?" I ask Jackie. I'm going to be late for first period. She's walking and dodging clusters of students so fast, it's hard to keep up with her. I follow her past the black box theater and through a narrow navy door I'd always assumed was for faculty. The small hallway we're standing in is lit by an amber light that's much warmer than the rest of the school's fluorescents. It's like we're not even in Grove High anymore.

"This used to be where the drama program did lighting and sound, before they built the new auditorium," she says, opening one of two doors in the hallway. "Ms. Sepulveda let us take over the space for PODER."

It's at least two classrooms long, and instead of a back wall, there's a large purple curtain that hangs from a high ceiling with exposed silver air ducts and lighting equipment. All the other walls are covered in posters, banners, and stickers. A black-and-white print almost as tall as I am says INTERSECTIONAL FEMINISM IS THE ONLY REAL FEMINISM. An LGBTQ rainbow flag is pinned to the wall next to another flag with blue, pink, and white stripes, and a postcard below it says #TRANS ISBEAUTIFUL. There are filing cabinets covered with stickers that say SAVE THE EARTH, SAVE OURSELVES. A pile of flyers for women's rights and voting rights are arranged in two tall, neat piles on top of it.

The room is a strange mixture of order and chaos. The far left corner looks like something out of the arts and crafts section of Target, stocked with letter cutouts, foam poster boards, and super thick Sharpies in every color imaginable. The smell of acrylic paint fills the air.

"Pretty cool, right? I know it has a very postapocalyptic bunker vibe, but we've been working on brightening it up." Jackie points to the beanbags and couches arranged in the center of the room. There are stacks of books on a square white coffee table, and a tall lamp with an extension cord duct-taped along the floor to the wall. "You can borrow any book you want."

"What is this place?"

"It's our center of operations," Jackie says nonchalantly. "Ever since I nearly got expelled at the beginning of the year."

Oh. It's all starting to make sense now. "This is the space they gave you for your protest club?"

"Activist group. Though we do protest sometimes. It's not a bad word, you know. You don't have to whisper it, Mariana."

She smiles in this oddly maternal way that makes me feel like a naive freshman.

"No, I didn't mean it like that. I just . . . didn't know."

"It's fine. I get what you mean. And yeah, I think they figured if they tucked us away to some forgotten corner of the school, we'd go quietly. It's worked out really well, actually. They stay out of our way and Ms. Sepulveda is super supportive when we need her. She was at the first Women's March in DC, and now she helps plan the one here."

All I remember about the Women's March is that Papi took us all to church to pray the country would unite again. I was eleven, and after mass, we stayed home with the TVs off, as if the power had gone out. Mami checked her phone several times, though. I saw her sneaking glances at it in the pantry.

I'm about to ask Jackie why she brought me here when the door opens and two students I've never met before walk through. One of them is an Asian girl carrying a purple duffel bag and the other is a Black guy with a stack of white postcards that he hands to Jackie.

"Here. Registered eleven at last night's game. And senior pictures are starting next week, so we're gonna set up a booth there," he says.

"'Kay. I'll drop these off after school. Mari, this is Didier." Didier waves with one hand, then Jackie points at the girl standing next to him with the duffle. "And this is Cristina." Cristina smiles but doesn't really look at me.

"It's Mariana," I say.

"Right, sorry," Jackie says, looking like she's on the verge of smiling. "Crissy and Didier have been registering students to vote too. You probably saw them at the booth the other day."

"Oh. Maybe . . ." I wish Jackie hadn't brought that up.

Cristina smirks and I realize she probably already recognized me. She's wearing shimmery eyeshadow that sweeps a fine dust of glitter across the tops of her high cheekbones. It's the perfect shade of lavender against her light brown skin.

She opens the duffle bag and Didier starts going through its contents, which crinkle and crunch. He's nearly as tall as my dad, but much leaner, and the way he goes through the bag reminds me of a dancer, because even when he's bent over, his posture is perfect.

"Oh my god, Crissy! You got Sublimes?!" Except he says it in a Spanish accent—su-bli-mez—and pulls out a square candy bar wrapped in silver with dark blue letters. He grins and I notice he has a thin, stubble-like mustache, and his jaw muscles bounce in and out as he chews.

"I have a whole maleta-full back home," Crissy says. "Take as many as you want. Here. Try one, Mari. They're from Peru."

"It's Mariana," Jackie reminds her.

"Whatever, sorry." She holds the candy bar out to me, but I'm too worried I'll be late for class to eat anything.

"No, thanks. Did you just get back from vacation there?"

She takes a deep breath and seems to hold it inside. Every time she smiles it looks pained and fake, like she secretly hates me. "I was born there. And my brother was just . . . he lives there."

"Oh, I didn't mean—"

"It's fine. People always act surprised that there are Chinese people who are Latinx."

"No, I get it," I say. "My great-great-grandfather was part Chinese and Irish. And Cuban." Crissy tucks a loose hair behind her ear and raises one eyebrow as she smirks at Jackie. Oh god, I'm making this awkward, right? "It's nice that you get to visit. I don't even know what kind of candy is Cuban candy."

I try to imagine a childhood full of trips to my grandparents' birth country. Papi always says the only things his mother brought with her were the clothes on her back and a few pictures of the family standing outside their house. It's a different kind of leaving when you can't go back. Meanwhile Crissy has luggage stuffed with so many sweets even her friends have their favorites.

Didier shakes his head. "Your dad really took the whole assimilation thing to heart, didn't he?"

"Dude," Jackie says.

"What? I'm not saying it's his fault. Just that it's sad, that's all."

"My dad's really proud of being Cuban. And American," I say. Papi says this catchphrase all the time, though sometimes it's reversed, depending on where he's giving his speech. I'd never thought about that until now.

"Don't tease her. She's been through enough today," Jackie says.

Didier covers his mouth and gasps. His eyes turn soft as he looks at me. "Shit, I totally forgot. Honestly, whoever took those pictures should be in jail for like, child pornography or something. And the blog that published them?! Ooh. Your family should sue them."

Crissy takes out her phone and starts scrolling as she pops a hard candy into her mouth. "You know . . . I doubt that would work. This gossip blog posted them, and they'll probably take them down but by then everyone will have screenshots. And any journalism outlet with half a legal team wouldn't dare publish them. But they're reporting on the fact that they happened because, well . . . it *is* newsworthy. I mean, it's the elections and you're—"

"Okay, we get it, Miss Future Pulitzer." Didier turns his attention to the nutritional facts on his chocolate bar wrapper.

"Crissy's on the newspaper staff. She's one of my best writers," Jackie explains.

My face grows warm just thinking of the blog post headlines. I feel like I'm back in Joe's car, smelling the green pine of his air freshener, seeing my pixelated body on display for the whole world. "I wasn't naked!" My voice cracks. "And I was trying to make them go away. They made it look like, like I was . . ."

But I can't finish.

"Asking for it?" Jackie whispers.

I still can't believe I'm talking to her. About this, of all things.

"Besides, even if you *were* naked," Crissy says.

"I wasn't!"

"Okay, but I'm just saying. Even you shouldn't be shamed for your own body."

Even me?

"Look," Jackie says. "I just wanted you to know we've got your back. And that you're not alone. What you're going through sucks, and it's not your fault." A timid look flashes across her face, and then it's gone, replaced by that same steeled expression she carried when she rescued me from Patrick Franco and Jorge in the hall. A week ago, nothing scared me more than the thought of being a target of Jackie's scrutinizing eye. Suddenly now she has my back?

I look around the room. It's Papi's version of a nightmare. To him and Mami, Jackie is la malcriada que anda metida en problemas. They think she goes looking for trouble.

"What does PODER mean? I mean, I know it's Spanish for *power*, but does it stand for anything?"

"It's short for People against Oppression Demanding Equality and Resisting," Jackie says proudly.

"It's *so* one of those acronyms you make up after you've chosen the word," Didier says.

"Cállate la boca," Jackie says, except she's smiling as she shuts him up.

"Pa fè sa. Don't act like you don't know."

"You're Haitian?" I ask Didier. I don't understand what he said just now, but I know enough words—like *eleksyon* and *byenveni*, from when my parents vote at our precinct and all the signs are trilingual—to know he's speaking Kreyòl.

He nods and Jackie loops her arm under his and rests her head on his shoulder. They have an ease about them that reminds me of Vivi and me. "You speak Kreyòl too?" I ask Jackie.

"I mean . . . a little."

"You don't spend as much time at my house as Jackie and Crissy do without my mom teaching you a few phrases," Didier says.

It's sweet. I think of how Zoey could pick up on some Spanish around Vivi and me if she really wanted to. The only time she's ever showed interest was before midterms, when she needed help with her Spanish homework. By help, I mean she asked us for all the answers. I pretended to be clueless, but Vivi started messing with her by saying the most Cuban phrases she could think of instead of the more "proper" Spanish her teacher was looking for. Zoey got the hint, and she never asked again. It's really annoying, though, being treated like I'm her translator on demand.

It makes me think twice about asking Didier what he just said. I'll figure it out eventually.

"So, what are you going to do?" Crissy asks.

"I don't know. I haven't talked to my parents yet."

"Your parents? No, she means, what do *you* want to do? About the pictures and everything?" Jackie says.

"Nothing. I just want them to go away. I want people to forget about me."

"Oh, Mariana." Disappointment drips from Didier's voice.

"What?"

"It's just . . . people are watching you."

"I know. That's why it sucks."

"No, you don't get it," Jackie says. "I mean, yes, it sucks now. Because it's not on your terms. But you can use this. You have a platform so many of us don't."

A platform? Jackie sounds just like Joe, only thinking about what she can get out of a situation.

"Is that why you brought me here?"

"You skipped out on your father's interview."

"That was actually a pretty bold statement," Crissy adds.

"No it wasn't. It was me staying out of it. Or trying to. It was a nonstatement."

"See? Te dije." Crissy gives Jackie an I-told-you-so look.

"I'm just gonna go," I say, reaching for my bag.

"Don't let Crissy get to you," Jackie says. "It's just, there's no such thing as a nonstatement. Even saying nothing says a lot."

So I say nothing. I just walk out of the room without looking back.

eighteen

It's a miracle I get through the day without having a complete breakdown. I had to get a tardy slip for first period and on my way to class I got a text from Amarys telling me to stay strong, and though I brushed off her words at first, I ended up repeating them to myself all morning: when I walked into Ms. Walker's class and everyone went quiet, like they'd just been talking about me. When my bio teacher had to tell everyone he would not tolerate cell phones or distractions, because he obviously knew the kids behind me were looking at the pictures. Zoey gave me an indecisive hug-kiss to try to make me feel better, but it just made me wish Vivi were here instead.

Stay strong, Amarys texted. Call us if you need to talk.

But I don't want to talk to anyone.

At the end of the day, I wait for Joe to pick me up after school. This is the worst part of my being grounded for skipping out of the interview last week; my parents agreed it'd be Joe's job to take me straight home as soon as the bell rings. It's like a trap I can't see a way out of. Is this what my life will be if Papi wins? Some hired guy in a suit following me everywhere, dropping me off and taking me home from some bullshit school for famous people's kids?

I'm trying to make sense of this realization when Mami

calls. It's 2:34 p.m. exactly and I've been ignoring her and Papi's messages all day. They keep warning me we'll have a serious conversation about my behavior soon. The last text Papi sent was in all caps: DO NOT TALK TO ANYONE. HAVING PRESS CONF ASAP.

"Hello? Mami?" I can hear her voice but it's directed at someone else, something about a schedule change, and then there's a lot of rustling and the sound of her quick footsteps and then dead quiet.

"Hija." Her voice is scary calm. "Your father and I were gone one day. One day. Y mira lo que pasó. What happened? What were you thinking?"

"I didn't . . ."

"It's time to take responsibility for your actions, Mariana. First the running away. Now this. I want to know why, with the primary coming up so soon, you thought it was a good idea to tan nude."

"I wasn't nude! I had my top on. You talk like I stripped in public or something."

But it's like she's having a conversation without me.

"Your father is hurt that you'd be so thoughtless, Mari."

So much for not freaking out. I search through my backpack, trying to find my sunglasses. "*He's* hurt? Did he ever bother asking how I feel? Did you?"

She lets out a deep sigh. "You're right. I'm sorry. How are you feeling with all this?"

"How do you think?"

"Don't take that tone with me. You may not notice, but I've

been working very hard to protect you from all of this ugliness. Pero dime, how many more times will your father and I have to clean up after your mess?"

"My mess? I was in our backyard. That's private, remember? Or obviously not anymore, since you're the ones who let cameras into our home in the first place."

"Ya no puedo más." Mami sounds breathless, like she's walking somewhere fast. "Tonio, talk to your daughter. I can't with her anymore."

I brace myself for my father's anger, but all I hear is him talking somewhere nearby, calling me a malcriada and saying that the pictures make me look like a—but he stops short of saying it. I can tell Mami's covered the phone because their voices become muffled, and finally she says, "Unbelievable," though I'm not sure she means me.

"Mari. We have to go. Your father will talk to you later."

Just then, Joe's orange Subaru pulls up to the curb. I open the door and look in on him.

"Why the face? I don't see half-naked pictures of *you* going viral," I say. "Thank god."

Surprisingly, all he does is hand me a box of tissues. "Just get in. The Senator's presser starts any minute now."

He does that sometimes when he talks to me—calls Papi the Senator—like he's forgotten I'm his daughter. It never bothered me much until now. I get into the passenger seat and slam the door with all my might.

"Watch it! This is a new car."

I turn away from him, smirking as I lower the window. Joe

starts speeding the second we're out of the school zone, and within minutes we're standing in the kitchen with the TV on. It doesn't take long to find a station; they're all broadcasting an image of an empty podium with Papi's logo on it. I hear footsteps coming from down the hallway where Gloria's room is. She has a handful of laundry that she starts folding on the kitchen table as she watches with us.

"¿Cómo te sientes?" she asks me.

"I'm fine. I don't really want to talk about it."

"Shhh! They're starting," Joe says. Sure enough, there's my dad on TV, standing tall behind the podium. Seconds later, Mami appears and slips her hand into his.

"My wife, Juliana, and I are here under circumstances that no parent should ever have to find themselves in. When I chose to run for president, we decided, as a family, that we wanted to show America who we are—free of pretense and gimmicks —and welcome the American people into our home. It's only fair, after all. In asking you to make me president, we are asking you to welcome us into your homes and lives.

"But what happened to my daughter this week is not fair. Not at all."

My breath catches. He pauses and I realize I've stopped breathing, waiting for what he'll say next.

"We became aware of the"—he clears his throat—"pictures that were taken of my fifteen-year-old daughter while we were traveling through the great state of North Carolina.

"These pictures were manipulated to make it appear that something perfectly normal for a teenager like herself

—tanning in the privacy of her own backyard—was more nefarious. Those responsible should be ashamed, along with the blogs that published them and bullied my child. This is truly a new, unimaginable low. My family is hurt and disillusioned by today's events. We ask that you respect our privacy during this time, and respect the decision we've made, for our own children's protection, to no longer have them joining us for any events where press will be present. Thank you."

My father walks off camera, ignoring the string of reporters' questions that follow him. They want to know if he plans on pressing any charges and to what extent the pictures were manipulated. I wished he'd answer. I wonder if he's thought about protecting me, or just himself. His words echo in my mind though I know they're the work of a speechwriter; words he repeats instead of words he means.

Perfectly normal for a teenager like herself.

I hear them in someone else's voice. I can't recognize him in them.

Joe turns off the TV, practically stabbing the remote control with his thumb. "See? You win, Mariana. No more press. Isn't that what you wanted?"

I can't believe this is what it took for Papi to listen to me. What I wanted never mattered unless it could somehow help him. I cover my mouth, tired of feeling like everything inside of me is always on the verge of pouring out.

"Leave her," Gloria says, louder than I've heard her say any words in English.

nineteen

Despite all my recent absences, my parents think it's best I stay home from school the next day. Mami says it's so that things can calm down, and that hopefully students will have fresh gossip by Wednesday. It makes me think of how Papi always says to wait a day when things are looking bad —there's usually something else coming up in the news cycle, and people's attention spans can only handle so much. I wonder if we ever really grow out of it, if all of life is just an endless chain of chisme, and maybe all I have to look forward to when I graduate is a grown-up version of high school with higher stakes and higher ratings.

The first text I get in the morning is from my dad, a picture of the sunrise in Savannah.

Es un día nuevo, he writes.

It's this thing he's done on the road ever since I was little. Before I got my first phone, he'd email me sunrises and sunsets from wherever he was.

They're all different, and yet all the same.

It was supposed to remind me that even though he was traveling, he was never very far. This morning I take it as a pseudoapology. A new day.

OK, I text back. It's easy for him to say; it's not his body that's gone viral, turned into memes and caption contests. I spend most of the day in bed, sucked into their vortex. *When you're running for student body president but you take the whole thing literally,* one of the most shared memes says. I shouldn't read the comments, I know this.

But I do. Of course I do.

It's not the LOLs or emojis that get to me. Or the ones posting fake campaign slogans that are nothing but boob jokes. Some people are nice enough to defend me. *She's just a child,* they say. But the ones who fixate on my body, on how it's ugly, on how it's hot, on how there are so many things they'd do to it. They make me want to jump out of my skin.

How could people be so sick and cruel to someone they don't even know? And how could Papi just be moving on? He's always talking about how he would never let anyone hurt me or my brother, but here I am, scared to climb out from under my bedsheets for fear of the public, for fear of all the people he's spent his whole life serving. I guess they matter more to him than me.

I doze off and when I wake, Gloria's tapping lightly at my door, insisting I have to at least eat something, and Zoey's texting me today's homework assignments. I thank them both even though I just wish they'd leave me alone. I wish everyone in this whole country would leave me the fuck alone.

At the beginning of the year, when Jorge broke up with Vivi because he needed time to decide if they were long-term or not, Vivi used to talk about how nothing felt real anymore. How she felt like she was walking around in a daze, watching people hang out and laugh como si nada, completely oblivious to her broken heart, and it made her realize that we never really know each other at all.

I know it's not the same thing, but it's exactly how I feel now that I'm back at school. I feel detached from everyone, like I can't really trust them. The only person I want to talk to is Vivi, but for some reason she hasn't been answering her phone.

By Thursday it's like Mami said it would be; people have gone back to their own lives, but I'm still walking around with this ball of shame in my gut. I can't look at Patrick Franco without thinking of his slimy smile, the way his teeth gleamed when he looked at me. Even talking to Zoey is hard because she's so worried about me she second-guesses every word she says. I offer her some of my potato chips at lunch and she shakes her head as she takes out a bag of baby carrots.

"I'm trying to be good. With swimsuit season coming up. Not that it's bad that you eat them. You look great in a swimsuit. I mean, not that it matters . . ."

I cut her off before she can dig herself in deeper. "It's fine. What exactly is swimsuit season, anyways? It makes it sound like there's a whole harvest of bikinis you could find at farmers' markets all of a sudden." I don't know why but her comment just grates on me. Who's she trying to please by eating carrots and being "good"? People are going to be super mean no matter what.

I pretend to finish my meal and tell Zoey I'll see her in fifth period. We still have twenty-five minutes left of lunch but my appetite is nonexistent. I walk around campus and end up in the hallway outside the PODER office, watching a group of students rehearse a dance routine led by Didier. He's counting out in sets of eights and doesn't miss a beat as he smiles and waves at me to pass through. I mouth him a silent thank you as I make my way inside. The first thing that hits me is the smell of church coming from an incense burner on the couch. Two feet in black-and-white Adidas are propped up on the armrest, and suddenly Crissy sits up looking excited and then immediately deflated.

"Oh. I didn't think you'd come back. Jackie!"

I don't even try to hide my face as I roll my eyes. I'm growing tired of caring what people I don't even know think of me.

From across the room, a familiar voice yells, "Mari—ana!"

I don't get why Jackie keeps wanting to call me by my nickname.

"It's so good to see you. How have you been? How are you feeling?" She emphasizes *feeling* like I just got over a horrible illness, and it dawns on me that I don't know how to answer. Or maybe I don't know how to answer *her*. I look around the room in hopes it'll make me look like I came here with an actual purpose instead of just a rage-fueled, blank stare.

That's when I see them. The sea-green flyers she was

handing out that day at the library. Talking about my dad and how we'd be electing a new president soon, and how people urgently needed to get involved. They're face down on a table by all the paint.

"What is the deal with you always writing this stuff about my father?"

"What stuff? Wait . . . is this about my article on his bubble statement?"

"That. And the one you wanted to interview me for. And your tweets and, and this." I finally grab a handful of the flyers and wave them in her face.

"Those," she says, slowly and confused.

I flip one over. It's a flyer about the elections, all right. The elections for new PODER officers. At the end of May the club will be choosing a new president, vice president, secretary, and historian, and the flyer is meant to get students signed up to run.

"It's just, Crissy and I are graduating," she explains. "So we need to be sure it's left in good hands, you know? And Didier can't do everything on his own."

I feel so stupid. This whole time I thought Jackie was campaigning against my father when it wasn't really about him, or me, at all.

"And the article you wanted to interview me for?"

She shrugs like it was years ago. "I mean . . . everything's so focused on him. I figured no one's asked you what it's like, you know? But I get it now. I hear you. You want to lay low and

I don't blame you. You're welcome to hang out here anytime you need to get away from all that." She points in the direction of the door. We both know she means the school courtyard beyond it, but just then the room grows really quiet and all we can hear is Didier counting down *five, six, seven, eight,* and the bass from his speakers kicks in and Crissy runs outside to watch him and his crew rehearse.

I can't help smiling at Jackie. I honestly don't know what I'd do in a space like this, except maybe work on my community service project. They seem to have a whole corner dedicated to environmental issues, full of posters and pamphlets to get people to donate to different organizations.

"For what it's worth, I'm really sorry we made you uncomfortable the other day," she says.

"Thanks. I'm fine now. I mean, I'm not, but I will be."

"I know."

She goes back to watching something on her laptop while I settle into the couch and try to finish eating the sandwich and fruit salad that Gloria made me. I'd packed everything up so quickly to get away from Zoey that I hadn't noticed there's no napkin today. Everyone's being so distant lately. Even Vivi still hasn't gotten back to me.

You ok? Hellooo, I text her.

No answer. The bell rings and I tell Jackie, Crissy, and Didier that I'll see them tomorrow. When I walk into fifth period and sit next to Zoey, both of our phones go off at the same time.

Sorry MIA. Abuela got food poisoning yesterday. Was in ER with no service. Fine now. Big scare for nothing.

So glad she's OK, I respond. Then I message her back privately. MISS YOU. Sleep over my place Sat?

Vivi sends back a party hat emoji and a bunch of the lady-dancing-in-red-dress.

twenty

Lately I feel like I'm watching things happen from under-water. It's a weird kind of peace: quiet but suffocating. My parents head back out on the road again on Friday. Ricky's so upset I got us banned from Papi's campaign, he's stopped talking to me. And every time I see Gloria, she's on the phone. Twice I've heard her whispering in her room, probably talking to Amarys. I haven't wanted to eavesdrop, but it's hard not to notice they've been arguing. While she gets ready to catch the Metro I hear her say, "I can't. I won't," before hanging up.

Saturday morning I give her a kiss on the cheek goodbye and say I'll see her on Monday. I ask if she's okay but she only smiles and says, "I will be."

"Tell Amarys I said hi?"

"Of course."

They must really miss each other during the week. It's like they're in a long-distance relationship in the same city.

When Abuelo gets back from dropping her off at the station, he starts doing his crossword in the living room. "What a mess," he says as he scans the clues. "You look at it and think, coño, who could ever make sense of this?"

I play along. We take a minute reading all the clues. I know he knows most of the answers by now, but he's pretending not to.

I point at the clue for sixteen down. "'Persona famosa; brillante.' Estrella."

He counts out the letters and lets out a gasp as he fills in the squares. "Muy bien. See? There's always at least one with a simple answer. Start there and you can figure out the rest."

We work out a few more answers together, but I can't stop looking at the clock.

"What time is Vivi coming over? So I know when you'll abandon me," Abuelo adds with a smile.

"Her mom's dropping her off in about ten minutes."

"How is Lily?"

Abuelo knows all about the divorce, about how Vivi's mom got locked out of her house from one day to the next.

"I don't know. Vivi and I haven't talked much, with everything else that's been going on."

All I know is that she's not in a good place right now, and it doesn't help that I haven't really been there for her. That's going to change today. I've decided that the only way I'm going to get through this campaign is to block it out. I haven't checked the news all week. I haven't checked the trending hashtags on Twitter. I haven't asked my parents or Joe about the latest poll numbers and they haven't brought them up either. I spent my last two lunch periods in the PODER office, making posters about protecting the environment and reading books about climate change in their library, and it was nice to focus on something other than my problems or my dad's campaign troubles for once. The Florida primaries are in a week and a half so Jackie, Crissy, and Didier have started urging the seniors to vote, but they know better than to try to bring up the subject to me. Instead they've been helping me with my project, pointing me in the direction of reliable sources on the Everglades and sea level rise and proofreading my papers. Even Crissy took a moment to look everything over, and she told me that I have a pretty good report, but now I just need to take action.

"You have all this information. Now what are you going to do about it?"

Which is actually a really good, really overwhelming point. Of course I had to go and pick the one issue that's so much bigger than me, it feels like I can't possibly make much of a difference. Sometimes I think I should've committed to petting puppies like Justine. (Making dogs happy? There's a task you can't mess up.) But then I think of my dad and all our trips to the Glades and our beach cleanups, and I know it'd be harder for me to give up than keep going. So I'm figuring things out. Kind of. Slowly.

Abuelo mumbles under his breath as he realizes an answer he already wrote into the puzzle is wrong. He's using one of those erasable pens that don't really erase at all. "No importa." He folds the paper shut and changes the subject. "Qué bueno that you and Vivi will have plenty of time to catch up."

Two days and one night doesn't seem like plenty of time after the week we've been through. When Vivi arrives, we run up to my room and shut the door before Ricky can come in. He's had a thing for Vivi all year long.

"Let's go for a jog." She pulls out a pair of yoga pants and sneakers from her duffel bag.

"A jog?"

"It'll help with my stress. You don't understand. Going to school on the beach is crazy, Mari. Everyone's like, super stuck-up. This one group, all they do is brag about their parties on Star Island, or Hibiscus Island . . . I don't know, I can't keep track of all their private little enclaves anymore. If their parents are so rich then why the hell are they in public school, you know?"

She gets quiet all of a sudden. We both know my parents sent Ricky and me to public school because they thought it'd look better for the campaign.

"Trust me, you're so much more laid back than them," she says. "This one girl drives a BMW M3. Her parents practically live in Brazil so she has a house on Fisher Island all to herself. It's so gross how all the kids suck up to her."

"Have you talked to her?"

"No. I ran into her on my second day of school and she looked me up and down, super long, and then pretended she hadn't seen me at all."

"That's how the women at my father's fundraisers look at my mom. She acts like she doesn't notice, but I know it bothers her."

"Screw them," Vivi says. "Are you going to change into your workout clothes or not?"

We go for a walk/run. We stick to the back roads in our neighborhood because Abuelo warned us that he's going to the post office in a bit, and if he sees us on Red Road he'll pull over in the middle of traffic and take us home. My father partly blamed him for the drone fiasco last weekend, so now Abuelo's being extra overprotective.

It's so humid I feel drops of sweat on my upper lip not even minutes after we take off. There are still puddles along the sides of the roads from the afternoon rain. They spread over the gravel into people's front yards, forming semicircles of tiny swamps with grass poking out of the water's surface.

Vivi sprints forward and back while I speed walk to keep up with her. We pass houses that are four times bigger than ours and driveways that look like jungles, full of overgrown palm trees and bushes thick as walls. Trees with roots like claws line the sidewalk and stretch over the roads, leaning into one another to form a shaded canopy.

I'm out of breath and cramping by the time Vivi slows down. It's only then that I notice she's taken us to her old neighborhood.

"Oh. We're here." By now even the lizards scattering across our path are moving faster than I am.

"I had to see it for myself," Vivi says. Her house is the second one on our right. It's a pretty plain one-story that's shaped like an L, with a long stretch of windows along the front lined by hurricane shutters. There's a big red and blue FOR SALE sign on the front yard, and a black placard that says PENDING on it.

"He really didn't waste any time. Out with the old, in with the new. Just like Mom said."

We go right up to the front door, where there's a lockbox hanging from the knob so realtors can get the key. Vivi fidgets with it, sniffling uncontrollably.

"I can't even get into my own house."

Through the windows we can see it's been staged. Strange paintings and photographs hang from the wall where her parents' wedding portrait used to be, and the gray couch in the living room looks stiff and sterile, like no one's ever sat on it.

"Did he get rid of our furniture? What about my room? My mom's grandmother's dining table?" She runs around the side of the house toward her bedroom.

"Vivi! Wait."

She's already jumped over the wooden fence. The gate clicks twice and she opens it for me. "Just real quick," she says.

We don't make it as far as her bedroom. We don't have to. The blinds in the garage window are wide open, and instead of her father's car, it's filled with everything that used to be in Vivi's house. The beige, flower-patterned couch where we used to watch movies on weekends until we passed out. The baby piano Vivi never learned to play anything on other than "Row Row Row Your Boat." There are stacks of boxes scattered everywhere; they look like the uneven skyline of Brickell, with all of downtown's in-progress construction. They're labeled things like VIVI'S and LILY'S and MISCELLANEOUS. I picture Vivi's father throwing stuff into them without a second thought. Everything's tucked away, as if any indication of Vivi's life would be damaging evidence in her father's plans for the future.

Plans that clearly don't include her or her mom.

Vivi tightens her jaw and slides her fingers off the window glass. "Come on."

She takes one look into her bedroom—now a gender-neutral baby nursery—and sprints off the property so fast I think we've been caught. I run after her.

"Vivi! Wait! Wait up!"

She doesn't stop. Instead of heading back the way we came, she runs straight toward Red Road, the busy two-way street Abuelo told us to stay away from.

Cars speed past us, not bothering to slow down for the puddles on the road's edges. We try to dodge their splashes, but it's no use. By the time we reach the house, our legs are covered in muddy splatters and clumps of dirt are caked onto our skin.

In my room, Vivi sits on my desk chair and spins slowly side to side. She stares into nothingness.

"I really thought this was temporary," she finally says. "I didn't think he'd actually sell the house."

"It said 'pending'," I offer. "Nothing's final yet."

But we both know things are moving faster than we imagined, with a force beyond our control.

twenty-one

The next morning I'm woken by the sound of Vivi texting. The tiny taps of her keyboard had been blending into my dreams until I remembered she'd slept over. She's always up long before I am. I roll over without opening my eyes and stretch.

"Morning, sleepy. Didn't mean to wake you."

"You know you did," I mumble.

"I'm bored. And hungry."

"You sound like my brother."

"Come on. We only have six hours before my mom takes me back to the beach." She sits up and holds a pillow against her chest, like she wishes it would protect her. At Grove High, Vivi was always the quirky girl, the one who couldn't care less about cliques or trends because she'd decided from day one that she was going to pick and choose, on her own terms, who to hang out with and what she liked.

Going to a new school in the middle of the year takes away all of that. You don't get to decide anything. All the rules have been set before you got there and, what's worse, you don't even know them well enough to choose if you want to follow or break them.

Not that Vivi would normally care.

"Is it really that bad?"

"I haven't even been able to pick up the rest of my clothes from my dad's," she says. "I keep washing and wearing the same three outfits. Everyone thinks I'm a freak."

"They're such jerks," I say, remembering the look on people's faces the morning the pictures of me came out. They were practically animalistic, so quick to pounce on a victim so long as it kept the attention away from themselves. "Do you think they ever grow out of it?"

"Doubtful. Just look at all that happened with you and your dad and Gloria."

"Gloria? What do you mean? What happened?" I sit up in bed and Vivi immediately starts going through her toiletry bag. Her cheeks turn red and she won't even look at me. "Vivi?"

"It's nothing. I just meant how all the media surrounded her apartment the night you snuck away."

"But . . . that was it, right?"

"You really haven't been reading the news? Like, at all?" She shakes her toothbrush at me in disbelief.

"I told you. I had to block it out." I'm beginning to think that was a huge mistake. If Papi were here, he'd remind me that problems only get worse when you ignore them.

"It's just . . . trolls with nothing better to do, that's all. Harmless BS gossip about Gloria and her girlfriend."

"What kind of gossip? Gloria never mentioned any gossip." My phone charger snaps as I pull on my phone, tipping a cup full of pens and papers off my desk. They scatter all over the floor, but I ignore them.

Vivi puts her hand over mine. "Don't. They really haven't told you anything?"

"No. And now you're scaring me."

"Then it's probably not a big deal. If it was, they would've said something. You were right to block it all out."

"I should at least check Twitter . . ."

"Trust me. Don't get into it. Just talk to Gloria. She'd tell you if it was bad."

That's exactly the problem. Gloria has said like five words to me all week. Is this why she and Amarys have been fighting so much? Is this why she's been avoiding me?

"I'll just text Amarys to see if they're okay." My phone is still in both our hands. Vivi gives me a disapproving look, hesitating to let go, when it vibrates. Out of instinct we look down.

It's Jackie.

Having a meeting today. Urgent. You'll want to be at this one.

"Zoey mentioned you've been hanging out with Jackie lately. What's she like? Did she really douse Principal Avila's car with paint that one time?"

"What? No." Jackie's practically a living urban legend. Only she would have rumors that actually make her look good. It's like she defies every law in the universe. "She's just intense, is all."

"I can't believe you're becoming friends with Jackie Velez."

"We're just hanging out—"

"Tell her to come over!"

"What?"

"I want to meet her. Zoey says she's been shutting down anyone who talks shit about you."

"She has?"

"She overheard Jackie asking people if they'd bothered questioning their sources or if they believe every little thing they read online."

"That's really cool of her."

"Zoey's been defending you, too, you know."

"Really?"

"I know it's probably really awkward without me, but give her a chance. She's the kind of person who's there for you when you need her."

"I wasn't *not* giving her a chance." Maybe I've skipped lunch with her once or twice, but I've been busy with my community service project.

Which was supposed to be *our* community service project. Oops.

My phone buzzes again. Jackie sends a bunch of question marks.

"Ohmigod. You should invite her and Zoey over. Tell your grandpa it's for school."

"I don't think that's a good idea."

"Please? I miss Zoey. And I want to be part of whatever this is," she says, signaling at my phone.

Whatever this is, Papi would kill me if he knew I invited Jackie Velez over. He's convinced she's what's wrong with kids these days—not drugs or teen pregnancies or violence, but their radical ideals.

What's the meeting about??? I text.

The environment. Sewage in the water.

I show it to Vivi.

She nearly chokes on her own saliva. "Yes. Ohmigod. That shit's still in the water on the beach. The doctors at the hospital said my grandmother had gotten food poisoning, but honestly, what if it's something she drank? What if my aunt's right about the water?"

She's talking almost as fast as Abuelo when he speaks in Spanish, barely catching her breath between words.

"Okay, okay. I'll tell them to come. But only for like half an hour. So they can tell us what this is all about."

"Okay, great," she says, looking like a million little gears are turning in her head at once. She runs into my closet and yells, "Can I borrow a shirt?"

"Do you even have to ask?"

Vivi comes out wearing a white boat neck top covered in a blue zebra pattern that ties in a small knot on one side. It's one of those things I bought a while ago and then decided I couldn't pull off. It looks perfect on her. "You should take a bunch of outfits with you. For school."

She gives me this proud mom smile, like she's in awe of the gesture.

"You're better than a little sister I never had, you know that?"

"Because all our clothes are the same size?"

"Basically."

It's crazy how you can miss a person even when they're

standing right in front of you. My parents will probably punish me for the rest of the year when they find out about Jackie coming here, but if it makes Vivi as happy as she is right now . . .

Screw them and the campaign and the way things look. Whatever happened to caring about the way things are?

twenty-two

I'm super anxious when Jackie, Crissy, and Didier first arrive. For one, they come in carrying a truckload of paper rolls, paints, posters, and wooden sticks, and before anyone even says hi, Jackie wants to know where to put everything.

"Help us unload the trunk?" she says to Vivi, as if they already know each other. Vivi looks momentarily confused, but she grabs a giant container full of brushes and Sharpies anyway.

"¿Y esto? ¿Quién los mandó?" The way Abuelo asks, you'd think they came out of nowhere. "No, no, no, no . . . pa'fuera. No painting in the house. Your mother will kill me if you get paint on the couches." He shoos us into the backyard. Through the glass door, I can see Ricky staring at us with his hands cupped over his eyes, his breath fogging the view.

Vivi's phone beeps and she starts texting someone. Her keyboard is still super loud from when she was trying to passive-aggressively wake me up this morning.

"You mind putting that on silent?" Jackie asks.

I guess we're skipping the introductions and going straight to making things weird.

"Can we just . . . can you wait and tell me what this is all about?" I ask as Crissy and Didier start covering the patio tiles with newspaper.

Crissy puffs up her cheeks and makes a sound like the air coming out of a tire. I decide to go into the kitchen to get us something to drink. I grab a few cans of Materva, fill a couple of glasses with water, and leave the rest filled with ice on the table for everyone to help themselves. It's so humid out that the air drips onto our skin, and the glasses soak the newspapers and construction paper with their condensation almost instantly. The doorbell rings just as I finally sit down.

It's Zoey.

"Ohmigod! You're here!" Vivi jumps up and hugs her like it's been forever. Maybe to her, it has. Maybe when you're the one who's taken out of your school, rather than the friend who's left behind, time passes more slowly.

I try to introduce everyone but end up just mumbling their names as they each nod.

Jackie picks up a glass of water. Instead of bringing it to her lips, she holds it over her head and examines the bottom.

"Is this tap?" she asks.

"Yeah, but it's filtered," I say. "I can get bottled . . ."

"No, no, I didn't mean it like that. It's just that, this is why we're here," she says, setting the glass down on the table. "We're not going to be able to drink our water soon. Any of us. The contamination is out of control . . . haven't you seen the news?"

"You mean the sewage leak on the beach?" Vivi says.

"Well, no. I mean, that's a whole other mess, but that's . . ."

not what we were talking about," Crissy says. "We're talking about the Biscayne Bay aquifer on the news. Almost all of Miami gets its drinking water from it." She opens up her laptop and types something real quick, then flips it over so we can get a look. A map of Florida with nearly the entire southern tip from Boca Raton past Homestead is covered in yellow and gray lines.

"That's the aquifer," Didier says. "It's a whole layer of limestone that runs underground."

"And it's been getting pumped full of sewage water for years now."

Zoey practically spits out her Materva. "What?! That's ridiculous. They wouldn't literally have us drinking pee."

"It gets treated," Jackie says. "Through the limestone and all sorts of cleaning mechanisms. And then it has to meet federal drinking standards. But look." She takes the computer back from Crissy and switches to another screen. "*The Miami Herald* has been working on an investigative report on it for months. They found out about these tests that came out this week . . . the water's still full of drugs from people's waste. And carcinogens and metals. And like, a shit-ton of Viagra."

"People are freaking out," Didier says. "You seriously hadn't heard?"

"I've been avoiding the news this week," I admit.

"How nice for you," Crissy mumbles. Jackie shoots her a nasty look and she quickly apologizes.

"They're saying the mayor will issue a boil-water warning by tonight," Didier says.

"This can't be right." Zoey is still not getting it, and I'm not really sure I am either. "Aren't there, like, laws to keep this kind of stuff from happening?"

Jackie sighs. "You would think. But the Florida legislature passed the bill that allowed for this years ago. They claimed it'd help us avoid water shortages. Especially with all the salt water contaminating the ground water because of sea level rise. And they needed a better way to get rid of the sewage than just dumping it into the ocean."

"Why waste perfectly good toilet water if you can also drink it?" Didier says.

Zoey gags. "That's disgusting."

Vivi nods like this is all finally making sense. She sits back in her chair and rests her foot against the table. "So it's all tied together. The sewage. The water. The sea level rise on the beach every full moon."

"Exactly," Crissy says. "And all of it goes back to—"

"Not now." Jackie puts her hand in the air and nods just the tiniest bit in my direction. "Mariana? You okay?"

"I'm fine. It's just a lot." I didn't think it was possible to feel so grossed out, angry, and helpless all at once. "What can we do?"

As soon as I ask, Didier and Crissy both cross their arms and turn pointedly to Jackie.

"You guys are assholes," she says, half laughing, but serious. She lets her voice trail off as she begins to mumble. One thing I've learned about Jackie this past week is that she's always thinking of a million things at once. Sometimes those things contradict each other, so she ends up talking to herself a lot, working through her own arguments. I've decided not to interrupt her when she does this. It's her process.

"Okay, here's the thing," she finally says. "As ridiculous as this all sounds, the bill only passed all those years ago because building developers were pushing for it."

"Greedy conchudos," Crissy says.

"But . . . why would they care?" Vivi asks.

"Because it makes it easier for them to build new condos and homes. They keep water supply levels high with access to sewage everywhere, and now they're not restricted by where to treat it. They can basically build wherever they want."

I nod, though I feel my stomach begin to tighten. "So do we, like, start a bottled water donation drive?"

It seems like such a small and futile plan, now that I say it out loud, but I'm not Jackie or my father. They're always focused on making things happen when, so far, all I've done is make things not happen: no Home Invasion interview, no more press appearances, no being seen or heard anywhere. Things just work out better when I stay out of them.

"Collecting clean water is a start." Jackie's voice cracks from how gentle she's trying to be, and then, for the first time since we've met, I catch a note of exasperation in it. "But you especially . . . you have so much, power, Mariana. You don't even know it."

I can't help but laugh. Me, power? Even Vivi and Zoey

aren't buying it—they exchange their best *Did you hear what I just heard?* looks.

"Trust me. I'm grounded till probably the end of the school year. The last thing I am right now is powerful."

"If you're already grounded, then you have nothing to lose," Crissy says in a singsongy, nonchalant way.

"What's that supposed to mean?" I ask.

They do that annoying thing again where it's clear that the three of them know more than I do.

I wait. "Jackie?"

"I'm really, really sorry to ask you this. I've been feeling kind of sick about it, honestly. But it's just that . . . there are lives at stake, and we need to do something big. Something that'll get everyone's attention, and not just here in Miami. Look what happened in Flint, with all the lead in people's water—we can't let the government keep getting away with this. That's why we're making these signs." She tries to hand me a blue poster board. I let it hang in the air between us until it sags. "We're doing a walkout at school on Friday. We'll have the whole week to get as many students as possible to join us."

"That should be easy," Didier says. He shows us an e-flyer he posted online that heavily relies on the water drops + poop emojis. "It hasn't even been an hour and I have a shit-ton of likes. Sorry. Pun not intended."

"But FCAT prep." All this time Zoey hasn't said a thing, and now that she does, her words don't even form a complete sentence. "The sophomores are doing FCAT prep."

"Even better," Crissy says. "So we interrupt their precious

standardized testing. The whole point of protest is it's inconvenient."

"Protest?" All at once, it hits me that this was a mistake. The second Papi finds out what they're planning here, he's going to kill me. "I don't understand how this has anything to do with me."

"We want to do speeches," Jackie says. "We'll stream them, of course."

"I'm not allowed to post anything online. My parents are super paranoid, with everything that's happened in the campaign and all."

"Again, that's kind of the point," Didier says.

"You want her to post video of herself online? Talking? After everything she's just been through? Did you *not* see the news last week?" Zoey's heard enough, I guess.

"Yeah, I'm sorry. That's not happening," I say.

Jackie rubs her left temple and closes her eyes. "You don't understand . . ."

"I get it. Really. But not all of us are used to just putting ourselves out there like you are," I say.

"That's not what I meant."

"You do it. You're the one who can go on for hours about this stuff."

"Look, I know it's not fair. I know it's a lot to put on you . . . but it'll matter more coming from you," Jackie says.

"No, it won't. I'm not my father, remember?"

"Mariana. Mariana!" She yells so loud that out of the corner of my eye, I see Abuelo and Ricky turn their heads. They've been sitting in the living room this whole time, pretending not to pay attention to us, but now they don't bother pretending and stare through the glass door. Everyone goes quiet.

Jackie sighs, and there's a sadness in her eyes that I've never seen before. "Your father's the one who sponsored the bill. When he was state senator. It was his idea to allow sewage water in the aquifer. And the property where all the water testing came back contaminated this week . . . the developer . . . he was pushing for the bill too. It was Harrison Irving."

Oof. I feel like she just shoved me against the wall.

"Your father's biggest donor," Crissy adds.

"I know who Harrison Irving is," I manage to say.

twenty-three

There are promises my father makes to the people and promises he makes to me. Sometimes those things are different.

Like when he says he wants all families to have access to jobs and the pursuit of happiness that they deserve, but then he's late to dinner if he makes it at all.

Or when he says that we need real, experienced people running the country, not millionaires turned reality show stars, but then he has Joe tell me and Ricky exactly what to say and do when there are cameras around.

It's like he's two different people. I used to be okay with this, because it meant one of them was a father we got to keep all to ourselves.

The guy who'd insist we don't talk politics at home.

The guy who'd make me playlists and audio messages of jokes he thought of while he was out of town.

The guy who'd curse in Spanish, a mile a minute, anytime he got cut off in traffic.

The guy who still sleeps in the volunteer T-shirt we got for helping clean up Biscayne Bay.

That guy.

That guy couldn't possibly have known about this.

Could he?

I check the watch on my phone. It's been way more than half an hour since everyone got here, but I'm not about to remind them it's time to leave. Not until I get to the bottom of this.

Crissy pulls out her laptop again and begins reading from the website of Harrison Irving's newest real estate development. "Erban—get this, it's spelled with an E, so obnoxious—is reinventing luxury living in South Florida."

"It's a monstrosity." Jackie scrolls down to the architectural sketches of the property. It looks like a shimmering chunk of green-tinted glass stretching toward the sky, surrounded by lily-white concrete renderings of a street. Young couples walk their dogs along the sidewalk and children grab ice cream from a vendor.

"Just a twenty-five-minute drive to the beach . . . Bull. Shit," says Didier. "This Irving guy is straight up lying. Maybe a twenty-five-minute drive at four in the morning with no traffic." Out of all of us, Didier is the only one who has his own car. He loves to remind us of this, in subtle and not-so-subtle ways, anytime he can. Like right now, his car keys are in the center of the table instead of in his pocket. Aside from the clicker for his Honda, he's got a metal Haitian flag for a keychain and a plastic yellow tag labeled with his name in all caps.

"Can we focus?" Jackie says. "We need to organize."

They set up a new Twitter account and begin retweeting the latest news reports using #DumpIrving to promote the walkout. They announce the date and time: Friday at noon from Grove High. Any other Fla students want to join from your school? @ us.

I watch them through a haze, feeling like every crevice in my head might explode from too much pressure. They've decided to make a scapegoat out of Irving—already the local news retweeted them and they're talking about his ties to Papi's campaign. I imagine the team is in crisis mode, trying to control the way the press will spin this, and only days after they've finished spinning me.

Not a single thing about this feels right. Not the water. Not my father. Not them being here, plotting against him, in our home. I want to ask them to leave, but I don't. Even though the mayor of Miami hasn't issued a boil-water advisory yet, news stations show reporters at Publix asking shoppers if they plan to stock up on bottled water. Abuelo leaves for a quick run to the grocery store minutes after. I check my father's campaign accounts to see if he's issued a statement. His last tweet is a generic, "Thank You to the people of Tallahassee for a fantastic event," sent just minutes before the news of the water contamination broke this morning.

"He must not know this is happening," I say.

"He knows," Jackie says, placing her hand over mine gently. "It doesn't matter now, anyways. It only matters what he does next."

"He'd never support this."

"Never support what? Irving or the walkout?" Zoey asks.

"Both. He thinks the environment needs to be protected. He's told me so a hundred times."

Crissy clears her throat.

"Oh ti cheri," Didier says in an overly sugarcoated voice. "That might be what your father's told you privately, but . . . I mean, you've seen how he votes, haven't you?"

I keep my face straight, trying hard not to cringe. I don't understand why people keep calling me sweetie. And even worse, I've never thought to look up my dad's voting record. Why would I need proof that my father is doing all the things he said he'd do?

They're all quiet, waiting for me to answer. "Of course. I just meant that's how he talks about the future. He has plans, you know?"

"It's more like . . . Irving has plans, and your father follows," Jackie says. "I know it's hard to hear. But just think about it."

Didier shakes his head and mumbles something about how much money Irving's company has donated to my father. It's loud enough for me to hear, but low enough for him to pretend I wasn't supposed to.

"I'm going to talk to him," I decide.

"Of course. Whatever you want. But can we count on you for the walkout?" Jackie says.

"I'm going to talk to him," I say again. "Maybe the walkout won't be necessary." But it's clear they don't believe me. They finally pack up all their supplies. Jackie gives me a hug and apologizes profusely before she goes.

"Believe me, I hate that it's come to this."

That makes two of us. But I don't respond.

Crissy doesn't even say bye as she walks out of the house and waits for them in Didier's car.

"What's her problem?" Zoey says.

I'm glad she asked. I've been wondering all week but haven't had the guts to say it.

"She has her reasons," Didier says. "Crissy was born here, but her older brother wasn't. He's a veteran and he still got deported to Peru last year."

"I don't understand. I mean, that's horrible, but what does it have to do with me?"

He looks at me wide-eyed and mouths, *wow*. "Maybe you should do your homework on your dad ASAP. At least know his stance on things."

It's only after they leave that I notice Vivi has been super quiet.

"What do you think I should do?"

She crosses her arms and shrugs. "I'm in shock right now, Mari. What if the water's what made my abuela sick?"

I tell her I'm sorry and give her a hug. There's so much to process all at once. While Zoey comforts Vivi, I head up to my room and open my laptop.

It's all so confusing. Searching for Papi's voting record online, all I find are spreadsheets and charts full of hundreds of bills and resolutions that he either sponsored, cosponsored, voted for, or voted against. None of their names make it clear what they're about. Resolution for Restoration of Health and Dignity or Martin Allan Jones Act don't exactly paint a clear picture. I close the computer and go into his office.

We're not supposed to be in here when he's not, but there's no one around to stop me. It's a small room with floor-to-ceiling dark wooden bookshelves and a matching desk that is almost as wide as the back wall. I sit in Papi's leather chair and try to open the drawers, but they're locked. His desktop has a pile of manila folders on one side and stacks of papers on the other. In the center, a cup full of hard drives sits next to a framed picture of Papi, Mami, Ricky, and me the night he won some election, I can't remember which. The air carries the faintest hint of his cedar wood and citrus cologne, just enough to make me feel like he's here, watching me.

I go through his stack, lifting the edges of the papers just enough to see their headings. Nothing catches my eye until I get to a thick, light-green cardstock—a blueprint for an office unit at Erban. This can't be right. I run back to my room and grab my phone, dialing the only person I know who could make sense of all this.

"Amarys? Are you busy?" I sink back into my father's chair just as she asks what's wrong. "Can you help me figure out Papi's policies?"

For a moment she remains quiet. I can practically hear the hesitation in her breathing, but instead of saying no, she says, "What policies were you wondering about?"

I ask her about the aquifer and tell her about Vivi's

grandmother. She tells me it's true that Papi voted to let the sewage be treated there years ago.

"But he didn't know, right? That people might get sick?"

"No sé, nena. Seguro que that's what people will be investigating soon."

Soon isn't good enough; I need answers now. "Then what about immigration? What about, like a vet who got deported? My dad's gonna fix that, no? When he's president?" The line is so silent, I wonder if we got disconnected. "Amarys?"

"Since your Papi's been a US senator, he's voted several times against immigration reform. Other times he doesn't show up to vote at all."

"What do you mean, doesn't show up?"

"Mari . . . I hate being the one to tell you these things. Your Papi has one of the lowest attendance records in the Senate."

"That's impossible. He's never home. He's always in DC."

"That might be the case. But a lot of times, he doesn't place a vote."

It doesn't make any sense. He's always saying that it's his biggest honor to work for the American people. If he's not going to bother showing up to place a vote, then what's the point of him being away for so long? What's the point of any of this at all?

My voice shakes as I thank Amarys for helping me. "I'll ask Papi about this when he gets home."

"Don't tell him I helped you. He'll accuse me of turning you into a progressive."

"I'm not . . . I don't really like to go by labels." I'm just trying to figure out what I believe in, and what my dad believes. I know I don't want people getting hurt. "I'm not trying to take sides or anything," I add.

"Nena, sometimes you have to choose a side."

twenty-four

My father has never been good at accepting rejection or failure. It's just not who he is. He doesn't let up even when things are going well. Back when he ran the smaller campaigns from our apartment, when the staff used to stay up late at night sending out emails for donations, I'd always hear him say, *We can go for a little more.* He'd dictate to them what to write. Something about the campaign not meeting their fundraising goal, about the next few hours being crucial, about needing everyone to chip in even four dollars more.

I know because I'd hear Papi whispering to Mami. *One more time,* he'd say. *We won't know if we don't try.* Maybe it was like a game to him, the rush of a gamble.

Everyone admired this about him. *The guy has no quit in him,* they used to say.

I guess it's true. Since I've broken my news blackout by searching for my father's Senate voting record, I decide to check how things are looking for them on the trail. I take my laptop to the family room, where Vivi is filling Zoey in on the situation with her parents, how her dad put the house up for sale without even telling them.

"Can he do that? Without your mom signing something?"

"The house has always been in his name. My mom just always trusted him."

Zoey gasps. Her parents don't even share the same last name because her mom kept hers.

I half listen to them, half read articles about Papi. It's crunch time now that only ten days are left until the primary election. Up until yesterday, his lead in Florida was up by a few digits in the polls, but now it's within the margin of error. *The margin of terror,* Joe always calls it, because it means, for all we know, he could be losing. People are saying that Ruiz's campaign has been all over the place, constantly in crisis mode with one thing after another. The Bubble Boy comment. Me running away the night of the Home Invasion interview. The drone pictures. They're saying if it wasn't for me caught sunbathing in our backyard, he might not have bounced back at all. People thought his decision to take me and Ricky off the campaign trail showed character. It made him look like a real family guy.

But now this new report about the water contamination is trending. I refresh his Twitter page—still no statement. I don't dare text him, Joe, or Mami.

Family first and families first, is what he apparently said during a speech in the Florida panhandle last night. It was the sound bite of the day until his silence on the aquifer became the big story. Now the news networks link to clips of footage from last night on Twitter. He's standing on a platform in a grassy field with Mami purposely in-frame behind him. His hair is parted to the right as usual, and he has one hand on the mike, the other pointing at the audience. The headline across the screen reads: RUIZ EMPHASIZES FAMILY TO FLORIDA VOTERS, NO STATEMENT YET ON WATER CONTAMINATION. Joe must be having a mild heart attack.

When Abuelo gets back from the grocery store, we help him bring four cases of bottled water into the kitchen. He leaves a fifth in the trunk to take home with him.

"See? It's just like preparing for a hurricane," he says.

Except you can't change the course of a hurricane.

No one says anything while he makes us sandwiches for a late lunch. We stay outside on the patio because a breeze has come in off the canal.

He checks his watch as we chew quietly. "They'll be home in three hours."

Abuelo knows that whatever happened while Jackie was here meant something. He has always had a good sense about storms coming. Actual storms. He's the first one to board up his windows with wooden planks when a tropical depression so much as forms in the Atlantic. While no one else takes it seriously until the local weather says it's at least a category 2, Abuelo has already bought a week's supply of canned food, water, batteries, and powdered milk for our house and his. He believes in being prepared for everything, so now he finally sits down with us on the patio and asks, "What do you plan to tell your father when he gets home?"

Vivi pushes herself just a few inches off her chair and pulls her legs in off the ground to sit cross-legged. "What do you think he'll say?"

Before I can answer, Ricky rushes over like he's afraid he'll miss something.

"Nobody called you," I say.

"I already texted dad that you had friends over to talk about him."

"You did what?!"

"Oh, Ricky," Vivi says. "What'd you do that for?"

"What? They wanted to know how we were doing."

That explains why they haven't texted me. I know Ricky probably meant well, but sometimes I wish he'd stop working so hard to please my parents.

"They shouldn't have given you that phone. You're too little."

"You got yours when you were my age."

"That was different. I didn't also have an iPad and a Play-Station and a TV in my room."

Ricky has no idea how good he has it. He thinks poor people only exist on television, the same way that white Christmases and huge brownstone houses are only things we see in movies. To him, there is no reality outside of our home and definitely not outside of Miami. I used to think it was sweet that he was so sheltered, but the world's going to hit him hard some day. One time, I heard him ask Gloria who cleans her house. She said she did.

"Nobody else does it for you?"

"No, papito. But it's okay because mine isn't even a quarter the size of this one."

Ricky practically got whiplash from the shock, and Gloria and I laughed.

Lately, though, it's not so funny.

"Can you take us to Sunset?" I ask Abuelo. I'm not in the mood to shop, but I need a distraction and we only have a couple of hours before Vivi's mom picks her up. Maybe the three of us can get our nails done.

Vivi and Zoey perk up.

He pretends to think about it. "I have to run more errands. I'll drop you off while I go." Ricky starts to get excited until Abuelo adds, "Tú vienes conmigo. I need your help getting more groceries at the other Publix."

Abuelo is the absolute best.

We take US 1 because Abuelo says two-way streets make him feel claustrophobic. I sit in the front while Ricky sits in the back between Vivi and Zoey.

This week, Abuelo is driving a thirty-something-year-old gray Mercedes with an engine that rattles like it's full of marbles. He changes cars like someone changes outfits, always trading in one vintage vehicle for another. He says it's like flipping houses but with less money.

This car has leather seats that are so creased, they feel like tissue paper, and the central compartment has an actual car phone that of course doesn't work. It makes me feel like we're in a time capsule.

"Did you ever use one of these?" I twirl the phone's cord around my finger.

"In Cuba when I was a boy, you just got on a horse and yelled." I never know if he's telling the truth or exaggerating.

All his stories about Cuba make it sound like the most far-off place in the world, even though it's ninety miles from our shore. In his wallet, Abuelo carries a picture of the house that Bisabuelo built and left them when he died. He and Abuela lived in it for just a year before the revolution began. On the back of the picture there's the date and address written in Abuela's perfect cursive. When I was little and learning to read, Abuelo used to show me the picture and quiz me on the address. He wanted me to memorize it. *For when we go back,* he said. *So you can always find your way home.*

He hasn't asked me to recite the address to him in years. Not since Fidel Castro died. We all thought things would change once he was gone, but aside from the parades on Calle Ocho, nothing happened. What do you do when your last hope turns out to make no difference at all?

We wait at a red light behind a bus that is covered in advertising for a local insurance company. The back looks like a comic book. A woman with huge breasts and a tight green dress is tied up to a chair like a hostage. The dress has dollar signs all over it, and her dialogue bubble reads, "Save me! Save me!"

"That's gross." I've seen the bus so many times, I can't believe it's never bothered me before.

"My mom said the same thing. She wrote a letter to the editor of the *Herald*, saying how it objectifies women's bodies," Zoey says.

"She did? I would've never thought to do that. That's really cool of her," I say.

"Totally," Vivi adds.

We keep going and pass a billboard with a woman's flat stomach and the bottoms of her breasts showing. Her skin is pale and smooth. The billboard is for a plastic surgery center, the same one with that annoying jingle you hear on the radio every five minutes. It says: *Electrolysis. Liposuction. Two-for-one breast implants.*

It's unsettling. It's like I've seen all these things before, but never really looked close. Now that I see them, I can't not see them.

"Did you know that the pictures of us tanning actually helped him?" I blurt out.

"What? Who?" Zoey says.

"My dad. After all the crap he gave me. Making me feel guilty, like it was my fault some creep decided to spy on me and Vivi when he was more than happy to have us on television any chance he got—"

"Hijita . . ." Abuelo says, pulling up to the rounded curb at the mall's entrance. Behind us, a couple of cars are already waiting for us to move forward.

"Those stupid pictures helped his poll numbers spike again. People thought he was some kind of hero because he stood up for his daughter. Isn't that what a father's supposed to do? Since when do you get bonus points for doing the bare minimum? He should be the one thanking *me*. Not calling me a malcriada and saying I looked like a cheap—"

"He said that? Your father actually said that?" The car jerks forward as Abuelo puts it in park. Two long, high-pitched horns go off, and I catch a middle-aged man flipping us off in the rearview mirror. "¡Vete p'al carajo!" Abuelo yells. I've never seen him so angry. He usually loses his temper during Marlins games or Miami Heat playoffs, but never at random people on the street. "I'm going to have a talk with your father. As soon as he gets back."

"It's okay, Abuelo." But he's not even looking at me anymore, just talking at the steering wheel, slapping his hand across it. Zoey and Vivi scoot out of the car as fast as they can, mumbling bye and thanks to Abuelo. He sighs and lowers his voice, rubbing both eyes with one hand.

"I've told him a million times. He needs to protect this family. Not just his career. Not just his position. He was supposed to make us proud. Do all the things we couldn't. ¿Y ahora qué? People are getting sick."

"I'm sorry, Abuelo. I didn't mean to upset you." I place my hand on the car's door handle but don't open the door. I don't want to leave him like this.

He shakes his head. "Escúchame, Mari. You never have to apologize for telling the truth. None of this is your fault."

Between Jackie, Crissy, Didier, and now Abuelo, it's the fourth time this week someone has told me that. I nod and tell him I understand. Maybe it's time I start believing it.

twenty-five

Since we only have about an hour and a half before Abuelo picks us up from the mall, Zoey and I get our nails done while Vivi gets a bikini wax. The salon is not my favorite —it looks like a bomb of cotton candy pink exploded and they tried to class it up with a couple of see-through tables and crystal chandeliers. It's really that cliché. But it's cheap and fast, and even though the polish never lasts more than a couple of days, it gives us something to do. While our feet soak, Zoey and I sit in the leather massage chairs and stare out the floor-to-ceiling windows. People walk through the outdoor courtyard with their designer sunglasses, holding shopping bags and cones of gelato.

Zoey and I haven't been talking much while the women do our nails, but now she leans in close and whispers, "So Vivi really hates her new school."

"Yeah, she told me. It's not like it's a secret."

"I know. I was just thinking. I'm going to ask my mom if she can move in with us. Just till the end of the year."

"There's no way her mom would let her."

"Why not?"

"Because . . . that's just not how her family does things.

Especially not with her grandmother being sick. I know my parents wouldn't let me."

"Your parents aren't exactly typical."

"Just trust me." I don't know how to explain it to Zoey. Vivi once tried to sleep over at my house two nights in a row and her mom gave her a huge guilt trip and told her no. I asked Papi if I could sleep over at Vivi's instead and he said, "What's the matter? You don't want to live with your own family anymore?"

And that was the end of that. Maybe it's a Cuban thing.

"Don't think I haven't thought of it," I add, just as Vivi comes out of one of the back rooms. She sits in one of the empty massage chairs while she waits for our mani-pedis to be done, and when it's time to pay, she pulls our wallets out of our purses so we don't ruin our nails.

"I'm starving. Let's grab a smoothie," Vivi says.

We're carrying our shoes in a plastic bag and wearing neon green disposable flip-flops that the nail ladies put on our feet before painting our toes. When we walk, we wobble like penguins.

It seems to take us forever to get to the smoothie shop, but when we do, it's closed. A printout on the glass door reads CLOSED DUE TO WATER ADVISORY. It's the same for nearly every restaurant in the mall; the only one still open has a limited menu.

"So basically, anything that's fried is fine and any dish with produce that needs to be washed is out," Vivi says after looking it over.

We don't really have time to eat at a restaurant anyways, so we make our way back to the entrance where Abuelo left us, which is right across the street from the Whole Foods and a row of two-story condos with several FOR RENT signs.

"Maybe you can move into one of those," Zoey says.

"Doubtful. This area's way too expensive," Vivi says.

"What? We're not even, like, twelve blocks away from your old neighborhood."

Vivi and I sigh in unison. Sometimes Zoey just doesn't get it.

"We might as well be in another world," Vivi says. Her house—well, her father's house, or whoever buys it—has always been one of the smaller, older ones in the area. While everyone around them kept buying property to demolish and rebuild a McMansion, Vivi's parents stayed put. They turned down all the offers on their house because Vivi's mom said that no matter how much they sold it for, it wouldn't be enough for them to buy another house nearby.

She was right. Now they're living in Miami Beach, which I know sounds glamorous, but it's not. Her aunt is in one of those older apartments with a window a/c unit and a kitchen smaller than my closet. I wonder how long until a developer pushes them out of there too.

"Let's just wait over here," I say, pointing at a bench by the intersection.

Vivi sits in the middle, just like we used to at lunch. Across the street, there's a huge, empty plot of land cordoned off by wired fencing. It's a construction site, and the ground's been dug several stories deep to make space for the foundation of whatever it is they'll put there. Probably another high-rise condo. I know because Abuelo taught me that the bigger the hole, the taller the building.

This one looks like it could swallow Vivi's house eight times over.

twenty-six

By the time Mami and Papi get home at night, the mayor has officially issued a boil-water advisory. He says we're safe to shower, but otherwise, all tap water has to be boiled before we cook with it or even brush our teeth. Abuelo already has two huge pots boiling, and Ricky has started worrying about the water he drank this morning, convinced he's already poisoned.

"It's fine. It's all just precautionary," Papi says as he brings in all their luggage. He and Mami are being followed by a crew of campaign staff and camera people who are shooting new real-time footage for the PACs to use, I guess, or not.

I ask them if we can speak alone.

"Shhh . . . be careful you're not in the frame," Mami says. She hasn't even kissed me hello yet.

"You could ask them to turn it off for two seconds," I say. The smile on her face vanishes instantly. Papi places his hand on my shoulder and brushes his cheek against mine. That's how I know he's still mad at me, because he kisses me without actually kissing me.

"What's going on?" he asks.

"Nothing. I just want to talk to you guys."

"Does this mean you're ready to apologize now?"

I take a deep breath. "It's about Harrison Irving."

That gets his attention. My father looks over his shoulder to make sure the camera guy didn't hear me. He tells the crew to take a break as he leads me into his bedroom. Mami drags along her carry-on luggage as she follows.

"What's this about?" she says when we're alone.

I don't know how else to say it, so I just blurt it out. "This whole crisis with the water being contaminated."

"It's not a crisis," Papi says.

"But . . . it was your bill, right? The one that let them dump the sewage into the . . . aquifer?"

Papi looks briefly stunned. "What are you getting at, hijita?"

That's a good question. My mind is both blank and overwhelmed by everything I've read and heard today. It was all making so much sense until I tried to say something.

"And Irving. He was all for it, too, wasn't he? Because it'd help him build more buildings . . . and stuff."

My father begins going through the mail Gloria must have placed on their dresser. "Where've you been getting your talking points, Mari? I thought we taught you better than this." He gives me a look—his *qué coño's gotten into you* look—like he doesn't even know his own daughter.

Maybe he doesn't.

"I'm serious, Papi."

"You think I'm not? You think I don't care about Miami Dade county's water? You think I'd sell out all my people for Irving's money? Is that what your friend Jenny's told you?"

"Jackie."

"Jenny, Jackie . . . Is she the one putting you up to this?"

"It's everywhere, Papi. I don't live in a box."

"No, you don't. That's exactly my point. Our growing population needs housing, Mari. We're all doing the best we can with the resources we have. This is . . . a really bad turn of events, but it's not the crisis you and your friends are making it out to be. Irving knows what he's doing. He wouldn't invest seven hundred fifteen million dollars in a flawed project."

"That's . . . a lot of money," I say.

"It is. He invests a lot in these properties. Don't you think he thinks them through?"

"Do I think he thinks about the money? Yes. The environment? Not so much."

"Cuidado with that tone." Mami's been pretty quiet, but she never misses a chance to tell me not to talk back to my father. It's like an instinct she can't control.

"No, it's fine, Juli. Mari's just voicing her concerns." He sits on the arm of the couch that faces away from their bed and crosses his legs, suddenly attentive.

"Please don't do that." It's amazing how fast he's gone from chewing me out to patronizing me.

"Do what?"

"I'm not a constituent you need to convince to vote for you! I'm just your daughter and I'm really upset right now."

"Okay. Calm down. And tell me why."

"I don't want to calm down! I don't understand how you can be okay with Irving doing this."

"Mari, it's not as bad as you think it is. Besides, Irving's business is Irving's business. I stay out of his and he stays out of mine."

"That's hard to believe."

"What did you say?"

Maybe Mami is right; I should be careful. "Nothing. It's just, it doesn't look good. He's your biggest donor."

And your bill only helps him, I want to add. But I don't.

"What do you want me to do? Give back money this campaign already spent?" As he raises his voice, mine feels like it's shrinking back into my chest.

"You said you would protect our environment."

"When did I say that?"

It's like he just threw a basketball at my gut. Could he really have forgotten? Or worse, could he be pretending to?

"The last time we went to the Everglades. On the boat? And every time we do beach cleanups?" I blink back tears and look away. The shirt he sleeps in literally says, THE EARTH IS OUR ONLY HOME. PROTECT IT.

"Oh, Mari." He gets up from the couch and sits next to me on the bed, placing his arm around my shoulder. "I'm sorry. I didn't realize you were talking about our trips."

"It's not just that. It's everything. Abuelo bought like eighty gallons of water, and Ricky is so scared he's going to die. It shouldn't have come to this."

"I know. You're right."

"So you'll talk to him?"

"To who?"

"Irving."

"These things aren't that simple, Mari."

"Then what are we supposed to do?"

"Well, we focus on winning this election, for one. You can't change things if you're not in a position to do so."

I watch the way he pouts his lips as he talks. He's said this all my life and I've always thought it was about empowering other people. What if it's just about empowering him?

"It's not even on your platform, though. None of the environmental issues are."

"Ah, so you're checking up on me now? You don't trust your Papi anymore?"

"It's not that."

"Look. These big developments that people like Irving plan, they're a necessary part of a city's growth. A city either grows or it stagnates, and then everybody suffers because that's how industries die and people lose their jobs and homes . . ."

"Vivi's losing her home. She and her mom can't afford to live here now that her dad's selling the house."

"What? When did this happen?" Mami stops emptying her suitcase and slumps back on the couch. "How's Lily? I should call her . . ."

"Yes, it's very sad," Papi interrupts. "But these are all normal growing pains."

Mami looks at him in disbelief and I shake my head. None of this makes sense.

"If these are normal growing pains, how come the only ones getting hurt are people like Vivi's family?"

"I can't believe I'm hearing this." He begins undoing his tie.

"I feel like I'm debating one of my opponents, except it's my own daughter!"

"Cálmate, Tonio. Stop treating her like she's the enemy," Mami says. "She's just worried about her friend. I am, too, now."

"Not just Vivi, though, Mami. What about people even worse off than Vivi? She's living at her aunt's because she can, but . . . what about people who are really poor?"

"I know," she says.

"So now you're both ganging up on me?" Papi says.

"Tonio, for once, think of someone other than yourself!" Mami's words rush out of her mouth, and then she seems to gasp silently before clearing her throat. "Hijita, give me and your father a moment alone."

He looks just as surprised as I feel. Mami hardly ever gets mad at Papi in front of me. Seeing her lose her composure, even for a second, scares me. It's another one of those things I can't pretend I didn't see, the kind that, one by one, changes everything.

twenty-seven

Every other Sunday we go to the 10:00 a.m. mass, which is in English, and then the next Sunday we go to the 11:30 a.m. mass, which is in Spanish.

The Spanish one always feels longer because the priest talks too fast and he's really long-winded, and as much as I try to pay attention, I zone out. I don't mind because on the one hand, I get to sleep in an hour later than I do for the English mass. On the other, Mami doesn't like us having breakfast before church—she says the body of Christ should be the first thing in our bodies. So on any given Sunday morning, I'm either sleepy or starving, and cranky either way.

It doesn't help that we never actually leave right after the hour is up. On the way out, Papi finds any excuse to linger around the church steps. He'll pretend to look for his sunglasses or check his phone for messages. He'll thank the Father for the day's sermon.

He hangs around to give people a chance to say hello to him.

Some will simply say, "You're Anthony Ruiz," and shake his hand when he smiles and says yes.

Others will tell him their problems: an illness that's left their family in debt, a job they lost months ago. Mami says

they just need to vent, except she says it in Spanish. Sometimes I translate her words back to English even when I know
there's no exact translation.

Se tienen que desahogar. *They just need to undrown.*

Papi lets people talk as long as they need to. He never
interrupts anyone except to introduce them to us. I smile and
pose the same each time. Eyes wide but no teeth. Hands in
front of me with my fingers interlaced.

This morning is different, though. This morning there was
a smaller tub of holy water at the church entrance because
the congregation is trying to conserve water. When it came
time to take communion, they ran out of Eucharist because
they only boiled enough water to make three-quarters of their
usual amount in time for today's mass. I guess even the body
of Christ isn't immune to whatever chemicals are in our water
right now. And before the service started, there was a line that
wrapped all around the church building, full of people waiting
to get a case of bottled water. Papi donated several cases. He
had Joe and his staffers bring them in this morning, and they
ran out within minutes. The camera crew filmed Papi handing
off a couple of crates and shaking hands with the priest as he
thanked him, and then they took the rest of the day off. All I
could think about was all these plastic bottles ending up back
in the ocean once they're thrown away. It's like we're incapable
of solving one problem without creating another.

Now we're standing outside on the steps, and the last
thing I want to do is play the proud daughter. A few people
have stopped to ask us if there's any bottled water left. Others

simply walk by with nothing but horrible looks in our direction. I can't decide what's worse: their silent stares or the look on my father's face when he says there's no more water. As if a sympathetic half smile from their senator is supposed to make things better.

"This is pointless," I say. "It's embarrassing."

Mami only clears her throat and straightens her shoulders. When my father's been standing and waiting long enough that it's excruciatingly awkward, he ambles back toward us.

"It's a pretty day out, isn't it?"

It's our last Spanish mass before Florida votes in the primaries a week from Tuesday. He'd probably anticipated this would be his busiest post-mass appearance yet, and the disappointment on his face is undeniable.

"Vámonos, Tonio. You'll only make it worse," Mami says.

"Make what worse? There's nothing wrong with enjoying the fresh morning air. People are in too much of a hurry these days." His voice is louder than it needs to be. He talks like we're hundreds of yards away instead of right in front of him.

Finally, a man about the same age as Papi walks up with a little boy holding his hand. I can't really make out what he's saying until the man raises his voice.

"My son needs clean water! When are you going to protect him? Grow a spine, Senator."

Papi's face is unwavering. You'd think he just received a compliment. He thanks the man for sharing his opinion as he walks away.

"It's not an opinion, pendejo!" The little boy gasps at his

father's language, and the few remaining churchgoers in the courtyard look our way.

Papi waves one more time, looking flattered. I wonder what it must be like to live in his head, constantly creating your own reality, and having enough people in your life play along.

"Can we please just go home now?" I say.

"Yeah, Mami said she'd make pancakes," Ricky says.

We make our way to the car wordlessly. Papi squints as he scans the nearly empty parking lot.

"People are just concerned. And we're all tired." Mami reaches slowly for his hand but he brushes it away. "Maybe take the rest of the day off. Descansa."

Un-tire.

"No, it's fine. People need to feel heard. I get it," Papi says.

But making them feel like you're listening isn't the same thing as listening, I want to say.

I don't. I'm scared the truth will hurt him, so I keep quiet and let it hurt me instead.

As he drives us home, Papi's breath practically whistles through his nose. He stops at a red light, resting his elbow against the window, and covers his mouth with one hand as if it were a napkin.

Mami turns the radio on but he quickly snaps it back off.

"Tonio, you're reading too much into this."

He shakes his head slowly. "Things were supposed to be getting better after . . . after all of this." He waves his hand over the center console, tossing the air behind him toward the back seat. Obviously, he means me. "Polls are unreliable, though. But people . . . people you can count on, until they stop showing up. And they've stopped showing up." He punctuates each word with a stiff wag of his finger.

"I'm sure it's not as big a deal as you think it is." I realize too late that these are the exact words he said to me yesterday, when I asked him about Irving's project. He'll probably think I'm mocking him.

"I don't want to hear another word from you. You might not care if I lose this election, but there are a whole lot of people who actually support me and who I don't want to let down."

What about not letting all *people down? What about Vivi's grandma and that boy who doesn't have clean water?* But I can't bring myself to say these words either. "That's not fair. I never said I don't care."

"Well your actions said plenty. I know what you've been up to, asking esa muchacha Jackie to come over to plan your little rebellion. Hashtag Dump Irving. Did you ever stop to think they might dump me too?"

If Jackie were here, she'd tell him *This isn't about you.*

"I don't want you seeing her anymore. ¿Me entiendes?"

"What?" I grab the back of Mami's seat and lean in close. "You can't tell me who to be friends with. Mami, tell him."

She sighs. "Tonio. She didn't do anything. They're just kids with ideals."

"What is that supposed to mean?" I know Mami thinks she's defending me, but her words sting. What, so Jackie and I are too young to be taken seriously?

"That's exactly the problem," Papi says. "People like Jackie, they go around thinking they can fix everything and just end up ruining everything."

"Okay, okay," Mami says. "No es pa' tanto."

"You've never even heard her out. You've never even heard *me* out," I say.

"Oh, I hear you all right. I get that you don't want me to win. Loud and clear."

He gets on the highway and speeds up so fast that Mami taps his shoulder.

"Ya, Tonio. Enough."

"I never said that I want you to lose."

"You didn't have to."

twenty-eight

When we reach our house there's an old silver four-door Civic in our driveway, and inside are Amarys in the driver's side and Gloria in the seat next to her.

They get out of their car at the same time we do, and when I catch Gloria's eye, her chest rises like she's taking a deep breath. It makes me nervous to see her nervous. I give her and Amarys a hug while Ricky and my parents stay behind. They wait for Gloria to introduce them.

"So this is the famous Amarys," Papi says to them in Spanish. I wonder what he means by that. It must have something to do with the online gossip Vivi told me not to worry about. I got so caught up in the aquifer crisis, I forgot to Google them online. "You didn't have to keep her hidden all these years, you know," he says to Gloria.

Amarys looks like she's about to laugh, but instead she scoffs. "We like to keep our work and personal lives separate. I'm sure you can understand."

The thing about switching to Spanish when you've been speaking in English is that everything sounds more polite and formal to me. This would be fine under normal circumstances, but today it just makes Papi sound condescending and Amarys passive-aggressive.

Mami gives her best hostess smile and gestures toward the front door as if it's the first time they've been here, which I guess for Amarys, it is.

"It's so nice to finally meet you," she says.

"Yes, it's good for us to know who our daughter runs off to when she can't stand being with her family," Papi says.

I want to die. I want to summon one of those sinkholes that are always happening in Central Florida and slowly crawl into it.

"It wasn't like that," I say. "They didn't know I was coming."

"Did you really kidnap my sister?" Ricky says. "Is she going to have a girlfriend, too, now?"

"Ricky!" Mami says.

Amarys laughs and bends down so she's eye to eye with him. "How old are you?"

"I'm eight."

"Eight! You're way too big to listen to fairy tales and silly chisme."

Papi's face turns hot pink as he fumbles for the keys.

"I don't know where he heard that," Mami says. "We try to shield them from all the campaign gossip. But sometimes the kids at school, you know . . ."

So those are the rumors Vivi was talking about. A bunch of conspiracy theories about Gloria and Amarys abducting me and homophobes talking like being gay is contagious.

"That's really what they're saying?" I say.

"It's nothing. It's a bunch of trolls on Twitter," Amarys says.

"But you did get a couple of requests for interviews, didn't you? From the papers?" Papi says. "My publicist told me a couple of writers reached out to me for comment. Said that they planned to be in touch with you too."

"We ignored them, señor. Out of respect for your privacy," Gloria says.

He nods approvingly, and it makes me want to scream, *What about Gloria and Amarys's privacy?* They didn't ask to be brought into this. I mumble something about how ridiculous it all is, but neither Gloria nor Amarys responds.

Inside, the house is dark as a patch of cloud cover makes its way across our backyard. Tiny bits of light poke through, glistening through the glass door into the dining room. That's when I notice that Gloria is not only carrying her usual overnight bag, but a couple of empty suitcases too.

"What's that for?" I say.

"I'll tell you after I talk to your parents, okay?"

They make their way toward the kitchen. Mami tells Ricky and me to go to our rooms but I sit, curling my knees into my chest, in the middle of the stairway.

I hate that this is how Amarys is meeting my parents for the first time. Why couldn't they have met years ago, on a random Sunday evening when Amarys dropped off Gloria? They could've talked about stupid things like the weather and Miami traffic. We could've invited her in for a late night cafecito instead of whatever the hell this is now.

But I know that's too much to ask of Papi. What would people think, he'd say. He would've been too deep in his personal politics to treat Gloria and Amarys like people. Maybe they were right to stay away from him, but I hate that they ever had to.

I don't hear any plates or cups being taken out. No one offers them something to eat or drink. I hear the bass of Amarys's voice, but I can't distinguish any of her words. Slowly, I take off my shoes and make my way back down the stairs. I stop just shy of the slanted ray of light emanating across the tile from the kitchen.

"We had always planned that this would be temporary for Gloria. Just until I finished law school," Amarys is saying.

"And she graduates in May—" Gloria says.

"Congratulations," Papi says flatly.

"Thank you. We just thought, with everything going on . . ."

"It'd be better if we're out of your way," Amarys says pointedly.

I hear Mami sigh and tsk. "Ay, Gloria. You were never in our way. Nunca." The bangle bracelets she's wearing clink against the glass of the table, and I picture her reaching across and rubbing Gloria's forearm, the way she used to do to me when I was little and wouldn't eat my vegetables. She had such a soothing way about her. I wish I could be in there right now, just to see it again.

"De todas maneras," Papi adds. "Some notice would've been nice. This is terrible timing, with the primaries in a matter of days. We won't have time to find a replacement, and God knows Juli could use the help around the house."

"Tonio. I'll be fine," Mami says.

But he's not listening. He's off on some rant about how after all these years, after everything we've done for her, this is how Gloria leaves us, just one day to the next.

"That's not how this went down, and you know it," Amarys says.

"I guess I can stay through the elections, if you need me," Gloria says.

There's a lot of stirring. Amarys's voice lowers to a whisper until finally Mami says that won't be necessary.

Papi tries to argue, but Mami only repeats herself. "That won't be necessary. You need to do whatever's best for you both. Right, Tonio?"

My father doesn't say anything.

"That's exactly what we'd discussed," Amarys says.

"It wasn't an easy decision," Gloria adds.

This is worse than I ever imagined. Gloria's leaving us. Today. Soon she'll pack all her stuff into the suitcases she brought and her room will be left empty like she was never even here. And it'll all be my fault.

The tears come fast and quiet and unashamed. I can't blame her for wanting to leave. A part of me never understood why she would want to live in our house and work for us when there are so many other jobs that wouldn't keep her away from home all week. I even asked her once and she said, "Not everyone gets the same options. Some of us don't get to do what we want. We just do the best we can."

For years I tried pushing what she said out of my mind. It

made me feel guilty to think that, as much as I loved having Gloria around, for her, it was something she didn't really want to do.

Now she's leaving because things I've done made it unbearable.

They start coming out of the kitchen and there's no time for me to move without them seeing me, so I step inside and face them.

"I'm so sorry," I say through tears. "If I hadn't run away and Amarys hadn't ended up on the news with me, none of this would be happening."

Papi nods and says, "Now you see there are consequen—"

But he's interrupted by Amarys's laughter. It's guttural and musical and contagious. "Mari! You should be congratulating us, not apologizing! Do you know how much I've missed Gloria?"

I wipe away the wet mess I let drip all over my face. When I meet Gloria's eyes, she's beaming.

"I'll miss you," I say as I hug her.

"Well, you know where we live now," Amarys says. "And our door is always open to you."

I can tell my father is silently fuming. I love how little Amarys cares. She leans in to wrap her arms around both me and Gloria and I let out a laugh that turns into a sob.

I can't imagine not seeing Gloria every day, but a part of me is relieved for her. This is going to be different now. This is going to be better.

twenty-nine

Our school has been shut down. And not just Grove
High either. Classes on Monday are canceled across all
Miami-Dade County public schools and a bunch of private
ones because of the boil-water advisory. There's an air of con-
fusion everywhere, like we're all trying to prepare for a hurricane that already came and did its damage.

"I don't get it," Ricky says. "I mean, I'm glad that class got
canceled but . . . would we get contaminated if we went inside?
Are the schools unsafe or something?"

"It's logistics," Mami says. "Look how much longer it takes
me to make your oatmeal, or wash a handful of strawberries,
just for you and Mari's breakfast. Now multiply that times several thousand students and all their breakfasts and lunches.
The school district needs time to figure out a plan B, that's all."

I'd never really thought about how much of our drinking
water we rely on for more than drinking. Even brushing my
teeth, I keep forgetting to use the bottle that Mami left next
to our sinks. And Zoey—poor Zoey—texted me and Vivi this
morning that her fish died. Her freaking fish. Then eight minutes later Vivi texted back that her grandma was in the hospital again and Zoey apologized like five hundred times. I told
her not to feel bad, that she couldn't have known. And besides,

it's okay to feel bad about more than one thing at a time. It made me wonder what's going to happen to all our wildlife if the prescription chemicals in the aquifer somehow seep into their water. I keep thinking about the shrinking alligators in the Everglades. And what it'd be like if Papi and I never went back to spend time on the boat together. There's no place quieter. No other place he ever acts like himself.

I stir my oatmeal in its bowl. "Now is he going to issue a statement about the water crisis?"

Mami shrugs and lets out a tiny huff. "I don't know. It's likely. That's what I hear, anyway. His speechwriters were working on it all night."

"You're not writing it?"

"No, not this time. But your father really likes them. He says they've gotten him this far." Her voice drops on the word *says*. She doesn't sound too convinced.

Sometimes I wonder what Mami would've done if she hadn't decided long ago that her job was to be Papi's rock. That's what he's always calling her. *My rock, the strongest person I've ever known. The woman who has made all my dreams come true.*

But he's never talked about her dreams.

Mami raises the TV volume and points at the news with the remote. They're reporting on the school shutdown, how they're anticipating it'll only last one day.

"Only," Mami repeats. "You know, not everyone can afford to take time off from work. Even if it's *only* for a day."

Ever since I can remember, Mami has reminded us of the

different ways we're lucky. I've always thought it was a count-your-blessings kind of thing. That we have food on our table. A roof over our heads. Two parents who are still together, who love and support us. Today it makes me think of Vivi, how she no longer has her home or her parents to really count on, and none of it is her fault. It doesn't seem fair that we got to be so lucky while she's so *un* . . .

We finish breakfast and I start putting the plates in the dishwasher while Mami cleans the table. My brother dashes off to his bedroom without even clearing his dirty plate. Of course. I'm about to say something but when I glance at Mami she looks exhausted, like her body is aching just holding itself together.

"I'm going to lie down and watch an episode of Lucy," she says. "¿Quieres verlo conmigo?"

"Of course. Do you even have to ask?"

In her bedroom, we watch the one where Lucy and Ethel switch places with Ricky and Fred. They go looking for jobs while the men take over things at home, and Lucy and Ethel end up working at the chocolate factory. They can't keep up with how fast the truffles keep coming out of the terminal.

I lose it when Lucy starts stuffing her hat and shirt and face with chocolate. It's a classic, and it never gets old.

"Ayyy," Mami says, in that high-pitched, soft way she sighs when she's been laughing too hard. "The things she gets herself into just to prove a point."

I tell her that it's my second favorite episode, after the one where Ricky promises Lucy she can be in his show if she can learn the choreography.

"He doesn't think she can handle it. And she almost doesn't. But it's one of the few episodes where she finally gets to be in the spotlight, and she's so good. She just needed Ricky to get out of her way."

Mami rests her head on her hand and tousles her hair. "It's timeless. Do you know how they were in real life? Lucille and Desi?"

I shake my head no.

"She was crazy about him. They were going through some tough times in their marriage, so when this opportunity for the *I Love Lucy* show came around, she insisted that they cast Desi as her husband, because she didn't want them spending any more time apart. The studio didn't think a Cuban would be a good fit for the role. They thought it wouldn't be American enough. But Lucille told them she wouldn't do it without him. She put everything on the line so they could be together."

"That's so romantic," I say, though it also makes me sad. It reminds me of Mami, how she's sacrificed so much for Papi, but people only see him.

Mami looks distracted. "Maybe after all this is over we'll take a trip to California. See the original studio. Just us girls? Ricky and Papi can go to Miami Beach for a week while all the tourists are gone."

I'm not sure I heard her right. It takes me a moment to piece it all together, and I wonder if she even knows what she's just said. "You mean, this summer?"

She stiffens. Her smile is replaced by the one she wears for the press and, I now realize, for my father. "In the fall, of course. Sometimes I forget about the election and make plans as usual. But you and I can still go to California. And Papi and your brother . . . well, they can spend the day getting to know DC before we move."

I thought I was the only one who's been trying not to think about us moving to DC. I told myself it's so I wouldn't jinx anything; Papi's always saying we should never assume a win is in the bag. But I can't get over how relieved Mami sounded when she said *after all this is over*. After all this is over in the summer. After all this is over and life can go back to normal. After all this is over and he's lost.

"I guess. Yeah, that's fine," I say.

"¿Cómo está Vivi? I tried calling her mom but I got her voicemail."

I shrug and look down at my arm. I press my finger against a mosquito bite and make a little curved cross with my nail. "Not great. Nobody will talk to her at her new school, and her Abuela's not getting better . . ."

"¿Qué le pasa?"

"A lot of vomiting. A lot more than last time. She almost got dehydrated. They sent her back to the hospital this morning so she can get an IV."

"I see. And how are you?"

"I miss her."

"But you're making new friends. With Jackie and her little group?"

"They're not that bad, Mami. Jackie just wants to make a difference. You'd think Papi would love that about her."

She lies back on her pillow and looks up at the ceiling. "Maybe. If things were different."

I'm surprised she's not fighting me on this. It's like one version of her left for the campaign trail this weekend, and another, more laid-back version came home. We binge several more episodes and though Mami insists I take the extra day off school to catch up on my homework, she lets me bring my books and binders to her bed and keeps the show on in the background. The theme song comes on for the fifth or sixth time when Didier texts to ask what I'm up to. He and the crew are shopping for a new sound system for the walkout on Friday.

We're passing by your house in 15. Come with?

I sit up in Mami's bed. "Can I go to Dadeland Station with Jackie and them? Didier can pick me up."

She reaches for her phone and holds it against her chin.

"Did you finish your homework?"

I nod. I have one more reaction to balance for chemistry, but I'll be done with it by the time they get here.

"I'll have to talk to your father." She hurries out of the room toward the bathroom with the phone already pressed to her face. I wait for what feels like forever, convinced that Papi will say no, in which case, I'm screwed. The unspoken rules have always been that if Mami says yes but Papi says no, it's no. If Mami says no and Papi says yes, it's yes. When I was little this system usually worked in my favor. Thinking about it now, I'm embarrassed that I used to laugh whenever Papi overrode Mami's decisions.

When she comes out of the bathroom her face is flushed

and her eyes are bloodshot, but she gives me a huge smile and says, "Okay. Bueno. You can go—"

I squeal. Even though I'm worried about her, I can't help it.

"But," she adds, "but I need to meet everyone first. Por lo menos un par de minutos."

A couple of minutes saying hello in the driveway? "Yes, totally. That's fine. Thank you, Mami!" I give her a hug and rush up to my room to change and text Didier to come get me.

thirty

Mami loves to tell the story about how Abuelo grilled the first boy that came to pick her up for a date when she was fifteen. First, he leaned into the driver's-side window and asked to see the kid's license. Then he told him to come inside for a few minutes.

This isn't a bus stop. Bájate del carro and come inside and say hello.

"He wasn't about to let me just hop into his car and drive away," Mami always says. The story goes that Abuelo told the kid all about how in Cuba, he'd had to ask Abuela's parents for permission to take her out, and even then, they had chaperones. Abuela spent the whole night daring Abuelo to kiss her in front of the chaperone, just to see the look on her older cousin's face. And that's how he knew he would love her forever.

Here Mami was, on her first date, and Abuelo was talking about falling in love for eternity. Mami was mortified.

I hope she remembers that as Didier's car pulls into our driveway. Obviously it's not a date, but it's the first time I'll be riding in a car that a friend drives. None of my other friends are seventeen.

Thankfully, Mami's changed out of her bathrobe into a

pair of jeans, flip-flops, and a long, flowy cardigan that she pulls tight across her chest as we step out of the house.

From the passenger's seat, Jackie waves hello as she undoes her seat belt. The three of them get out and give Mami an air kiss on the cheek as they introduce themselves. "I've heard so much about you," Jackie says.

"Likewise," Mami says.

I don't remember telling Jackie much about my mom at all, but I assume she's just being polite. The five of us stand next to the running car, waiting for my mom to dismiss us.

She breaks the silence in the worst way possible.

"Didier. Can I see your driver's license, please?"

I start to protest, but Didier takes it out of his wallet without question.

Mami takes a few seconds to study it. "A Scorpio, huh?"

"Yes, ma'am. Honest and passionate." He giggles as Mami hands him back his license. Jackie rolls her eyes and smiles at Crissy. I'm just glad this can't possibly get any more awkward.

"Okay," Mami says. "Where's your phone while you're driving?"

I guess I was wrong.

"Out of sight and out of mind," Didier says, without missing a beat.

"And if someone texts you?"

"I wait until I've pulled over."

"And if someone calls?"

"I have Bluetooth?" he says, less sure of himself this time.

"Fine, but stay focused. This is my baby's life in your hands."

She pulls me so close, I feel my cheek smoosh up against her chest.

"Ya, Mami. Por favor."

"Have fun and make good decisions."

I dart into the car before she can say another word. And she doesn't: instead, she mimes putting on a seat belt through the window, just in case my humiliation was incomplete.

Didier pulls out of the driveway slowly. Everyone stays quiet until the moment my mom's waving figure disappears from the rearview mirror.

"Your mom's cute," Crissy says. "Not at all like I thought she'd be. I mean, she always seems so serious on TV."

"She has her moments," I say, not wanting to reveal that I'm just as surprised as Crissy that Mami let me go out with them.

"How's she doing with all of this?" Jackie asks.

I shrug and say she's fine. "Why'd you tell her you'd heard so much about her, though? She's going to want to know what I've told you about her."

Jackie looks confused. "I didn't mean you. I just meant I've heard about her and her work. With the wage gap? Oh my god, tell me you know about this." She turns in her seat to face me. I have no idea what she's talking about. "Your mom was, like, one of the biggest pushers for making it illegal to pay men more than women for the same job."

"Oh my god, Mari, how do you not know about this?" Crissy asks.

"Back in, like, 2002?" Jackie says.

"You mean, before she was born?" Didier says.

I'm so grateful for him in this moment. "That was a long time ago. My mom never really talks about that stuff."

"That's super sad," Jackie says, sinking back into her seat. "She should be proud of herself. So should you."

She's right, of course. It's like discovering Mami once had this whole badass alter ego, an alternate universe I never even considered. I try to ignore the guilt that washes over me as we pull into the Dadeland Station parking lot. I could've asked my mom, just once, what her life was like before she met Papi. I could've asked her what was wrong this morning, as she lay in bed looking exhausted and broken. But she would've dodged my questions and pretended everything is fine. I gave up trying to be real with her years ago.

We meander through the parking lot behind cars that take forever to pull in and out of their spots. Dadeland Station is always packed, and parking is a mission. There are a few restaurants and nail salons leading up to the entrance of the shopping center, but other than that, it's just a tower made up of several big-name stores like Michael's and Best Buy and Target. It's not exactly bursting with personality, though there's a huge Romero Britto sculpture right outside the main entrance trying its hardest to make up for that. It's a cartoon figure of a man wearing white-and-blue striped pants and a polka-dotted tux, spreading his arms and legs wide like a starfish. I don't really get it.

Didier doesn't bother looking for a spot on the first floor. He heads straight for the spiral-shaped driveway at the edge of the parking garage.

225

I spot a couple of empty spots and point them out, but he doesn't slow down.

"You'll see," he says. "We always go to the top."

When we get there, the lot is packed full of black and gray SUVs with dealership stickers on their windows. Didier parks in an empty spot by a yellow partition in the corner.

"This is the lot the dealership across the street uses . . . but look," he says, nodding at the windshield with his eyes fixed on the sky. In the few minutes it's taken us to get here, it's turned bright orange. I get out of the car and feel a cool, strong breeze against my neck and shoulders, the kind you usually get when you're closer to the beach. We're higher up than I'd realized. When I look over the edge of the building I can see the terra cotta–tiled tops of houses in South Miami, the clumps of tall, lush trees I didn't even notice were there, and bursts of palm trees everywhere. From this high up, the canal looks as calm as an empty street after the rain, curling through the backs of homes and under bridges.

"It's so peaceful," I say.

"My ex-boyfriend used to bring me here to watch the sunset," Didier says. "It's too pretty not to come back. Now I bring just the three of us."

"And then Jackie and I cross the street to take the Metro home," Crissy says.

I nod like this is the most natural thing in the world, like I wasn't completely clueless about riding the Metro before the night I snuck away to Gloria's apartment. Papi always talks about it like it's too dangerous, but maybe like everything else he does, I see now it's just another way of controlling me. I envy their independence, how easily they seem to get around town whenever they want.

"We should go look at the sound systems. I have to pick up my mom from work in an hour and a half," Didier says.

When we turn and begin walking toward the elevator, I notice there's one more car parked in the lot than there was before. It's impossible to miss. A bright orange Subaru with the engine turned off and the tinted windows rolled up.

I squint as I walk closer, my breath accelerating with each step.

It can't be. It has to be a coincidence.

Through the dark glass I see that the driver's side looks empty. I hear Jackie and Crissy calling after me, asking what's wrong, and I'm about to tell them it's nothing when I notice someone stirring.

The driver's side looks empty only because the seat is pulled all the way down.

Lying on his back, looking right at me and trying to stay perfectly still, is Joe.

thirty-one

"You had me followed?!" I scream so loud into the phone when Papi answers that my voice bounces off the concrete walls. I pace back and forth. The elevator arrives and the doors slide open, but Jackie, Crissy, and Didier stand with their arms crossed, staring down Joe in synch.

"Cálmate, Mari. Cálmate."

Is he serious right now? Who in the history of the world has actually calmed down by being told to calm down?

"You sent Joe to spy on me. Do you know how creepy that is? Do you know how creepy *he* is? One time, he asked me if I had body piercings in places he couldn't see."

"Stop exaggerating, Mariana. You read too much into things," he says. "You're always being too sensitive."

"And you're never sensitive enough!"

He takes a deep breath. I don't know if that means I've gotten through to him, or if he's just preparing himself to berate me. I don't wait to find out.

"You said you wanted people to respect our privacy, but you only care about yours. My privacy doesn't count to you."

"You're fifteen, hija. You don't get to make decisions about things you don't understand."

"You don't get to tell me what I don't understand."

"That's enough. I made a decision. I don't have to defend it to you or your mother."

I gasp. "Does Mami not know you did this?"

"I can't talk anymore. I'm going into a meeting."

"Does she know?" I ask again.

I'm not surprised when he hangs up without answering. Joe inches toward me with his hands tucked in his pockets.

I call back the elevator and signal to my friends.

"I'm taking you home," he says.

"I'd like to see you try." No sooner have the words left my mouth that Jackie, Didier, and Crissy gather around me. They don't say a word and they don't have to. We step inside the elevator and the doors slide closed with a loud, high-pitched chime, encasing us in glass. I keep my eye on Joe as we descend, and soon all I see is his torso, then his knees, then his worn brown leather shoes.

It's Crissy who breaks the silence. "You okay? We can go somewhere else if you want."

I shake my head. I wave my hand over my face and start pacing back and forth, three small steps at a time. They all press their bodies against the rail to give me space.

"He doesn't care about anyone but himself. This is all a huge ego trip for him. It's all about power, and staying in power, and no matter how many times he says it's for the people, it's only for one person—him. I feel like such an idiot."

I dash out of the elevator the second the door opens and the three of them follow. I only know because I can hear their hurried steps keeping up.

"Get the hell away from her!" I hear Jackie say.

Joe's riding toward us on the escalator, breathless.

"We'll make a scene," Didier says, holding up his phone. He shakes his head and pouts, sucking the air in through his lips. "Please make us make a scene. I'm begging you."

Already, there are people stopping and staring. Joe slows down and reassesses the situation. He shakes his head at me and puts his arms up, revealing navy sweat stains on his baby blue shirt.

"You're costing us everything, you know that?"

I hear my father speak through him, as if Joe just borrowed his words and his voice and threw them at me like spears. I actually stumble back a few steps, and Jackie grabs me by the shoulders and holds me.

"Don't listen to him," she says as he finally walks away. "He's just trying to wear you down."

If that's true, it's working. I'm tired of feeling like I've done nothing but fight and argue and plead for things. Like all I've really done is stand against a dam and keep it from bursting open, but that hasn't stopped all the commotion from the other side from wearing me down.

"I keep making things worse," I say.

"That's not true," Jackie says.

"I asked him about Irving. He said I'm making this a bigger deal than it is, and that you all are overreacting."

"He's totally gaslighting you, Mariana. He's just trying to get into your head so you're too busy doubting your own judgment to question his. So typically toxic." The way Didier says *toxic* slices the air in half. Holy crap. This is literally what my father did on the phone just now, when he said I was being too sensitive.

We begin ambling toward the Best Buy. The entrance smells like BO and plastic. Someone in a blue shirt and khakis greets us as we walk past the receptacle for recycled printer cartridges and batteries.

Almost immediately, Didier and Crissy have flocked to the Nintendo display, and they each grab a controller and start a new game.

"We'll catch up to you in five," Crissy says.

Now it's just Jackie and me, walking through the aisles full of sound systems. She grabs one of the mikes that's next to a speaker. It has a cream-colored elastic cord that keeps it attached to the display, and when she blows into it, it makes no sound.

"How are we s'posed to test them if they're not on?" She tries several more, and each time, I can tell she's super disappointed.

"Can I ask you something?"

"Hmm." She nods, not looking up as she reads the back of a box.

"You don't ever get nervous. About speaking?"

"Well, yeah, but . . . not enough to stop me. Why? Do you?"

I half shrug, embarrassed to admit that it's always made me freeze.

"But you were awesome just now. With Joe?"

"That's not the same thing."

"It totally is. You spoke up. You didn't take shit from him."

"But he's only one guy. That doesn't count. I mean, like, speaking in front of a crowd."

"It's not that different. A crowd is still made up of individuals. You have to imagine you're reaching one person at a time."

"You honestly don't get nervous?"

She stops in the middle of the aisle, so abruptly I almost bump into her. "Of course I do, Mariana. But . . . how do I explain it? You have to use it. Nervousness is still energy. It can either stop you or it can push you."

"You sound like Jamie," I mumble, disappointed.

"Who's Jamie?"

"No one. Just a friend of my dad's."

She crinkles her nose, deep in thought. "Maybe it's more like, it's about what you have to say. Like when you believe in something so much, it becomes a part of you. It's constantly running through you. And when the moment comes, even though you're scared, you kinda just find strength and trust that the words and ideas that flow through you will also flow out of you. Like water."

"Like water," I say.

She gives a satisfied nod and turns her attention back to the sound systems.

"This is all overpriced BS. You know what, fuck the mike," she says. "We'll just have to make a ton of noise."

thirty-two

I don't want to go home.

I'm in so much trouble it won't make a difference if I get home in an hour or eight. I've ignored five calls from Papi and thirteen texts. Mami's left six messages every time I sent her call to voicemail.

I don't feel like listening to them while I'm still with my friends, so I take a quick look at the transcriptions of Mami's voicemail.

It's all gibberish. Random sentences like *Mary Ana soul carry savor Kate stays vein.* This is what happens when my mom leaves a message in Spanish and it gets transcribed phonetically to English. Nothing ever makes sense.

"Are you guys hungry?" I ask, by which I mean that I am.

I suggest the Pan-Asian café off to the side of the entrance. The hostess hands us a modified menu and tells us that if we'd like water, we'll have to buy it bottled. We all ask for iced tea instead, but she responds that there's no ice.

"Then can I get a sparkling water?" Crissy asks. "Fair warning: It makes me burp like crazy. I'm not responsible for whatever noises come out of my mouth next."

Jackie, Didier, and I all lock eyes and start giggling. We're all thinking the same thing. Crissy set herself up way too easily.

"Very funny," Crissy says.

Jackie orders the pan-fried noodles while Didier gets the Lemongrass Chicken. I ask for the most expensive dish just so I can charge it on my parents' credit card. Spoiled rich girl move, I know, but it's the only one I've got right now.

"You're not eating?" I ask Crissy.

She glosses over the menu and sets it aside. "My mom made arroz chaufa last night. Even her leftover fried rice is better than this stuff."

"Oh. Well, you can have some of my mine if you change your mind."

"I don't get what your father thought he was going to accomplish by having you followed," she says, ignoring my offer. "What did he think we were going to do? Steal shit? Kidnap you?"

"Or worse," Didier says. "Turn you into a liberal."

"He didn't want me to come out with you guys, but my mom let me anyways."

"Really?" Jackie asks.

"She hasn't been acting like herself lately. Not that I'm complaining," I say.

"Honestly, I used to think your mom was kind of a sellout, but now that I've met her, I don't know. She looked nothing like the pictures and video I always see of her with your dad. Kind of the opposite. Maybe she still has a little bit of fire left in her."

I always thought Mami's public persona was a way of protecting us, so we could see our private lives and campaign lives as separate things. It never occurred to me she might've been protecting herself too. I change the subject and ask about the walkout on Friday. So far, none of them has asked me outright if I'll be joining them, though I'm guessing it's because they're assuming I will.

Crissy pulls out her phone. "You haven't checked our stories?"

"I'm not really supposed to be on Instagram," I mumble.

Didier waves his hand in the air. "It's nothing you don't already know. Oh, and we were trending on Twitter today. And also twelve other schools in Miami agreed to walk out too."

Oh, and also Jackie decided she's running for president, he might as well have said. I'm missing everything because of my parents' dumb rules.

The food comes too fast. Even before I take my first bite, I try to think of things we can do next.

"Do you guys want to go see a movie?"

They look completely uninterested. Didier reminds me that he has to pick up his mom soon.

"They're just playing the same tired movies anyways," Crissy says.

If Vivi were here, she would already be getting tickets for whatever rom-com or action movie was playing next. She loves going to the movies because she says they're either awesomely good or epically terrible—the only ones that suck are the in-betweens. I wish she were here now. Things seemed simpler when she was still going to Grove High.

By the time we're done eating, Jackie and Crissy have to run or they'll miss their train. Jackie kisses me and Didier goodbye, but Crissy just smiles and grazes my cheek with hers. We watch them cross the street toward the Metro station.

"Do you think she'll ever not hate me?" I ask.

"Who? Crissy? She's getting there. Slowly. You haven't noticed?"

We head back toward the parking garage and I step onto the escalator. "For what it's worth, I wish my dad would do more to help people like her brother."

"Yeah, but he won't. He doesn't feel the need to. It's different when your community isn't directly affected." He puts both arms on the railings and lifts up his body, letting it sway over the escalator steps.

"He's a son of immigrants. He does care."

"Yeah, but . . . when his parents came over from Cuba, they got their green cards fast because they were political exiles, because of Castro. And even up until a few years ago, Cuban refugees who touched land got to stay. Nobody did that for Haitians. We had dictators and coups too. We got on boats and risked drowning, and we still got sent back."

"You did?"

"Not me literally, Mari. I was born here. But . . . how do I put this?" He brings his fingers to his lips and squeezes. "You ever notice in your dad's speeches, how he only says 'exiles'

236

when he's talking about your family, but 'immigrants' when he's talking about refugees from Honduras or Haiti or Mexico?"

I step off the top of the escalator, embarrassed to admit I'd never paid attention.

"Crissy just hates that he doesn't use his privilege to help others. And I'm not saying I wish Cubans had it as hard as Haitians do . . . I just wish we could've all gotten the same opportunities. But you know, now it's just a shitshow for everyone. So maybe your dad will come around one day. Or maybe not. Who knows."

We walk across the parking lot with just the sound of Didier's keys clinking in his hands. It's only now that I realize we've never hung out alone together. It's always been him and Jackie and Crissy, the way that Zoey and I were never together without Vivi.

Crap. Zoey. I forgot that she texted me to ask if I'd go to the pet store with her.

"Where am I dropping you off?" Didier says. "I have a feeling not at your house."

"Is it that obvious?"

"Kinda. Just make it someplace close. I only have like fifteen minutes."

"Where does your mom work?"

"At Publix. She's a floor manager there," he says, nodding in the direction of US 1.

"Oh my god. I know where you can take me."

Didier doesn't ask whose apartment it is when we pull up

to Gloria and Amarys's a few minutes later. He simply puts the car in park and leans in close to the steering wheel to get a better look at the second floor.

I thank him for the ride and he fist-bumps me. "I'd say anytime but . . . it's probably the last time I'll have the car in a while."

"What do you mean?"

"My mom flipped when she found out I'm skipping class for the walkout. She said if I still do it, I may as well kiss using her car goodbye."

"Oh. I didn't know you shared it."

He nods. "As long as I keep my grades up. Not like I ever haven't. If I get so much as a B she starts threatening to ship me to Haiti. You know how it is. When your parents sacrificed everything to come here, the least you can do is make it worth it."

I'd never thought of it like that, but hearing Didier say it out loud, it feels true. I used to think Mami and Papi were trying to make me feel guilty whenever they brought up all the things my grandparents left behind in Cuba when they emigrated. But what if they were trying to repay their parents somehow? What could be more overachieving than becoming president and first lady of the United States?

"So you're still doing it? The walkout?"

He looks at me like the answer is obvious. "This stuff matters too. In a way our parents can't understand."

I nod as I snap off my seat belt.

"But also . . . Jackie will probably kill me for saying this, but you don't have to do a speech. I mean, if you want to, awesome. But if you don't, then don't. It doesn't really help us if you're not feeling it."

His words sting, even though I know he doesn't mean it like that. I mumble, "Thanks," and smile as I leave. Walking up to Gloria and Amarys's apartment, I wonder if I'll get them in trouble by coming, but then I remember Gloria doesn't work for us anymore.

I knock three quick times, and then, when no one answers, twice more, louder. It's not until I'm about to knock a third time that I realize there's no light coming through the blinds of the window.

Why didn't I consider they might not be home? They could be grocery shopping, or watching a movie, or having dinner with friends. I'd never really thought about Gloria's life beyond our home.

I rush back downstairs in hopes that Didier is still there, but he's already gone. It's dark and quiet; none of the motion sensor lights outside the building are turning on, no matter how hard I wave my arms across them. Exhausted, I sit at the top of the stairwell and finally check my phone.

There are no new messages, but somehow that makes me feel worse. Ten, twenty minutes pass, but still neither Gloria nor Amarys comes home.

My phone buzzes in my hand, sending my stomach halfway up my throat.

It's a text from Mami, the only one she's sent all night.

Just come home and we won't have to talk about it until tomorrow. I promise.

I reply with two words. And Papi?

He's asleep. Big day tomorrow.

"Of course he is. Heaven forbid we wake the Senator," I say to the darkness. I tell her I'm at Gloria's and wait.

thirty-three

Driving home with Mami is like carrying a cup of coffee that is filled to the rim across a crowded room. I try to be quiet and steady, but all it'd take is a wrong breath or sudden movement for everything to spill and burn me.

I can feel the heat in her gaze fixed on the road. She fidgets with the a/c vents as we wait for the arrow to turn green. Even though it'd be faster if she crossed the highway and took the back roads home, Mami makes a left onto US 1. Might as well torment me as long as possible since I'm literally strapped into a metal box with her. When she pushes down on the accelerator, it feels like an invisible weight is being pressed against my chest.

"You're the one who said I could go," I finally say. She nods and raises her eyebrows in a kind of hesitant agreement. I guess she's taking this promise-we-won't-talk-about-it thing seriously. She starts scanning the radio and briefly stops at the mention of my father's name on NPR.

"Ruiz, who until recently was considered the front-runner in a tight primary race, may be in trouble in his home sta—"

She switches the station. A small scoff escapes her in the brief silence between the newscaster's voice and a song.

So she *is* mad at him too. "Papi's the one who went behind our backs and had me followed."

"What did I say? WHAT DID I TELL YOU WE WOULD NOT TALK ABOUT?"

I jump as her voice fills the car. "I didn't . . . I'm just saying, I'm mad at him too."

"Did you ever consider, for once, that this isn't about you? That maybe your father's world doesn't revolve around you, or me, or any of us? Did it never enter your mind? Or maybe you got so caught up in believing all the things he says, over and over, without realizing he's not saying them to us, he's not promising me, he's promising them. *They* are all that matter, Mariana. Not you. Not me. Not Ricky. Them. We're three people and one vote. Nada más."

We jolt to a stop at a light. A small vein runs between the creases of her forehead, and the glow from the red light fills in all the little cracks in her skin. It looks like an outline of the pain and hurt she's been holding in, finally wanting out.

"Mami? Are you okay?"

She covers her mouth with two fingers, as if she were holding an invisible cigarette to her lips. The light turns green and half a second later, a car behind us honks.

"Mami?"

"Ya. That's enough, Mariana. It's nothing." She sits up straight and turns the wheel.

"It's not nothing. What did Papi do this time?"

"Please. I can't do this right now. Not when your father and I, we're so close—"

"I get it. Florida votes in seven days. No one ever lets me forget."

"Stop talking about things you don't understand. You promised me, remember?"

"Stop telling me I don't understand! I know when he's lying. I know when you back him up. I know you're angry that he doesn't listen to you anymore, that we're not the team we used to be."

"Cállate."

"No. I'm tired of being told to shut up when you don't like what I say and to speak when you need me to lie. I'm not his personal microphone you turn on and off."

"¡Coño! We're so close."

"Close to this being over? Thank god—"

"Close to everything falling apart!"

She slams the brakes at a yellow light we could've easily taken. A black SUV behind us swerves into the next lane and swishes past.

"I didn't know. I'm sorry," I whisper.

"Just—no more, Mariana. Te lo ruego." She presses her hands together and looks past me, begging for silence.

To our right, there's a small plot of land littered with campaign signs. Some are the usual red, white, and blue, but others are coral, turquoise, and mermaid green, like our skies and the Art Deco buildings along the ocean.

Instinctively, I search for my father's name, but it appears only twice. It looks so small. Four simple letters and one syllable.

thirty-four

When we step into the kitchen from the garage, Mami switches on the lights and begins making up excuses.

"I don't want you worrying about what I said. Things are not that bad, we're just all under a lot of stress. We're fine. I shouldn't have said anything."

I go through the refrigerator in search of something to drink.

"So what's Papi's big day all about? Tomorrow?"

She slips her purse off her shoulder, practically letting it topple over the edge of the table. "He has several important meetings. With some donors."

"With Irving?"

"Ay, Mari," she says. "And if it is? What are you going to do?"

It's not really a question. She's obviously decided the answer is nothing. I don't bother responding as I start filling a glass with water from the filter on the refrigerator door.

"Mari . . . el agua."

"Sorry. I forgot." I empty the cup down the drain and pour myself a new glass from the jarful of water that Abuelo boiled and let cool this afternoon. "So much for things not being that bad."

"Now you just sound spoiled. People all over the world boil their water every day, ¿sabías? You're lucky that—"

"Oh my god, ya! I get it, okay?" Except I don't. I don't understand how simply knowing others are worse off is supposed to make anyone feel better about their problems. What good is valuing what we have if others can't have it too?

Even after I've showered and gotten ready for bed, I'm unsettled. I've got all this pent-up energy and nothing to do with it. The day's events are like a roller coaster that has left me motion sick. There's a part of me that still wants to relish riding in my friend's car for the first time: the music Didier played on his phone, the way the wind felt coming through Jackie's window up front. It felt like the city was ours, because we could've gone anywhere without asking anyone, and there was no one to tell us otherwise.

Except there was Joe, and there was my father. They took this moment away from me and now I'll never get it back. What other firsts will he steal if he becomes president? I picture Ricky and Mami and me being followed 24/7 by Secret Service agents who look like different versions of Joe. It dawns on me that I might never be alone again, and that strikes me as the loneliest thing in the world.

I open up my laptop and check my apps for something to watch. Nothing catches my attention. Instead, I launch the browser and type in Harrison Irving.

His company website is the first hit. I click on it and right away a video fills half the screen with the letters ERBAN.

I scroll down. Along the bottom of the screen there's a section for the company's latest news and acquisitions. A familiar image catches my eye.

No way. It's Vivi's old neighborhood.

There's a row of five houses with hers in the middle, looking like the youngest child in a portrait with taller siblings. The neighborhood looks bigger than it is, as if the picture were taken by an ant looking up at it. A caption below reads: IRVING CONSTRUCTION ANNOUNCES PLANS TO DEVELOP TEN-UNIT LUXURY VILLAGE IN THE HEART OF SOUTH MIAMI.

The press release goes on to say that with the recent purchase of the last house on this centrally located street, construction will now be under way in as little as two weeks. The units are available for presale from the low 900,000s.

So this is why Vivi's father was so quick to sell their house. With Vivi's mom out of the picture, he was finally free to take whatever deal the latest developer offered.

And that developer turned out to be Irving. The man responsible for leaving my best friend without a home *and* her abuela in the hospital. The man leaving entire neighborhoods without clean water. The man who basically finances my father and who my father would never cross.

Even though it's late, I text Vivi the link to Irving's latest property:

This explains a lot.

When she doesn't respond, I send it with no comment to Zoey.

Damn. That explains a lot, she writes. Does Vivi know?

I sent it to her.

Does this mean you'll join the walkout? With Jackie and them?

I don't know. I'm sorry I didn't get back to you about the pet store.

I wait for her to respond. The dot-dot-dot on the screen lights up and dims for several seconds, but when her text finally comes through, all it says is: It's fine.

Which it obviously isn't. I try to think of another way to apologize when she adds:

What if I do it with you? I can help, you know.

I stare at her text for several seconds. I don't know why, but it makes everything feel a little less scary. For the first time it feels doable, like it's not just me versus everybody, but me and Zoey and all the rest of us.

That'd be awesome, I write.

Ok. We'll do it for Vivi.

K.

Papi always says to create change you need three things: People, purpose, and ganas. I have the first two, and Irving just gave me all the determination I need.

thirty-five

Everything kind of spirals after our school reopens on Tuesday, and not just at Grove High. The mayor still hasn't said how long we'll be under a boil-water advisory, so all our sports games are canceled ("indefinitely" is the word they keep using) because no one wants to risk student athletes dehydrating in this heat. Even prom in May is kind of iffy, and it seems like all the seniors except for Jackie and Crissy, who say they were planning on boycotting it anyway, are pissed the school can't just find a new caterer and venue with stockpiles of ice, water, and food that doesn't need washing. Then there's the school water fountains. Everywhere we turn, they've been cordoned off with red tape and signs that say DO NOT DRINK! They look like mini crime scenes randomly scattered across campus.

To top it all off, Papi won't stop interrogating me. Before leaving for West Palm Beach, he asked if I planned on participating in the walkout. "Of course not," he said before I could answer. "You wouldn't do that to your own family, would you, Mari?"

On Wednesday, just as he grabbed a cup of coffee on his way out the door, while I was having my cereal, he outright forbade me to do it. I didn't argue with him then, either, and the most amazing thing happened. He didn't know what to do. His whole chest collapsed, like he'd been bottling up a lungful of arguments, and now they had nowhere to go. We stared at each other, holding the air between us, and I swear I felt something shift. The flinching look in his eyes gave it away. He was losing power, and I was gaining it.

By Thursday, he'd decided I wouldn't be allowed to go to school on Friday, period. By Thursday evening, he realized that would only make things worse. Everyone would know he kept me from going.

"What are you going to do, hijita?" he pleaded.

"What are *you* going to do, Papi? People need clean water."

He gave Mami a look like his eyes were about to jump out of his face. "Will you reason with your daughter, please?"

All this time, Mami has stayed out of it. She put one hand on her hip and said, "*Now* you want my opinion?"

He left it at that and set off to his fourth meet-and-greet in three days.

By the morning of the walkout, Jackie's tweets have been hearted by Chrissy Teigen and Zendaya, and the hashtag #PODERforchange has been trending nonstop. Last I checked, students from thirty-four other Florida schools plan to participate.

All week long, Jackie's been taking calls from reporters who want to interview her—and me, but she's kept me out of it like I asked.

"They sound bummed, but they don't push it," Jackie told me during lunch. "Sometimes they ask what our relationship is."

"Our relationship?"

"Yeah. Like if we're BFFs, acquaintances, just two students in the same club . . . stuff like that. They're always wanting to know what to label people."

"Oh. What do you say?"

"No comment," she said, with an odd grin that made me wish she had answered the reporters, just for my own curiosity.

Now it's only a matter of hours. Standing inside my closet, I put on a pair of black-and-white Adidas, my loose-fitting jeans that Mami hates because they have holes in them, and a dark-green spaghetti-strap tank layered over a white ribbed top. The tops ride up a little, exposing an inch of my midriff. For half a second, I worry my teachers will tell me to change, until I remember I'm planning on walking out of class anyway. It's not like people don't dress like this at school. It's just that I never have. Papi's always insisting we look presentable at all times—whatever that means—in case we're caught on camera. As a last touch, I put on a pair of gold-plated hoop earrings Vivi gave me for my birthday. It's the first time I've worn them because Papi thought they were too big and loud. I think they're perfect.

Yesterday, Jackie, Zoey, and I made a few extra posters during lunch in the PODER room.

Mine says: SAVE WATER, DRAIN IRVING.

Zoey made one calling out how the words *climate change* were banned from use in the Florida legislature. From top to bottom, her poster reads:

CLIMATE CHANGE.

CLIMATE CHANGE.

CLIMATE CHANGE.

CLIMATE CHANGE.

She used our entire supply of the blue and green glitter, but no one had the heart to stop her.

"Until I have a vote, this is how I'll be heard," she said.

"Word," Crissy said.

So much has changed in the past couple of weeks since Vivi left. Sometimes I think if she were still here, if she hadn't gotten kicked out of her house and her abuela weren't still sick (probably because of Irving), maybe I wouldn't care as much. Maybe I wouldn't be marching. And then I feel bad because that means I'm exactly like the people Jackie says are part of the problem: the ones who are happy to do nothing about injustice until it affects them or someone they love.

I grab my backpack and make my way down the stairs. Mami and Papi have already taken off for the day, leaving a note on the fridge that Joe will be taking me to school. I crumple it up and throw it at the table. After everything that's happened, I still have to put up with Papi's wannabe secret agent. I'm so ready to be done with this.

With Gloria gone, the house feels like an empty store after closing hours—all the usual lights and sounds are missing. I make myself some pan cubano with guava and ham and leave the plate in the sink. Not even a minute later, a high-pitched car horn goes off in our driveway. I know without looking that it's Joe.

"Does your mom know you're going to school dressed like that?" he says the second I get in his car.

"Does my mom know you're paying so much attention to how I'm dressed?" I say right back. This shuts him up quickly, but only for a few seconds.

The whole way to school, Joe lists reason after reason why I shouldn't protest, but I just nod and smile. It drives him bananas, so by the time we pull up to Grove High, he just mumbles something about staying out of trouble. I'm out of the car and slamming the door before he can even finish.

I'm honestly surprised that Principal Avila hasn't tried to keep us from protesting. We've seen it happen before—administrators who lock the doors before students plan to leave, claiming they're not allowed off school grounds unsupervised. A couple of years ago, a school let kids walk out when they marched for gun control, but then they wouldn't let them back in.

I find Jackie, Crissy, Didier, and Zoey in the math hall before first period. They're talking to Dania, whose mother works at Channel 7 and leaked the fact that I'd run away from the Home Invasion interview to the press.

"Do you think they'll come?" Crissy is saying.

Dania grimaces. "How should I know? You think the

world's going to stop what they're doing to watch you walk across the street?"

"There's going to be tons of news crews," Didier assures her.

Jackie stares down Dania, then she closes her eyes and sighs. "She's right. We didn't think this through."

"No, Jackie. We planned everything," Crissy says.

"We need something bigger. Otherwise, everyone will just ignore us and move on to the next story."

I don't think I've ever seen her this worried. "We're doing fine," I say. "Just ask my dad . . . he's been freaking out all week."

"Oh my god."

"What?"

"Oh my god. I can't believe I didn't think of this sooner." She drops her backpack to the ground and pulls her phone out of the front pocket. As she types something into the GPS, she begins bobbing her head as if she were at a concert. "Mari . . . please don't kill me."

"Why would I?"

"We have to march to your father's Senate office."

Didier laughs like it's preposterous. I'm glad I'm not the only one who thinks so. "All the way off US 1? That'll take forever. And not everyone can walk that far," he says.

"No, I know, but not everyone has to. We can set up stations. We'll need students holding up signs by the school entrance, so that we can maintain a presence here at Grove High. And we have a whole group staying in the PODER office to live-tweet the latest news and monitor our hashtag. But for whoever's marching . . . we need a destination with a real purpose. This way, we can leave the senator our demands."

"The senator is my father," I say. "I can't just . . . march up to his office."

"Why not?" Jackie says. "If he won't listen to you, then what chance do we have?"

I try to imagine it. There's a security guard in the lobby of the main floor; he'd probably be the first to come to the door. He'd tell us this is private property, and that we're welcome to congregate at least fifteen feet from the entrance. He'd take one look at me, and maybe, for half a second, have a hard time recognizing me. Then he'd immediately call Mami on his walkie-talkie. She'd run out of the elevators, through the revolving glass door, and yank me into the building by my hair. In front of everyone. Probably on national television.

I shake my head. "I never signed up for this."

The bell rings, signaling that we have five minutes to get to class. "It's fine. I get it," Jackie says. "You have to do what you're comfortable with."

Something about the way she says *comfortable*, though, rubs me the wrong way. "I don't think you understand how far out of my comfort zone I already am."

"You don't have to explain."

"No. You don't get to judge me just because I don't feel like betraying my father."

"Mariana. I'm not judging you. I promise. I get it. This is as far as you can go right now. And I don't mean that in a blaming way. Just that, everyone's in different places. Everyone has something different to contribute. I can't begin to understand what it's like to be you right now. I don't know what I would do either."

Somehow, her sympathizing with me feels worse than if she actually got upset, and I can't place why.

"I have to go," I say, afraid that if I say anything else, I'll burst into tears in front of all of them.

thirty-six

We're only a few minutes into second period when Principal Avila's voice comes through the PA. There's a lot of rustling and throat clearing, and the muted sound of other voices in the background. She speaks slowly, as if she's being fed lines in real time.

"We understand that today there are . . . plans for a student . . . demonstration. While we strongly support students' First Amendment rights, our interests are first and foremost your safety and education." All around me, there's a lot of eye-rolling, and everyone begins texting under their desk. "Any actions that disrupt your time in the classroom, or put students in harm's way, will be dealt with accordingly. Students must remain on school grounds during school hours. Those who leave the grounds will be marked absent."

Mrs. De la Torre, before she was interrupted, was about to have us interview the student sitting next to us and write a short story about them. There are almost forty of us and the whole class begins talking at once. Kids get out of their seats and call across the room, "You think you'll go?"

"It says to meet at the tennis courts."

"Will you help me make a sign?" Justine pops out of nowhere

and sits in the empty seat next to me. I've never heard her say a word except for when she shared that her community service project was to help shelter dogs. "I think it's really brave what you're doing."

"It's mostly Jackie's thing." I sit up, alarmed. "Are they saying I'm the one behind all this?"

"I mean, we just assumed. Because of your dad and all."

I check my phone and realize I have a barrage of messages.

None of them are from Papi, Joe, or Mami, though. The oldest is from Dania saying that she told her mom we're going to his office.

Jackie wants me to know everything's going to work out fine. Better than fine, you'll see.

Crissy wants to know if I'm okay, which makes me wonder if she texted the wrong person. Since when does she care if I'm okay?

Didier has sent me a bunch of laughing emojis. Avila's announcement lol.

And there's a stream of messages from numbers I don't recognize, people I've texted for a project or a party but whose names I forgot to save to my phone, saying they'll be at the tennis courts before lunch.

Let's do this!!! the last random person writes.

Crap. This is really happening. It's not just another one of Jackie's small protests; a few signs held by the school entrance, a few videos uploaded with #PODERforchange. Now all of a sudden the whole student body cares about clean water?

I mean, it's amazing.

But it's also terrifying. Because it means Jackie was right. They wouldn't care this much if they didn't think I was the one behind it. If it was just Jackie protesting Senator Ruiz, and not me protesting my father, they wouldn't be showing up. And yeah, probably some of them are just here for all the drama. But a lot of people think we have a real chance of stopping Irving from contaminating the water. They think we have a chance of being heard.

I have power. I didn't ask for it, but there it is.

See you at the tennis courts, I text Jackie.

She sends me back three lines of exclamation points, and a hug.

The two-tone bell signifying the PA system goes off again, and the class grows quiet.

"Mrs. De la Torre? Please send Mariana Ruiz to the office. Her mom is here to pick her up for early dismissal."

A collective gasp sweeps over the room, as if someone left a window open and a breeze snuck in. I feel them watching and whispering as I gather my stuff.

"You're not really leaving, are you?" Justine says.

I shake my head in disbelief. "I don't . . . know, it's fine. Everything's still going as planned."

The halls are empty as I make my way to the attendance office. A kid I'm not sure I've ever seen before gives me a nod as he comes out of the bathroom.

"Hey. See you outside."

I smile but don't say anything.

When I get to the attendance office, Mami is standing by the front desk, both hands on her phone and her big gray purse swaying from her elbow as she types. My whole body feels like it's sinking into sand.

She looks up and meets my eyes. She's got that look on her face again, the one that says *Don't you dare start with me right now*. Without saying a word, she walks out of the office and I follow.

She's waiting for the moment when we get into the car to say something, and each minute that passes only gives me more time to imagine the worst.

When we're finally inside, she puts her foot on the brake but stops short of turning on the car. In the distance, I hear the bell ring inside the school.

"We got a call. From MSNBC. They wanted to know if we had any comments about our daughter's plan to march to our office."

She pushes down on the START ENGINE button and it roars to life. "Of course, we thought it was a prank. Mariana has done some crazy things lately, but this? This would be . . . unimaginable. Not our daughter. Not the girl we raised."

"I didn't—"

"We're going to your father's office. And you're going to stay upstairs. And you're going to watch, quietly, while your father handles your schoolmates."

"They don't need to be handled. Just hear them out!"

We idle through the lot, making our way toward the exit, when she suddenly stops. A group of students—at least three or four dozen—crosses in front of us. They're holding posters and banners as they make their way toward the tennis courts. A couple of them meet my eyes through the windshield, which makes me want to crawl under the seat.

It'd be one thing if I were running away from all this; that alone would be pretty shameful. But to have my mom pick me up from school and drag me out of the fight?

Mami makes like she's about to honk the horn, then seems to think better of it. "Look what you've started."

"I didn't start it," I say, though now I wish I had. If none of this mattered, if we really were just a bunch of kids whose actions won't make a difference, then why is she so afraid? Why is Papi so dead set on stopping us?

All my life, my parents have said they wanted to shield me from politics, but that was a lie. They didn't want to shield me from politics any more than they'd want to shield me from air. They just wanted me not to notice what I was breathing. If every part of our lives is a decision that someone is making for us, then everything is political.

Even doing nothing.

Even staying in this car.

Crissy would say a nonaction is still an action. It enables things to stay the same. It's the opposite of change.

"Mami?" My voice sounds four years younger somehow. "Wasn't that you once? Didn't you work for things you believed in?"

Outside, the crowd is getting thicker, and the students show no sign of clearing a path for our car to pass.

"That was different," she says.

"How?"

"How do you even know about that?"

"Jackie told me. She thought you were a badass. Also Google." There were so many stories on the speeches she gave, the demonstrations she led. The Mami I never got to meet stayed silent for no one.

She places her elbow on the door and looks out the window.

"Why do you hide it? Why do you act like it's something to be ashamed of?"

"I'm not ashamed. It's just that it was nothing. It amounted to nothing."

"Is it because you and Papi got married? I did some digging. Some people think he made you promises he didn't keep."

"Things changed, that's all. We changed, and I made a strategic choice. I took a risk that—para. I don't want to talk about this." She stops. I can't see her eyes through her sunglasses, but in a quick motion she brings a finger to her eye, like she's wiping away an eyelash.

"I'm sorry. I just wanted to know what happened."

"Children are not supposed to see their parents' failures," she says. "We're supposed to protect you."

"From this?" I gesture to the students gathering by the tennis courts. They've begun chanting now, their voices rising through the air in four beats. I lower the window and it gets louder.

Our planet, our voice.

Our planet, our voice.

"Our planet, our voice!" I turn to see Jackie walking in front of our car, pumping her fist in the air. She moves slowly, her eyes locked with mine. I contemplate jumping out to join them. It'd be so easy.

Before I can make a decision, my window slides up. I hear the door locks click and see my mom's delicate fingers on the button.

"What are you doing?"

"Get out of the car."

"What?"

"Get out of the car. Go. Right now." She's saying it like it's a punishment, the way she used to do when Ricky and I would argue on the way home from Publix, and she'd threaten to leave us right there on the side of Red Road if we didn't shut up and let her drive.

I don't understand. I look at the door and realize the click I just heard was her unlocking it.

"Anda. Before I change my mind."

"What about Papi?"

"That's for me to deal with, not you."

I want to hug her, but there's no time. Jackie's kept walking and the crowd is moving fast. I push the door open and get out.

thirty-seven

I don't think I've ever seen so many students in one place unless there was a fight going on. I find Crissy and Didier by the portables on the edge of school grounds.

"You made it!" Crissy says.

"I got out of my mom's car when I saw you all walking out."

She looks impressed. "That's genius, Mari. Your mom checked you out of school so you're technically not skipping class. Meanwhile, they're saying the rest of us might get detention or in-school suspension."

"They said that?"

Didier nods. "Principal Avila called Jackie into her office and demanded she call everything off. So then she moved the whole thing up!" he says, giddily flicking his wrist in the air so that his fingers make a smacking noise against one another. He's holding a paper banner that drapes from his chest to his calves, pressed against his body by the wind like a skirt.

"Are you okay?" I whisper. "With the suspension?"

"I probably won't get to use the car again till summer, but . . . what can we do?"

"I didn't know so many people cared," I say. The crowd has grown past the tennis courts, past the science wing, and past the teacher parking lot to the front of the school, where a security guard stands next to the main gate. Which, as far as I can tell, is locked.

A couple of students start climbing over it, but mostly the mass of us moves slowly toward it, like a bottleneck of cars trying to get off a one-lane exit on the highway. People try opening the gate, shaking it to no avail, as they start yelling for the school to open it until the security guard finally unlocks the entrance. Maybe he sensed he had no other choice, that there was no stopping us. Students cheer and start trickling through, one by one.

The person directing the traffic? Jackie. Of course.

"Come on." I grab Crissy's hand and begin pulling her through the crowd. Didier takes hold of her other hand and follows. "Sorry. 'Xcuse me. Behind you." Everyone seems pissed that I'm trying to cut until they see it's me. They pull out their phones and begin shooting. Pretty soon, they've cleared a path for us. I keep my head down as we move forward. A light tap on my shoulder makes me stop and turn. It's Zoey.

"You're here!" I start pulling her with me.

Her face has specks of glitter all over it. She holds her sign over the back of her head and it doubles as a visor, blocking out the sun.

"Come on! We have to hurry."

When we finally make our way through, I reach through the gate to tap Jackie on the shoulder. "Oh my god, we thought we'd lost you!"

Everyone starts cheering. She pumps her fist in the air and yells, "We're doing this!" The crowd grows even louder and I join them. It's like the more I scream, the less alone I feel. My voice isn't drowned out because it becomes part of something bigger, amplified.

I look around, stunned that we managed to organize so quickly. Not everyone had time to make a sign, so some people hold up single sheets of paper, or notebooks where they've written things like #ITSTOPSNOW. Others pick up fallen palm fronds or banana leaves strewn across the sidewalk as we make our way down the road. We haven't even been out for ten minutes when I notice a small procession of cops on motorcycles.

"Shit," Didier says.

"Principal Avila said they'd show up if I didn't call off the protest," Jackie says. "She said they'd have to protect the students, and that it wasn't fair to local taxpayers. She's so full of it."

"Right. They're 'protecting' us," Didier says, using air quotes. He picks up his pace and edges toward the center of the crowd as he takes out his camera and begins filming.

I check my phone to see if he's streaming live. A text message from Mami covers the main screen.

Cuídate. Don't do anything you won't be proud of later.

It's weird. It's like I'm meeting a stranger but also finding a piece of her that was missing. They say parents live vicariously through their kids to make up for things that they regret.

Is this who she used to be? The person that I'm becoming?

We stay in a nearly single file to avoid spilling out onto the road. The wind picks up and the palm trees bristle over our heads. They sound like waves crashing ashore.

A cop wails his siren once, warning us to stay on the sidewalk. A white van with a giant red-and-blue seven painted on it speeds past and parks several blocks ahead.

"Ha! So they *do* want to watch us walking down the street," Jackie says. "Dania can eat it." In the distance, a four-person news crew climbs out and begins setting up equipment. A woman with big brown hair and a teal dress—Dania's mom, I assume—stands with a mike in her hand. Just the sight of her sends a tremble through my limbs.

"I don't think I can talk to them," I blurt out. No one seems to hear me. "Jackie?" I say louder.

"Yeah. You okay?"

I give several tiny, quick nods. "It's just . . . They're going to want to talk to me, right?"

"Probably. But you don't have to do anything you don't want to."

"I'm not ready."

"We've got you." She puts her arm around my shoulder and I wrap mine around her waist. Crissy catches up to us and gives me a silent look, as if to ask if she can join. I nod, and pretty soon, along with Didier and Zoey, we've become a human chain.

I turn my head to get a sense of how many we are now. There are students as far back as I can see. Where the road ends, several blocks behind us, there's a group setting up chairs and signs at the intersection, and a few other clusters of kids crossing, making their way toward the highway we're close to reaching.

Did the whole student body seriously just do this? We're a school of about twenty-five hundred and it feels like nearly all of us are participating. Of the thirty-four other schools that are walking out, two are meeting with our group at my father's parking lot. I look around, and it's hard to imagine there will soon be more of us. For now our noise feels like chatter, quiet chants in the distance, a woot here and there.

But we all know once Jackie says the word, we'll raise our voices.

thirty-eight

Without realizing, we've synched our footsteps, and as we pick up the pace, my heart beats faster too. It makes me feel like we're unstoppable, a determined force that will never be silent. Even after this ends, even when we all go home. This will change everything and we'll all be changed because of it.

We reach the news van and keep going. Dania's mother joins us with her microphone and cameraman in tow. She's wearing black three-inch heels that I guess seemed reasonable this morning. They crunch against the uneven payment and her breath spurts onto the marshmallow pad of the mike.

"Mariana, what are you marching for today? Are you sending a message to your father?"

I keep quiet, my eyes fixed on the space before me. If I ignore her, will she go away? Or will I end up on national television looking like one of those frozen iguanas that fall from trees in the winter?

"Mariana, have you thought about how this will affect your father's chances in Tuesday's Florida primary elections?"

A few arms lengths to my left, I hear Crissy yell, "Maybe he should've thought of that before letting Irving put caca in our drinking water!" Her voice nearly croaks from fury and a bunch of people bust out laughing.

Dania's mom doesn't seem to catch it. She asks Crissy to repeat herself, but the moment has passed. The five of us try to keep a straight face, but every time our eyes meet we can't suppress our giggles.

"They're going to think we're high," Jackie says, suddenly very serious, which only makes us laugh even harder.

Didier takes a deep breath and fans his face with his CLEAN WATER NOW sign to dry his tears. Zoey holds her poster over her mouth, but you can see in her eyes that she's smiling.

I want to tell them how amazing they are, how happy I am that we're friends, but I know that the second I say a word, the mike will be back in my face. Instead I keep my expression neutral and wrap my arm around Jackie's and Zoey's waists again, and a collective squeeze travels through all our bodies.

We reach the intersection between US 1 and Kendall Drive and stop to wait for the walk signal. There are so many of us that we can't help blocking traffic.

Car horns start blaring. People scream at us in both support and anger. A group of students standing in the middle of the previous block start cheering, raising their hands and signs higher.

It's a cacophony of chaos. The cops wail their sirens again, and it ends up sounding like a catcaller whistling at us as we pass.

"Mariana . . ." I'm beginning to realize that Dania's mom

starts all her questions to me by saying my name ". . . was shutting down US 1 part of your plan today?"

Shutting it down? A couple of cars are missing their green light, and she calls it shutting down?

"Mariana?"

I glance at Jackie and that's all it takes for her to swoop in.

"Protest is not supposed to be convenient." Even though the mike is right in front of her, Jackie has to yell for us all to hear her. "Just like our contaminated water is not convenient." She pauses and we begin cheering. "Just like buying crates of bottled water even though our taxes are supposed to pay for drinking water is not convenient." The cheers grow louder. "Just like making clean water a luxury affordable only to the rich is not convenient." It begins to sound like a concert now, a back and forth. "Just like children being poisoned for years in Flint, Michigan, while the government turns its back on the Black community is not convenient." Jackie's amazing. I'm in awe. Her voice rises with each of the word's three punctuated syllables, like a drum. *Con. Ve. Nient.* "Our health is more important than your convenience."

The camera is fully focused on her now. Jackie picks up the pace as she talks. She has no scripts or notes—it's like she's been preparing for this all her life.

"Our right to clean water is more important than any developer's profits."

Again, the crowd erupts. I stand next to her, clapping and yelling at every pause.

"We're not here to disrupt." Her voice takes a calmer but

still heavy tone. "We're here to be heard. If our legislators find our voices inconvenient, that's on them. They're the ones who disrupted our most basic rights first. They're the ones who need to fix this. Now."

She goes silent and Didier latches onto her last words, repeating them over and over in his deep voice until they're a chant.

Fix this now.

Fix this now.

Fix this now.

We walk in step until we've carried our message across the intersection and through the Metro's overpass, past the Wells Fargo bank, past the strip mall with the Old Navy and the BrandsMart, past the cluster of high-rises and developers' billboards of more to come, past the cars that keep honking and the sudden addition of camera crews from channels six, thirty-nine, and CN-freaking-N, past the parking lot of the tall, gray glass building that juts into the sky like it's out of place, until we arrive, out of breath but not out of words, at the door to the lobby of my father's office.

thirty-nine

"We've just reached Senator Ruiz's office." Crissy holds her phone at an angle over her face and begins recording. "Enough is enough. Our elected officials need to remember they work for us, not their donors. If they can't wrap their heads around this concept, then we'll vote them out."

Dania's mom, who up until now was interviewing other students, is suddenly at Crissy's side. "Excuse me, can you repeat that?"

"We'll vote them out."

"And how old are you?"

"Sixteen and a half," Crissy says, which of course makes her sound twelve. She cringes and we all smile at her to keep going—the fact that we've gone national is beyond, and I don't think any of us have had a chance to really process it.

"So then how do you plan on—"

"That's not the point." She recovers quickly. "I may not be old enough to vote yet. And there are millions of us who aren't eligible to vote, either, whether it's because we're undocumented or not yet citizens, but that doesn't mean our voices don't count."

"So what are you hoping to accomplish today?"

Crissy doesn't miss a beat. "We're putting people like

Senator Ruiz and Harrison Irving on blast. We see what they're doing, and we're not letting it go. They can never rely on our silence to protect them again."

The kids within hearing distance start to cheer, but I stay quiet. It's not that Crissy's words are surprising—I've heard her say some version of these things before—but now that we're here and she's saying Papi's name, I feel his presence emanating from the twelfth floor of the building. I wonder if he's watching me on television or from his window. I try to imagine what he must be thinking. That he'll ground me for months? That no longer carries the weight it used to. That his own daughter deceived him? I start to feel so guilty I have to remind myself he did it first. I can't place why this dark sense of dread is coming over me, like a fog over my head.

From the back of the parking lot, the faint, stilted sound of a chant begins to form. I can't make out what they're saying yet, just the five beats that rush toward us. People pump their fists in the air as the chant grows and gets to us.

"NOT MY PRESIDENT. NOT MY PRESIDENT."

I stumble a few steps back, right into Jackie's chest. I feel her hands land gently on my shoulders. "You okay?" Her voice is low, but we're standing close enough that I hear her words clearly.

More important, I hear what she's not saying.

"You're not chanting," I say, my throat suddenly dry. "You love chanting."

She looks side to side out of the corners of her eyes, then

smirks as she shrugs her shoulders. "Sometimes. If it's a good one. And anyways, I just think this is bigger than one election . . ."

But she doesn't finish what she was saying. Something over my shoulder has caught her eye, and her gaze travels upward as a mixture of amazement and maybe even fear spreads over her features.

"Senator Ruiz," she says, standing taller.

I turn around and there he is, not even a foot of space between us. "Papi."

"You wanted to talk to me, hija. So I came out to listen."

Everyone around us goes mute, their voices suddenly extinguished. Mine too.

forty

Before I can say anything, Papi has his arm around my shoulders and he's smiling right at the cameras. His palm feels warm and sweaty through my shirt, and everything else feels distant, separate. Pressure begins settling on my chest, so heavy that when I try to say something, the words get caught inside of me.

Papi looks into my eyes, and for a moment, it's just us, father and daughter about to finally have a conversation. He grins and I swear I catch a hint of encouragement in him, like the day we posed for that picture with the parrot at Parrot Paradise. It's the look that says *You can do this, I know you can do this.*

It flashes between us like the sun through a swaying palm tree, and then Papi turns away.

"I wanted to tell you all how proud I am of our youth for using their voices to champion the things they believe in."

He takes his arm off me and gestures at the crowd. He pauses when he gets to Jackie, then looks over Crissy, Didier, Zoey, and everyone standing behind them.

"It takes courage to do what these kids have done today."

He talks like we're not even here. Like he's not actually talking to us.

"This is how democracy works, and why I am so proud to have been elected to serve you. Hearing from my constituents —of all ages—helps me do my job better."

I blink back tears as he moves a few steps ahead of me. It's almost masterful, the way he's put me back in my usual place. Him taking center stage, talking over everyone. Me in the background, stiff as a prop, wishing I could be anywhere else but here. I'm frozen in place, powerless to stop him from stopping us. With a few quick words he's dismissed me, dismissed all of us.

Didier looks at me and nods as if to say, *don't worry.* "Fix this now! Fix this now!"

But Papi raises his hand to squash the chant before it spreads, and shockingly, it works. "If anyone has any questions, I'll be happy to answer them. But screaming back and forth at each other isn't going to help anyone. That's not how a conversation works . . ."

His words begin running into one another in my mind. How can one person say so much without saying anything at all? It almost feels violent. He's taking up space so that we can't claim it.

Jackie steps into the semicircle the crowd has formed around us. "Senator Ruiz, will you stop taking money from Harrison Irving and work to fix our water?"

No one hears her, and Papi pretends not to. The cameras and their mikes are focused only on him, so he goes on about how we have to listen to both sides, how no matter what you feel about something, we're all in this together . . .

He was banking on this. He knew I'd be afraid to talk back to him, let alone speak. He knew he'd be able to take control of the situation easily.

Don't enter a fight you can't win, he always says.

But what kind of father fights against his own daughter? What kind of father wants the children to lose?

I try to say something, but I'm afraid my voice won't carry. I feel it catch in my stomach, as if someone bottled it and tossed it away until it sank. I look to Jackie and Didier, whose faces are a mix of hope and desperation. I start to shake my head, but then they nod. I blink, take a breath, and lean into the numbness that's come over my body. I imagine all the tension and doubt and fear spilling out of it like water crashing ashore. I tell myself what Jackie said, to let my voice flow through me, but then louder still I hear Papi's own words on the day he taught me how to swim in the ocean. I was so afraid the current would take me under. He told me not to be afraid. *Swim with it,* he said. *Let it take you to safety.*

"No. You're wrong." The words feel thick against my lips.

And yet, their sound stops all others. The street suddenly goes quieter than a room full of test-takers. The eyes of all my peers, all the millions of people watching online or on TV, land on me.

Papi turns in shock. I can see the question form on his mouth, but he thinks better of it. Asking me to repeat myself would be giving up the podium. "I firmly believe that—"

"You once told me that of all the reasons to run for office, there's only one good one: to improve the lives of others," I say in a louder voice. "If that's still true . . . and I need to, I have to believe it is, deep down . . . then this is all really simple. There is no such thing as both sides when one side is drinking contaminated water and the other side is contaminating it. We don't need a debate. We need action. We need clean water. It's the most basic thing. It's biology. It's survival. What kind of society are we if we can't provide people with this?"

I'm almost yelling now; each word is a massive breath shaking everything inside of me. Beyond our semicircle, the students go wild. They raise their fists and banners. Their energy stretches before us like a rope that's tying each and every one of us together. I can feel when they're quieting down. They can feel when I'm about to speak.

But what I have to say now is not really for them. "Papi. I believe in you. I'm begging you to . . . no, I *know* you'll do the right thing here."

If his face were a puzzle, this would be the part where each piece tumbles out of place. Never, in all the times I've watched him onscreen, has he ever looked so lost. Every muscle in his body sags at once.

"Are you okay . . ."

He recovers and cuts me off with the subtle raise of his left hand. "You're right. I made you a promise. I intend to keep it."

With his back now to the news cameras, he takes a few steps toward me. I begin to move away, but then he slows his pace and reaches out a hand. He places it on my cheek and kisses me on the forehead.

Papi's lips are wet and warm, and I can still feel their

imprint against my skin, even after he's walked back into the building and the students have started chanting again. I feel lightheaded. I feel all my senses on fire. Sights and sounds burn and Mami's touch stings. Her hand is on my shoulder and I read her lips as she asks if I'm okay. I nod and lean into her as she wraps her arm around me. We enter the lobby and the glass walls do nothing to muffle the sound of the crowd. Everything is a blur.

Minutes later, I'm watching the crowd dissipate from the twelfth-story window of my dad's office. My phone is hot to the touch from all the texts and notifications coming in. I scroll through all of them without really reading until I come across one from Vivi.

I heard you speak! Omg I HEARD YOU SPEAK!

forty-one

They deposit me in an empty room that, from the looks of the binders and tape dispensers on the desk, used to be someone's workspace. Mami tells me not to go anywhere. She brings me a glass of water, a pastel de guava, and a couple of croquetas de jamón, then kneels in front of my chair. The way she looks at me, quietly and concerned, you'd think I just survived a car accident.

"¿Cómo te sientes?"

"Fine," I say. When she doesn't respond, I'm forced to really think about it. "I didn't know what else to do. People are getting sick . . ."

"Don't worry about that right now. You've done enough for one day."

I can't tell if she means that I did enough good or enough damage. She brushes two fingers over my forehead and wipes the sweat drops away.

"Just wait here, okay?"

The door doesn't make a sound as she leaves. Minutes later, the calm gives way to a commotion unlike any I've ever heard before. Multiple phones ring at once, followed by several sets of footsteps thumping hard against the carpet. An air of desperation emanates from the many voices that rise and fall, competing with one another for my ear. I only catch a word every few seconds or so.

His position.

Crisis mode.

No turning back.

This damn march.

His own fucking daughter.

I guess I can't blame them for freaking out. Papi made me a promise on national television. He said he intends to keep it. So, yes, maybe he didn't go into specifics, but that's probably what they're discussing now. It's a lot of work, changing policies so close to the primaries on Tuesday. But it'll be worth it.

They're so caught up that they don't notice me slipping out of my closet/office/dungeon. I stay close to the wall as I make my way down the corridor. Outside Papi's office, there's a desk that belongs to his secretary, who I guess is with him inside. I sit in her chair and scooch close to the door.

"It's fine. It's fine," says a voice that is unmistakably Joe's. "We just need to figure out how to spin this asap."

"You think I haven't thought of that?" Papi shouts.

"Have you talked to Irving yet?" asks a woman's voice I don't recognize.

"He's shutting down all operations in the Biscayne Bay Aquifer. Temporarily. We'll announce tomorrow that we're pushing for more extensive testing of the water."

"What kind of testing?" the woman asks. "The mayor has already ordered several tests."

Papi sounds annoyed at the question. "I don't know all the details. Does it matter?"

"It's just to buy us time. Just so these kids will back off until Tuesday," Joe says. "We'll deal with them after."

Deal with them? I can't believe what they're saying.

I hear the sounds of paper being shuffled and then finally my father clears his throat. "Just do whatever we need to do."

The room seems to spring into action. I rush off, hiding behind the first open door I can find. It turns out to be a closet full of boxes stacked as tall as I am with Papi's campaign kitsch: REBUILDING AMERICA yard signs and bumper stickers, vintage-looking pins with his face on them, and refrigerator magnets that say #RuiztotheFuture.

The air feels cold and fake in here. Every time I exhale, it hurts like a bruise I can't stop pressing down on. I take a few steps back, nearly tripping over an old paper shredder, but manage to keep my balance by grasping at the wall. My hand lands on something smooth and slippery.

It's a cardboard cutout of my father.

He's wearing a charcoal gray suit, a red tie, and an American flag pin on his left collar. He smiles like he's holding his breath and waiting for the moment to pass.

I lean into him on tippy-toes and take a selfie.

I group text my friends what I just heard go down.

Vivi and Didier both reply at the same time: I'm so sorry, Mari.

Zoey says, That really sux.

He was never going to change, Crissy adds.

And then finally in all caps, Jackie: IT'S FINE. THEY'RE SCARED. WE'VE GOT THIS.

I stifle a laugh, and only then do I realize there are tears in my eyes. They trickle down and hang from my chin like raindrops on an awning.

I send them the selfie of me and my cardboard dad.

This is about as real as he's ever going to get with me.

Their flurry of approving emojis makes me smile again.

I cut and paste the words into a tweet and attach the picture. I consider hashtagging it #RuiztotheFuture, but then I delete it.

Delete.

Delete.

Delete.

Delete.

Delete.

It's not worth it for now. The tweet would spread like wildfire but in the end, it'd only be me that got burned. Even Mami wouldn't defend me. She'd say I pushed her to her limits, and I can almost see Ricky's confused expression as he'd ask, "Don't you love Papi anymore?"

How do you explain this to an eight-year-old? That you can love someone but lose faith. That you can find things to believe in that are beyond him.

The thumbnail of the picture implodes on itself as I delete it.

It's better this way. I'm still angry, angrier than I've ever been. But Jackie's right. We've got this. Maybe not right away. Maybe not in the next few days. It's like Papi always says, important decisions take time and preparation. It's why he took so long to tell me and my brother he'd run for president. I finally get it.

Besides, my anger is too powerful to waste on hurting him. My anger is powerful enough for change.

forty-two

Since the walkout, Papi hasn't been home long enough to say a word to me. I've gotten zero texts to see how my day is going. No more than a quick peck on the forehead when he passes through the house. Papi avoids looking at me so purposely, you'd think I was the sun during an eclipse.

"I know what you're doing," I tell him the day after the walkout. He's heading out to his big press conference, the one where he'll announce Irving's plans to suspend operations on the aquifer for whatever phony test they probably aren't even going to do. "You're only pretending. Just enough for us to shut up before election day."

His jaw tightens like he just tasted something sour. He gathers a few files in his suitcase, never looking up once as he says, "I'm done trying to silence you. You betrayed me in front of the entire country. What is left for me to say to that?"

"You can try the truth, for once."

His suitcase snaps shut, and I jump a little at the sound. As if on cue, Joe walks into the room and Papi looks straight ahead to him, right through me as if I've disappeared.

"Ready. I'm done here."

This is the most we speak all weekend.

• • •

On the eve of the election, Papi is six hours away in Alachua County for one last push. He won't be home until the following morning, so Mami stays up all night. I know because I can't sleep either, and when I go downstairs for a midnight snack, there's light coming from the kitchen and she's got her laptop open and papers everywhere, all across the table. Her face is bare and glistening from the lotion she uses to take off her makeup.

"What are you doing?"

"Writing your father's speeches."

"Does he know?"

"He will. Why aren't you in bed?"

"Mami. Really?" I grab some milk and a box of leftover croquetas from the fridge. I take a bite of one without bothering to heat it up.

Mami looks at me like I just put a worm in my mouth. "Ay, Mari."

"What? It'll just get soggy in the microwave. And I'm too hungry to wait."

"You should've eaten earlier."

"Did you eat anything?"

She sighs. We both know we've been too nervous to eat. Now we're too anxious to sleep.

I sit next to her and glance over her notes. They're print-outs of nearly all the speeches he's given in the last year. She's highlighted some parts in yellow and put an X through entire paragraphs.

"I'm trying to tie it all together so it's like a journey: past, present, and future."

I offer to help and she gives me a highlighter.

"Just . . . anything he repeats a lot that sounds hopeful and determined."

There's so much.

I decided to run for president because I know that we are great, but that we can always be better.

Next I highlight: *When I look at my family, I see everything our great nation represents.*

There are plenty of lines I skip over because they're all the same: promise after promise. I grab another cold croqueta and the grease on my fingers leaves tiny transparent dots along the margins.

We work for forty-five minutes, until Mami has a rough draft. It's beautiful. It's the story of our lives, starting from the first campaign he ran when I was little, all the way up until now. At every opportunity, Mami writes that he's grateful for this journey, even the hard parts, because it's helped make him a better person.

This is our duty as Americans, to always strive to be better people so we can become a better nation.

This is why I'm announcing the end of my campaign today.

"Wait, what? This is a concession speech?"

She folds her computer shut and exhales. "It's just in case, Mari. It's common practice to write both. His staff has obsessed over the other one a million times. I just want him to be prepared for the alternative."

"Is it really that bad?"

"No. And it's not your fault, if that's what you're really

asking. Your papi's tracking numbers have been all over the place for a while, and the fundraising . . ."

Her voice trails off, as if she's suddenly remembered she's not supposed to say these things out loud. It sounds blasphemous, even to me.

I reopen her laptop and keep reading. In the next few paragraphs, as Papi explains his decision, Mami doesn't shy away from the walkout or the water. She writes, *Let me put the rumors and speculation to rest: there is no battle here, between father and daughter. If anything, what my campaign should prove is that we can and must love each other, no matter what.*

No matter what? That doesn't sound right, but I don't have the heart to say so to Mami. "Do you really think he'll go for this?"

She closes her eyes and her head falls forward. "We need to sleep. Vamos." We walk to her bedroom and I crawl into bed next to her, in the spot where Papi always sleeps.

forty-three

When I wake up, Mami's standing over me holding a black skirt and a red sleeveless blouse with a white lace collar decked out in pearls. "Toma," she says.

I groan and roll onto my right side, pulling the covers tight.

"Por favor, Mari. Don't make things worse." She's whispering, which can only mean Papi's around here somewhere.

"I didn't do anything," I say.

"Are we starting already?" Ah, so he's in the closet. I hear the clinking of his belt as he gets dressed. What time did he even get here? And where did he sleep?

"Come on, despiértate," Mami says, with a fake cheer in her voice that guilts me into playing along. I sit up and take the clothes from her. "Thank you. We leave for the precinct in an hour and a half. You and Ricky will wait in the car with Joe."

"We're not going in?" It's tradition. In every election Papi has ever run in, we've taken pictures with my parents as they cast their ballots. So the American people know we do this as a family, Papi always says.

"It'll be too much of a distraction. We're doing one picture of the four of us standing at the entrance when we arrive. No other press."

"Well . . . good."

She tightens her robe. "Yes, good."

I hold the blouse up to my torso in the mirror. "It's nice, thanks."

She sighs. "I'm glad you like it."

It's going to make me look like an old lady, but I don't have the heart to tell Mami this. I say the next best thing. "It reminds me of Ruth Bader Ginsburg." In the PODER room's mini-library, there's a biography of her called *Notorious RBG*, all about her life before she became the second female supreme court justice. I haven't finished reading it yet, but I've gotten enough of a gist to know that Mami probably loved her years ago. Maybe she still does.

Mami stares at our reflection in the mirror. Her face is full of longing, like she's looking at a picture of someone who's gone. "Go upstairs and get ready."

I lean in to kiss her. Before our bodies pull away I ask, "Is he still upset with you? For letting me go to the walkout?"

Her eyes dart between the closet and the bathroom, where he's migrated to. "He has eight hundred other things to worry about right now. I doubt he's even thinking about it."

That doesn't answer my question.

The plan was that after my parents cast their votes, we'd stop by Papi's campaign headquarters on Brickell, a first-floor office space they've been renting since last year. The only time I ever stopped in was months ago, when Papi surprised everyone by bringing in a stack of pizzas to thank them for volunteering. They were so elated to see him, the pizzas got cold while they took turns taking pictures with us. This was way before the Bubble Boy incident. Way before I knew anyone could hate my father.

Now Joe's saying there's no way we can go back there today. This is after Papi already told him to cancel the visit, but Joe loves to act like he's the one who makes decisions. We'll watch tonight's primary results at the Biltmore Hotel in Coral Gables, which is where we've spent Papi's last two elections—first for the state legislature and then for his Senate seat. Joe calls the hotel while we drive to the voting precinct in the campaign's black SUV. He sits behind me in one of those seats that folds up from the trunk.

Ricky is so excited he won't stop bouncing. He's wearing khaki slacks with a lavender guayabera that makes him look like a tiny version of Abuelo.

"Mami let me do my hair, like it?"

She actually just let him hold onto the comb, which he's been using all morning to keep everything in place. He's become such a ham ever since Papi decided to keep us away from the press. It's like he craves attention now that he's tasted life without it.

"It's just one picture," I tell him. "We're not even going inside."

"No thanks to you."

"Don't you have a game you're trying to beat on your iPad?"

"Don't you have someone else's life to ruin?"

"Wow. Really?"

"Everyone shut up!" Joe calls from the back seat.

We all turn, even Papi, who's in the passenger seat next to the driver.

"It's just . . . I'm on the phone with the hotel. They're setting up the war room," Joe says.

I've always thought that *war room* is such an interesting thing to call the room with all the reporters. If a free press is essential to democracy, why would we be at war? The look on Joe's face as he talks about the media makes me think of Gloria, how she once told me that telling the truth makes life harder for people who don't want things to change.

We arrive at the voting precinct within a few minutes. It's a small building, an old bungalow that used to be a clubhouse for the community and is now a historic landmark. A line of voters stretches halfway down the block. We climb out and wait for Joe to squeeze out of the back. There's a news van parked across the street, and he nods at a man with a camera just as he makes his way toward us.

"Okay. Rapidito," Mami says, putting her arms over Ricky's and my shoulders. With our backs facing the crowd of voters, the three of us move in an awkward shuffle toward Papi, who's already standing in the perfect spot, with the American flag in the background.

The pictures are quick, like they said they'd be. Behind us, people wave at my father and take pictures on their phones as they talk excitedly among themselves. I tune them out and head back to the SUV the second my parents say they're going in.

They cut ahead of the line. It doesn't take more than

fifteen minutes, and then Ricky and I are dropped back off at the house so my parents can head to meetings and interviews all day. Before she leaves, Mami hands Ricky and me their I VOTED stickers. I realize it's the first time we didn't cast a vote with the pretend ballots that Mami always makes us. That makes two family traditions broken.

I lie in bed and can hear Ricky blasting the news from his bedroom.

My phone vibrates twice in my pocket.

Hola, mami. You ok? It's Amarys.

Of course I know it's you, I reply.

Immediately, the screen goes off with a FaceTime call. She's sitting next to Gloria, in what I assume is their bedroom because there's a big cluster of magenta pillows in the background.

They wave hello and I sit up and cross my legs.

"Oh my god, you don't know how happy I am to see you!" I say.

"Well we've been seeing plenty of you, mami. Super proud of you, you know?"

"You showed up on Telemundo at eleven," Gloria adds. "With all the other kids. Are those your new friends?"

"Some of them. Like three of them. I still miss Vivi, though. And you."

"Nah," Amarys says. "You don't need us anymore. You've got followers now. You're leading a movement."

My whole body tenses up and my shoulders feel like they're in a brace. I've stopped checking all the follow requests on my social media accounts. Ever since the walkout, I updated my bio by telling people to follow PODER instead. Didier says they've blown up. "I don't really want to talk about it. My dad's never going to change. It didn't make the difference I thought it would. It just pissed him off."

"You feel that way now," Amarys says. "But change takes time. Hay que luchar."

"That's what Jackie's always saying. How've you two been?" I decide against mentioning that I stopped by their house the other night.

"Ahí vamos," Amarys says. "We've been looking for a new apartment. We have to be out of ours by the end of next month, así que . . ."

"Oh my god, what happened?"

"Nothing bad! Amarys got a job at a nonprofit downtown. So we want to be closer to her work."

"That's amazing," I say. "¿Y tú?"

"I'll find something around there," she says, not sounding very convinced. "How are your parents? Ricky?"

"Ricky's . . . fine. I mean, he hates me right now, but that's nothing new." I change the subject back to their new apartment. "So, like, where around downtown? You'll be so far . . ."

"It's not that bad, mami," Amarys says. "You can take the Metro."

"Amoris, she's not going to take the Metro."

I almost giggle but end up grinning really big instead. Gloria's nickname for Amarys is the most adorable thing I've ever heard.

"¿Y por qué no?"

"I can take the Metro," I say.

"Her father would never let her. Not after what she did last time," Gloria says.

"Déjala. Mari can decide for herself," Amarys says.

It's funny how she thinks I have any choice in anything. As we speak, Florida voters are deciding not only who they want to be the GOP's presidential nominee, but possibly the fate of the next four to eight years of my life. I check the clock. Three hours until the polls close.

Before we hang up, they wish me luck tonight. "Que todo vaya bien," Gloria says.

I no longer know what "everything going well" means. It used to be simple. It used to be my father winning. But that was when I thought we wanted the same things.

forty-four

The Biltmore Hotel is one of the most beautiful places in all of Miami. It's in the heart of Coral Gables, a city surrounded by lush green foliage. It overlooks a golf course on one end and faces a field dotted with palm trees on the other. The building resembles a sprawling, yellow Mediterranean villa, like something you'd see in a 1920s movie. A few blocks from the hotel is the little church where my parents—and, honestly, almost all the Cuban parents I know—got married. My father likes to remind me of this every time we turn through the traffic circle heading its way.

Tonight, though, he doesn't even look out the window as we approach. He stares at the dashboard with his hands held together, and we keep our voices down as he prays. I close my eyes and join him.

No matter what happens tonight, please let my family, and all the families affected, be okay in the end. Amen.

We pull into the terra cotta–lined entrance to the hotel. Immediately, a group of valets and press people swarm us. My father gets out first, waving his arm in a way that greets them but also keeps them at bay.

"Move, move, move it," Joe says as we climb out. "Left. Over here." He places his hand on my shoulder and we make our way through the arches in the lobby to the courtyard out back. There are cameras set up all over the place—by the water fountain in the terrace, by the coral steps that lead to the garden next to the giant pool. Everywhere I look, there's a reporter doing a sound check or recording a segment.

"We're here live . . ."

"Florida senator Anthony Ruiz awaits tonight's crucial results . . ."

"His home state . . ."

"A must-win for this campaign . . ."

Someone calls my name through all the noise. I look over my shoulder and see Vivi darting through the crowd with Zoey right behind her. We scream and run into each other's arms.

"How do you feel? Are you ready for tonight?" Vivi says.

"This is super intense." Zoey's breathless as she takes it all in.

"I'm just ready for tonight to be over," I say, perhaps a bit too loud.

Joe clears his throat. "Let's go. We gotta keep walking."

It's then that I realize I no longer know where my parents are. We cram into the elevator with Joe and a bunch of new-to-me people he makes a point of shaking hands with. Donors, I assume. Are they with Irving? Are they also condo developers? Could we be standing in this tiny space with the same people who will be building over Vivi's home?

"Sinvergüenzas," I mumble.

"What?" Joe says.

"Huh? Nothing. I just hate elevators."

We spill out into the penthouse suite, yet another space filled with people I don't know. There are flat-screen TVs everywhere. You can tell someone brought them in, so what used to be a pretty elegant room now looks like a sports bar tuned into all the news channels. The volume isn't turned up very high; the sound gets drowned out by the sound of everyone talking over one another. All around me, people are raising their glasses and making toasts. They point at the maps of Florida on the news—several of them from Central and North Florida have come in overwhelmingly for my father.

"Alachua!" someone yells. "Orange county!" They whoop and whistle as the numbers trickle in.

"Okay, okay," I hear Joe say. "Not a bad start. Not bad at all."

It's 7:31 p.m. The polls have only been closed half an hour, and it'll be another thirty minutes before the last polls in the panhandle close. What we're seeing now are the smaller precincts, the ones it took less time to count. I glance at the map and see that all of South Florida is still in a dead heat. Three percent of the votes have been counted, and Papi's ahead by 437. I take no comfort in this. My nerves are wound tight and I can't decide if it's from the possibility of Papi losing, or the possibility of him winning. I can't control any of tonight's outcome, but I hate knowing it'll control me.

Vivi, Zoey, and I make our way to the kitchen to get some sparkling waters.

"You're the senator's daughter," a woman in a navy skirt suit says to me. "I saw you on TV the other day."

I feel her eyes travel from my eyes to my toes and back. Vivi reaches across her to grab a handful of chips. "Okay. And???" *Crunnnch.*

"Are you happy? With what you accomplished?" She nods and smiles as she talks, but her words are coated so thick with politeness it makes them sound like poison.

"What do you mean?" I say, pretending to be clueless. I can't defend myself because it'd look like I'm the one who attacked her first, so I try to do the next best thing: make her explain herself.

She ignores me, though, and just keeps going. "That girl Jackie. Real opinionated, isn't she? Didn't she almost get expelled?"

Out of nowhere, Abuelo's deep, booming voice fills the kitchen. "¡Chicas!" The woman nearly drops her plate of celery sticks. "You look bored out of your minds. ¿Qué hacen aqui?"

"We were just leaving," Zoey says.

"Here. Take a pizza." He hands us a whole box. "Go enjoy yourselves. Someone should."

I stifle a giggle as we make our way to one of the bedrooms and shut the door. Inside, the whole bed is covered by men's jackets and women's purses. I sink into the overstuffed pillows and eat even though my stomach feels like a brick.

Now that it's just the three of us, I turn my attention back to my friends. "Tell me about your grandma. How's she doing?"

Vivi tilts an open hand back and forth. "She's okay. Not any better or worse, at least. Her neighbor just got admitted to the hospital, too, so now she has company, I guess."

"Tell her about the tests," Zoey adds.

Vivi shoots her a severe look. "Not now."

"What tests?"

"It's nothing," she insists.

"Will you just tell me!"

She sighs. "Just that they found some chemicals in her system, and they think that's what she's reacting to. And they match some of the chemicals in the water."

"Oh, Vi. That's terrible," I say.

"Nothing's confirmed yet." I can't believe she's trying to make me feel better, after all this. Vivi takes a bite out of her pizza. "I just wish she'd come home already. My aunt and I redid her bedroom for when she gets back."

It's the first time she's ever called her aunt's apartment home, and she doesn't even seem upset.

I think of Jackie, Didier, and Crissy, whom I haven't heard from all day except for a few thumbs-up, party hats, and tongue-out smiley emojis they sent a couple of hours ago. I know they're giving me my space tonight, but a part of me wishes I knew what they were up to. I'm sure they're off somewhere, planning next steps.

"We're going to fix this," I say, giving Vivi's wrist a reassuring squeeze. Outside our door, we hear another eruption of cheers. More good news for Papi. I try to imagine a future in which he has the power to make this right. I smile and clap twice, as if they could hear me. "Wow. That's great. Yeah."

Then everything goes quiet all at once. Our phones vibrate.

I can't look, but Vivi and Zoey check their alerts, gasping in unison.

"This early? Are they sure?" Zoey says.

Vivi nods. "The South Florida numbers just came in. That's a lot of votes." She scoots closer to me and loops her arms under mine. "It's going to be okay. Really."

That's when I know we lost.

forty-five

"How can you be sure?" I run out of the bedroom bare-foot. The carpet feels stiff and dusty. Everyone is either seated, slouched with their hands over their mouths, or standing with their arms crossed. No one looks at one another.

"Where'd he go?" I ask a man in a dark khaki suit, just as he's pouring himself a beer. He shakes his head and shrugs. His eyes are bloodshot.

The room fills with splashes of color from the television screens as the news stations announce the name of the projected winner in fancy 3D graphics.

"In a race that started out in his favor until Miami-Dade County's numbers came pouring in, Florida Senator Anthony Ruiz has shockingly lost the state's primary by a two-digit margin."

Two digits. So, more than 10 percent. It can't be.

"I'm sorry, Mari," Vivi says. "I know this was going to be hard no matter what the outcome . . . but that doesn't make it any easier."

"I just need to see my mom and dad."

We make it to the master bedroom. I'm about to walk in when something makes me hesitate. I knock three times, gently. I hear a couple of muted voices and then the unmistakable shrill sound of Ricky bursting into a long, escalating sob.

The door opens a crack. For a second Mami looks surprised to see me, then she stretches her arm through the small opening and pulls me through.

"Ven acá. Girls, give us a moment?"

Vivi and Zoey look at me for assurance that I'll be fine. I give them a quiet nod and step into the room.

I don't know what I'd been expecting. Maybe that Ricky would be sitting on Papi's lap while Papi tried to console him, telling him that there was no need to cry. Or that Papi would be standing by the window with his hands on his hips, jacket off, and tie undone, staring out at the Miami skyline.

Instead I find him hunched over the edge of the bed. It's unmade, with the white overstuffed comforter rolled into a giant wormlike shape. Papi's wearing only one shoe; his toe is pressed against the heel of the other foot, as if he started to take off the other one, but forgot what he was doing. He's frozen in that groggy way you get when you've just woken up and can't function.

"Is he—"

"Shhh," Mami says. "He just needs some space."

I hear Ricky wail again, this time behind the bathroom door.

None of this feels real. As conflicted as I was about the election, I never actually imagined a reality in which Papi lost. Not even the general election. Definitely not the Florida primary. Our own home state.

"There's still other primaries in other states," I offer.

Papi half laughs and half scoffs. "You heard what they said. There's no future for me if I don't win Florida. So congratulations. You never have to worry about me being president again."

Mami places her hand on my shoulder. "Tonio."

He straightens his back and looks up at me. "Your Twitter must be blowing up. Have you checked yet? Have you posted a selfie celebrating your victory?" He raises his eyebrows and holds his hands together as he speaks to me. I didn't know he was capable of being this cruel.

"That's enough! That's not fair," Mami says.

"*This* is not fair," he says, tossing his arm once in my direction. "We were so close. So close."

His words land sharp and cold on my body, and I can feel the pain spreading. I imagine it like an ink stain that just keeps growing until it consumes me. That would actually be better than this. At least then I'd disappear.

"Ruined by my own daughter," he says.

"I never thought you'd lose." As soon as I blurt out the words, I know they're true. I thought he was invincible, that he'd be able to handle everything that PODER or any of the other students tossed his way. I thought in the end, we'd somehow band together and he'd help us, save us. I thought we'd save each other.

But he's not the hero I thought he was. The hairs on the back of my neck rise as it hits me. I used to believe he could do anything. I begin to feel sorry for him, for all of this. Then he looks at me with the most unforgiving eyes.

"Of course you didn't. You never considered that your actions have consequences."

He, of all people, is telling me this. I want to punch the pillows and tear apart the comforter and scream that he's the one who acted recklessly all this time, when he thought he could get away with contaminating the water.

"Vivi got kicked out of her house because of Irving's new development. Her grandmother is still in the hospital because of the water contamination. Doesn't that mean anything to you?"

Mami tries to interject again, but Papi cuts her off.

"If we'd won, I would've fixed it."

"Prove it."

"What did you say to me?"

"Prove it. Fix it anyway. Now that you lost." I regret the words as soon as I hear them. They're too final, too real, and I'm the last person he wants to hear saying them.

I try to imagine what tomorrow will be like, but I can't remember what life was like before any of this. Papi always won, no matter what.

No matter what.

That was the problem.

"You should call the governor," Mami whispers. The governor of Georgia is the candidate who won Florida tonight. My shoulders tense as my body remembers what comes next. The losers will congratulate the winner. They'll make their concessions as soon as possible, with their families at their sides, before the winner can make his victory speech, so that no one has to compete for airtime. It's a professional courtesy, Papi told me the night of his last election. But that time, he'd won.

"Will we have to go out there too?" I ask.

"Come, I'll freshen you up," Mami says, leading me into the bathroom.

Inside we find Ricky sitting on top of the toilet with his feet dangling. His body sways like a tiny drunkard's as he tries to hold back his tears.

"What do we do now?"

His whole world is so small that this campaign engulfed everything. I sit on the edge of the bathtub and place him on my lap. "We're going to be fine."

"Will Papi have a job?"

We both look at Mami, but she's hyper-focused on the mirror, reapplying her lipstick with her mouth hanging open in a shocked expression. I can tell she's taking her time just to avoid answering the question. Papi's term was ending this year. He'd have to launch a new campaign for re-election. Could he just start over again? Would it ever end?

"There's still plenty of work to do," I say. "It's going to work out eventually."

I help Ricky wash his face. Mami redoes our makeup and by the time we leave the bathroom, Papi's pulled himself back together, suit and tie and everything. I'm guessing he made the phone call while he was alone, but now it's time to admit defeat in front of millions.

We head downstairs to the ballroom where his supporters have been waiting all night. There's a stage and a podium with his campaign logo splashed on the backdrop, the stage where everyone hoped he'd celebrate a win. A teleprompter displays the first few words of his speech, and they hover in place, waiting for him to begin. I recognize the words. They're the ones Mami and I wrote.

She takes Ricky's and my hands in hers. My father walks up the side steps ahead of us, and we wait a few seconds to follow. He waves and thanks his supporters, and then he turns to us and blows one big kiss. His arms hang open for half a second and then he slaps his hands together. It looks like a hug he's taken back.

"First of all, I want to thank all of you for your unwavering support. It got us further than you know, further than it feels tonight. But in the grand scheme of things, when history has turned its page, we'll look back and remember not defeat, but a beginning. A renewed sense of commitment to the beliefs that we will continue fighting for, win or lose, in the future that awaits our country."

He goes on to congratulate the governor on his victory. He wishes him strength and courage to mend our country back together, but eventually his words begin passing through me. I hear them as if they're detached from meaning, as if I'm underwater and all I'm aware of is my breath, how the air sits in my lungs, hurting. The edges of my mouth feel dry and cracked. The crowd starts applauding so I follow. He keeps talking, and talking, to a room full of strangers, for longer than he's ever talked to us. I scan the crowd and see Joe up front, nodding along. Next to him is Zoey, who tries to hide the fact that she's checking her phone, and next to her is Vivi. She has a look on her face that seems to live there permanently these days. It's pure worry, a deep, sad concern.

I tilt my head. My forehead creases like it does when I bite into something gross, in a way I can't control.

Mami clears her throat and nudges me. He's about to get to the part where he talks about the water, about a future in which we overcome our differences to care for one another.

Rebuilding America means we create a new foundation from which we can all succeed.

I see the line on the teleprompter. The scrolling stops, and the words are suspended midscreen, as if they, too, are waiting. Papi scoops his arm underneath the podium and grabs a water bottle. Drops of sweat drip from his forehead as he takes a long sip.

"Thank you. And God bless America."

forty-six

When he steps away from the podium, that's our cue to come forward and embrace him. He doesn't even look back, so sure that we'll come to him. Ricky is the first to take his hand, and then Mami is at his side for a kiss. They all turn to me at the same time and Papi mouths my name. Our hug is stiff and painful, like a handshake that crushes your bones together.

The voices all around us are loud but defeated. Every second that passes takes a bit of hope and happiness with it. Ironically, "Don't Stop Believing" blasts through the speakers as Papi begins making his way through the crowd to shake people's hands and thank them. I watch them smile like their faces hurt.

Soon he and Mami are walking through the crowd. Ricky and I sit on the steps to the side of the stage, and Vivi and Zoey join us. Within minutes he's asleep, his torso draped over my lap.

"What'll you do now?" Zoey asks.

I run my hands through Ricky's hair, careful not to wake him. "I don't know. They say he can still run for his same Senate seat. So maybe everything will go back to how it was before."

Which sounds so depressing, now that I say it out loud. The way things were before isn't good enough.

"She didn't mean him," Vivi says. "She meant you."

"I can't even think about me right now," I say. "Everything's still messed up. Your aunt's apartment will still flood every full moon, and the water will still be contaminated. Irving will still be full of it."

"We'll figure something out," Vivi says. "We have to." She puts her head on my shoulder and whispers, "You were awesome at the walkout. I liked seeing you on TV like that much better. Behind the mike instead of behind your dad. It suits you." She yawns just as she says *you*, not bothering to cover her mouth, and I don't know why—maybe it's because she looks so adorable, with her nostrils flaring open and her eyes squinted shut—but it breaks me. All the hope I'd had for my father—for his campaign, for all the things I wanted him to do and all the things he didn't—finally spills out of my body. Vivi and Zoey lean in closer, covering me so I can cry in private. Even though the room is huge it feels like it's just the three of us. Somebody switches on a block of lights, and they flicker on one after the other in random order. A heavy hush fills the space, followed by a collective gasp from across the floor.

A cloud of red settles over our heads. We stand and look up at the ceiling just as the last bit of net comes undone and releases thousands of balloons. I'd forgotten about them. They'd been sitting up there all night, waiting for the call of victory to let them loose. They were supposed to fall on an ecstatic crowd, but instead they float, slowly and uneventfully, onto the empty floor. I trace their lazy paths with my tear-filled eyes. "I guess they had to come down at some point."

I hear a pop, and then another and another. The sounds speed up and slow down like a bag of popcorn in the microwave.

"Joe!" My father's voice cuts through the noise. "Can you please wait till we've gone?" He emphasizes *please* in such a way that it's not a request. The stage vibrates as he walks across it one more time. "Vamos."

I kiss Vivi and Zoey good night. They head to the hotel entrance, where Vivi's mom is waiting for them. Mami takes Ricky into her arms, and even though he's getting big now, and he's still asleep, his body conforms to hers, making him seem weightless as she carries him. She rubs my shoulder with her free arm. As we leave the ballroom, I'm careful not to step on any pictures of my father that say RUIZ FOR PREZ.

We're a few feet from the elevator when the sounds of the balloons popping start up again. They're loud and angry in a way I wish I could be.

forty-seven

We don't ask not to go to school the next day, but we don't have to. Mami and Papi's bedroom door stays closed all morning, and when I pull back the curtains in the living room, the house fills with blinding light. I make my brother a late-morning snack—diced apples and water crackers with butter. He does this gross thing with his mouth, where he takes a bite but doesn't really chew, just waits for it to get soggy from his saliva. Then he smacks his lips and the little crumbly bits fall from his face as he swallows.

"Ewww. Qué asco," I whisper.

But he's like a zombie, not really here. He is the only one of us who doesn't hide his emotions. They pour out of him, pure and unfiltered, as if there is nothing worse in the world than this loss.

He starts to cry, his tears torrential but muted, and to my surprise, he lets me hold him. The concept that some people did not vote for Papi is soul-shattering to him. It's a betrayal I see written on his face, all the soft spots that turn hard as he tries to make sense of it.

"But . . . they said they would. Hundreds of them. I saw them."

He's thinking of the people who shook Papi's hand at

rallies, or the ones who took a picture with him for their Instagram, promising they'd get out the vote. Ricky didn't know it was a reciprocal transaction. I don't have the heart to tell him that people don't always do what they say they'll do.

Even after he's gotten the tears out of his system, Ricky doesn't turn on the television or his iPad; he just stares into the backyard. I notice the trees have sprouted new fruit, and since Gloria hasn't been around to keep track of them, the fruits just hang bright and heavy from the trees' limbs.

"Come. I want to show you something." I take off my sandals. Thick blades of grass tickle my toes and crunch beneath my soles as we make our way across the yard. Fallen mangoes lie along the roots of the trees, dotted with holes that birds and bugs left behind. I stretch on my tippy-toes to pick the ones still intact. They're yellowish green and firm, and splatters of sap cling to their skin. My fingers get sticky as I hand one after the other to Ricky. I spot our neighbor's papaya tree and banana fronds peeking over the fence. They've yielded nothing new, but what we have in our own yard is plenty.

"Will we lose the house?" Ricky asks. "At school, there's this girl Erica who's gone, and Andrew says it's because her mom lost her job and then their house."

"Papi hasn't lost his job. Not really."

Ricky stands in the middle of the yard with his arms full of fruit, staring at our home like it's a faraway place he already misses. I wonder if he knows what losing a house means, or if he's imagining that ours will float away and we'll be left stranded. I think of Vivi on the beach, miles from her home that used to be not even a mile from ours.

"We're not going anywhere. And even if we did, we'd still be fine."

"How do you know that?"

I go back to looking for more fruit because I'm not sure. I don't think I'll ever understand men like Irving, or the people like Papi who follow him. I don't know how they can be so obsessed with buying property and selling houses instead of making homes.

Last night during Papi's speech, he said he was looking forward to spending more time with his family. But when he finally comes out of the bedroom with Mami, it's only because Abuelo has arrived, and neither Ricky nor I heard the doorbell. The three of them come outside with their hands in the air, trying to block the sun from their eyes.

"Se van a quemar," Mami says. "At least come inside to put on some sunscreen."

In the kitchen, the local midday news is on, recapping last night's results. We pretend not to hear as we gather paper plates and disposable silverware for the bag full of chicken that Abuelo bought from Pollo Tropical. A second plastic bag from Publix is filled with avocados. I know they're from Abuela's tree—he'd never eat any others. As he cuts one open, careful not to let the blade pierce his skin, he smiles gently at Mami. "We have each other. That is the most important thing."

She squeezes his hand and I hear the familiar jangle of her

silver bracelets. It's like the sound of keys when you're heading home.

Behind us, the TV volume increases until a woman's voice fills the room. Papi is slouched against the edge of the table, holding the remote control.

"Earlier this morning, a five-year-old boy was admitted to Hialeah Hospital in what may be the youngest case linked to recent findings that the groundwater from the Biscayne Bay aquifer contains high levels of pharmaceutical contaminants. Doctors believe the boy's heart medication may have reacted poorly over time with the chemicals in the drinking water. No word yet on his condition or prognosis."

Papi sits in silence. I want to ask him if this changes things, if maybe now, for this boy at least, he'll take action. I'm angry that it's come to this; why do we need more victims for something to matter? Why can't we try to keep bad things from happening instead of doing damage control after they do? I start to move toward him but Mami places her arm softly across my chest.

"Not now, hijita. Soon. We'll have plenty of time for these things, I promise."

I think of all that time Papi said he'll be spending with his family. I wonder if it'll be days, weeks, or months before he's meeting with donors and constituents again. He can't change who he is. We all know he'd rather be running. For president, for senator, for anything. I wonder if now, maybe he'll run for me. But I can't wait for him to make a decision before I make one of my own.

As if she read my mind, I get a text from Jackie.

Sorry everything sux right now.

It's not your fault, I reply.

I know. But I'm still sorry. I wish things were different. All the things. The world.

You and me both.

I see her typing something and then change her mind. I wish I could just talk to her and Didier and Crissy. Putting my phone away, I start helping Mami empty out the dishwasher.

"I want to go back to school tomorrow," I whisper.

She also keeps her voice down, even though no one asked us to. "Are you sure you're ready?"

"Positive." Then I ask Abuelo if he can take me to see Vivi this afternoon once school lets out.

The streets of Miami Beach are worn along the edges. Bits of gravel collect in wet, black clumps in the places where the ocean water came and went. I catch glimpses of the crowded shore as we cross each intersection. Earlier today, city officials lifted the no-swim advisory now that the sewage leak cleared out, so people's arms and legs poke out of the waves here and there. We drive with the top down in Abuelo's newest old car, a 1999 Mustang convertible that he says he got for a steal because the air stopped working and the top won't go back up.

"So, pray it doesn't rain."

"Abuelo! You're joking, right?" There's no chance it won't rain this afternoon. Precipitation is the only thing that's ever punctual in our city.

I close my eyes against the breeze. When I open them, we're parked in front of Vivi's building and she's running toward us from the end of the street, having just gotten off the school bus. Last time I visited Vivi's aunt's apartment, we were eight and her aunt took us for ice cream on Ocean Drive after we'd spent the whole day in the sea. When we were done we chased lizards outside her building. They darted up ferns and palm trees, fleeing from the clusters of giant black-and-red grasshoppers in the hibiscus bushes.

I catch the sweet, light smell of hibiscus nectar as Vivi opens the gate to the building. She tells us that her mom brought her abuela home while she was at school today.

"Abuela!" she half shouts, half whispers as we walk into the apartment. The orange Saltillo tiles in the living room are almost entirely covered by cases of plastic bottles wrapped in plastic. "She might still be sleeping."

We poke our heads through a crack in the bedroom door and sure enough, her grandmother is out. Her lips are dry but they slowly pucker and part as she breathes, like a fish.

Vivi shakes her head as she closes the door. "They finally thought she had enough fluids in her system to let her come home. Isn't it crazy? The water made her sick but then she needed water to rehydrate. How can the thing that almost kills you be the same thing that heals you?"

I start to agree, but no. "It was never the same thing, Vi. Don't confuse the toxic with the good."

Epilogue

When you grow up in Florida, you don't just grow up on the land, you grow up in the water. It clings to the air you breathe. It falls from the sky almost daily, like clockwork, like someone was just flushing out the pipes. At the beach, if you dig a hole not even a foot deep in the sand, you'll find ocean there. Canals meander through neighborhoods. Ponds and fountains dot apartment complexes, manmade to mimic larger bodies. Almost everyone has a pool, or access to one in their building or a neighbor's. In the summer, newscasters track the moisture levels in the air as depressions turn into storms turn into hurricanes that make their way to shore.

Which is why no one is surprised when it rains nearly nonstop in the days after the election. It's the kind of spring rain that windshield wipers can't clear. On the way to dropping me off at school, Mami drives below the speed limit through the flooded streets, squinting through the window. It looks like someone ran a hose down the glass. I jump out of the car and run as fast as I can across the school courtyard. I feel every drop of water on my skin turn to ice as I walk indoors.

Nothing keeps the water out. The school lays extra drying mats, but we still drag mud and water into the hallways. In first period, the rain seeps in through the windows and Ms.

Walker plugs the leaks with a purple and green beach towel she got from her car. I can't stop staring at the towel during class. It's hard to imagine her lying on it in the sand, tanning in a bikini. I bet when she does, no one sends a drone to spy on her.

Days when it rains like this, everything goes quiet. Like life and all its noise can't make it through the dampness. We walk around being careful not to slip. And maybe it's because we like hearing the raindrops against the building, or the rumbling thunder, but no one ever raises their voice.

The calm feels nice. I let it settle me. I know it'll pass, but for now it helps me piece myself back together.

The day after I go back to school, PODER holds its first meeting since the walkout. It's not just the five of us anymore; it's standing room only and people stay so long that we pool our money together to order pizzas. Jackie brings out her stack of green flyers again and reminds everyone to run for offices of PODER. I hold one in my hand, folding over the edges into tiny triangles.

"I think I'm going to run. For *vice* president," I whisper, turning my head to smile at Didier. With Jackie and Crissy graduating, we've all known Didier will run for president. I'm still figuring out how I can help as I go. He puts his hand out in the air for a quiet fist-pump, and Crissy squeezes my arm as she rests her head on my shoulder.

We brainstorm what's next for PODER, writing our plans on a whiteboard calendar that Ms. Sepulveda bought after Jackie's first televised interview. It's filled with color-coded tasks that people can volunteer for. There's something for everyone: some of us will text our members of Congress, others will call or write letters. Zoey wants to protest outside the mayor's office while Didier is choreographing a gratitude demonstration for the senator (the other one) who released a statement in support of us after the walkout. Students from other schools have reached out in solidarity, so we're planning to FaceTime to exchange ideas. There's even talk of us forming our own PAC—we'll raise funds only for candidates who'll support passing laws for clean water and climate change prevention. I wonder what Mami will say when she finds out about that.

"We're revolting," I say once everyone except the five of us has gone, half to myself, half hoping someone will get my *I Love Lucy* reference. It's from the "Pioneer Women" episode, when Lucy makes demands for a dishwashing machine.

Didier smiles at me inquisitively.

"No more than usual," I add in my best Ricky impersonation. No one but me laughs at the joke, but it doesn't matter.

In the coming weeks, Jackie, Crissy, Didier, and I will take interviews with the kind of big media outlets my father rarely turns down. Every day after school we go over what we have to say. We'll tell them this is just the beginning. That our health and the quality of our water are not for sale. That it's way past time our elected politicians looked out for our interests instead of developers'. Always, we'll remind them this is nothing new. That Flint, Michigan's drinking water has been poisoned for years, and where is the influx of stories about the kids who've been demanding clean water now? Little Miss Flint was eight when the crisis started, and she hasn't stopped raising her voice. Her name is Mari, like mine. We don't pronounce them the same, but our messages aren't all that different.

"You're supposed to be the adults," I tell the *Times*. "You say you want to leave us a better world, but you're leaving us to clean up after your mess."

"And what does your father have to say about that?" the reporter asks. It's after school, and I'm sitting on the PODER couch with my phone on speaker, my friends quietly listening and cheering me on.

"I don't know. You should ask him," I say, knowing he won't respond to a request for comment. Papi is on what Joe calls a "listening break," which means he hasn't said a word to me. But last night I heard him and Mami arguing about my interview. They probably thought I was asleep. Mami told him not to get in my way, that he shouldn't stop me from becoming the person I want to be.

Her words filled me with both warmth and terror. I wanted to yell down the stairs that sometimes I don't know who that person is, the one I want to be. Then I caught sight of the moonlight glistening against the canal in the backyard, nearly still on the smooth water, and it felt like a slow exhale. All I'm sure of is that I want to be the one to choose, in my own time. I want to be the one who gets to have her say.

The reporter asks me if there's anything else I'd like to add before we hang up. There's so much. There's always more I feel I should be saying or doing, maybe because I went so long without realizing I could. But for now I tell her no. There's Vivi waiting for me at her apartment, and Abuelo outside because he promised me a ride.

By the time he drops me off, Vivi and I have an hour left before sunset. We walk along the boardwalk, its wooden planks creaking beneath our feet, and then we take off our flip-flops and step onto the sand. Today I can't decide if it's the sky or the ocean that's the more beautiful blue.

"It makes me feel so small," Vivi says, as if she read my mind.

"I know," I say, but then I breathe in the breeze. I think of the name my parents gave me, Mariana. The sea it holds. The way its power stirs inside me.

I run toward it and jump in.

Author's Note

The law that Mari and her friends march in protest against was inspired by real events. In 2018, the Florida legislature introduced a bill that would allow companies to dump treated sewer water into the state's aquifers. Supporters and critics of the bill used similar arguments to those mentioned in this novel. The bill passed in both the Florida House and Senate, clearing the way for it to become law. To the surprise of many, it was ultimately vetoed by the governor of Florida. It took one veto —and the voices of those who called their lawmakers, testified, and spoke up against the bill—to make a difference.

Acknowledgments

This book started as a spark, a *what if?* that was immediately met with genuine enthusiasm from my agent, Laura Dail, whose excitement was contagious and sustained me in moments I most needed it. Thank you so much, as always, for your unwavering support.

My endless gratitude to my editor, Jennifer Greene, for pushing me to get closer and closer to the heart of this story with each revision; I'm a better writer for having worked with you. Thank you also to Alex Cabal, for taking my breath away with your artwork and illustration of Mari, and to art director Sharismar Rodriguez, for having such a clear-eyed vision for this book's cover and bringing it to life in ways beyond my wildest dreams.

I wrote early parts of this book during my time at the Las Dos Brujas Writers' Workshop; every prompt, exercise, and reading that Cristina García shared with us unlocked a window into my characters. Mil gracias, Maestra, for the inspiration and empowerment. To every brujx in our workshop: I'm blessed to be in a community with you. My deepest gratitude to ire'ne lara silva for always reading my first words and seeing them not just for what they are but what they'll become. Demery Bader-Saye, Everlee Cotnam, Kate Cotnam, Barbara

Sparrow, and Raul Palma, I can't thank you enough for your invaluable feedback and encouragement along this book's journey. Each of you played such a uniquely meaningful part.

I finished later drafts of this book during my time as a writer-in-residence at the Betsy Hotel in Miami Beach. Thank you to Deborah Briggs and everyone at the Betsy for providing me with such beautiful time and space to write.

My love in every thought, word, and story goes, always, to my parents and my sister: Ceci, Ramon, and Ursula. Gracias, Nonnita, for the gift of poetry and words from a young age. Thank you also to my family in-love: Odalis, Ily and Lissy, Rey and Kathleen for your beautiful and loving support. I also want to give a very special thank-you to my Nonno and to Lolo, two amazing men who inspired so much of Abuelo in this story. Finally, and always, Eric. Every day I wake up smiling, full of love for you, and in awe that we found each other. Sharing this journey with you makes everything possible.

To anyone reading this who's ever felt their voice deep within, wanting to come out: You are an inspiration and a force.